T0196820

Evil by the Sea

The By the Sea Mystery Series by Kathleen Bridge

Death by the Sea
A Killing by the Sea
Murder by the Sea
Evil by the Sea

Evil by the Sea

A By the Sea Mystery

Kathleen Bridge

LYRICAL UNDERGROUND
Kensington Publishing Corp.
www.kensingtonbooks.com

LYRICAL UNDERGROUND BOOKS are published by

Kensington Publishing Corp.
119 West 40th Street
New York, NY 10018

All Kensington titles, imprints, and distributed lines are available at special quantity discounts for bulk purchases for sales promotion, premiums, fund-raising, educational, or institutional use.

Special book excerpts or customized printings can also be created to fit specific needs. For details, write or phone the office of the Kensington Sales Manager: Kensington Publishing Corp., 119 West 40th Street, New York, NY 10018. Attn. Sales Department. Phone: 1-800-221-2647.

First Electronic Edition: May 2020
ISBN-13: 978-1-5161-1001-8 (ebook)
ISBN-10: 1-5161-1001-3 (ebook)

First Print Edition: May 2020
ISBN-13: 978-1-5161-1003-2
ISBN-10: 1-5161-1003-X

Printed in the United States of America

I dedicate this book to my agent, Dawn Dowdle. It has been a wonderful journey of discovery. Thank you for being by my side as my advocate and friend. Every writer should be as lucky as I am. XO

Acknowledgements

To Elizabeth May, my editor at Kensington/Lyrical, for her insight and support. I want to thank all the cozy mystery readers and bloggers that promote cozies. Where would we be without you? To my amazing family for giving me the time away from them to do what I love most—write. And to Lon Otremba for his fabulous recipe contributions in both of my series. Soon we will have enough to make a Hamptons Home and Garden and By the Sea Cookbook!

We have lingered in the chambers of the Sea
By sea-girls wreathed with seaweed red and brown
Till human voices wake us, and we drown.
—T. S. Eliot

Indialantic by the Sea regulars who live on the grounds:

Liz (Elizabeth) – Amelia Holt, writer
Aunt Amelia Eden Holt – Liz's great-aunt, 1960s television character actress
Fenton Holt – Liz's attorney father and Aunt Amelia's nephew, engaged to Agent Charlotte Pearson
Ryan Stone – Liz's boyfriend, private investigator
Chef Pierre Montague – Indialantic's chef, lives at the Indialantic
Betty Lawson – teenage mystery writer, lives at the Indialantic
Greta Kimball – housekeeper/cook, lives at the Indialantic
Captain Clyde B. Netherton – skipper of the Indialantic's sightseeing cruiser, lives at the Indialantic
Susannah Shay – assistant hotel manager, lives at the Indialantic

Pets:
Barnacle Bob – Aunt Amelia's macaw
Caro (Caroline Keene) – Betty's black-and-white cat
Killer – Captain Netherton's black-and-white Great Dane
Venus – Greta's sphinx cat
Bronte – Liz's gray-and-white kitten
Blackbeard – Ryan's mixed-breed puppy

Indialantic by the Sea shopkeepers:

Kate Fields – Owner of Books & Browsery by the Sea and Liz's best friend
Pops Stone – Owner of Deli-casies by the Sea and Ryan's grandfather
Minna Presley – Co-owner of Home Arts by the Sea, mixed-media artist
Francie Jenkins – Co-owner of Home Arts by the Sea, expert seamstress
Ziggy Clemens – Owner of Zig's Surf Shop by the Sea and Aunt Amelia's boyfriend
Brittany Poole – Owner of Sirens by the Sea, women's clothing shop

Chapter 1

"My daughter wrote the book on superstitions," Dorian Starwood squeaked. Her long, almost waist-length lavender hair fell in waves around her attractive, albeit wrinkled face. Entwined in her hair were long glittery strands of metallic green, pink, and gold, like tinsel from a mid-century Christmas tree. "Amelia, lovely Liz," Dorian addressed them, fear in her pale gray eyes. "I swear my dream was as vivid as this fine tea table in front of us. I stumbled; I tell you. I stumbled on the way to the altar and flopped smack to the ground. When I'd glanced behind me, I saw why. I'd grown a mermaid's tail. It wasn't a pretty tail with iridescent shades of aqua, blue, and violet. Instead of rose petals, brown scales fell in my wake as I slithered toward the altar. I knew I'd been out of the water too long, but I couldn't decide whether to climb back into the sea or advance toward my true love?"

Liz and Aunt Amelia exchanged glances. Dorian Starwood had been Liz's great-aunt's psychic-on-call ever since Liz could remember. She'd always admired Dorian for her calm, grounded presence, even when she came across a murky crystal ball and had to deliver bad news. Liz wasn't sure she was a believer, but Aunt Amelia had three notebooks filled with Dorian's prophesizes that had come to fruition. Who was Liz to judge someone else's spiritual journey? Especially her eighty-year-old great-aunt's. She was still trying to find her own way since moving back to her family-run inn, the Indialantic by the Sea Hotel and Emporium, on a barrier island in Melbourne Beach, Florida.

Aunt Amelia opened her mouth to speak but before she could, Dorian cut her off. "It's bad luck for the bride to stumble, especially at the sacred

Litha Midsomer's Eve altar my beloved is bringing all the way from his sanctuary at the Sunshine Wiccan Society."

"Litha?" Liz asked.

"Litha is another name for the celebration of the Wiccan Sabbat or the summer solstice. I tell you, my dream was as clear as this gorgeous day. In my vision..."

"Was it a dream, dear Dorian, or a vision?" Aunt Amelia asked, reaching over and patting Dorian's hand. "I would think in your case there would be a big difference."

The nuptials between psychic Dorian Starwood and Wiccan leader, aka white warlock Julian Rhodes were scheduled for Sunday to coordinate with the Mystical Merfest and the summer solstice. Tomorrow would be the rehearsal dinner on the hotel's sightseeing and ecotour boat captained by full-time hotel resident Captain Clyde B. Netherton.

"You're right. I'm being a silly psychic."

Liz watched Dorian's hand tremble as she put her cup to her lips but didn't drink. She quickly set the cup down. The clattering against the saucer was like an exclamation point to her distress. "That's exactly the problem, my dears. I don't know what it was! I was in a fugue state. Not here nor there. The Indialantic's bell tower was ringing. I heard it echoing across the Atlantic—akin to a siren luring sailors to a rocky shore. A harbinger of doom, I tell you. The bell clanged to the tune of the wedding march." She pointed a sparkly blue fingernail up at the Indialantic's stucco bell tower visible from the hotel's open Spanish style courtyard.

They looked up. Even Barnacle Bob, who minutes before had protested about being caged on such a magnificent June day, turned his featherless head up to the sky.

There had been a good reason for the macaw's incarceration. The reason was wrapped around psychic of the rich and famous and the bride-to-be Dorian Starwood's neck like one of the boas Aunt Amelia had worn on the set of the '60s TV show *The Wild Wild West*. The same boas Liz and her best friend Kate used to play with as children.

"Pop goes the weasel," Barnacle Bob sang, "Pop goes the weasel." He raised his leg, aimed it at Dorian's neck like he was holding a pistol, then squawked, "Bang. Bang. Pop goes the weasel."

The ferret didn't open a beady eye, just stretched and waved its tail in annoyance, causing Dorian to sneeze.

"Bless you!" Aunt Amelia and Liz said in unison.

Dorian laughed. "Farrah always knows how to get me out of one of my moods." She looked down. "But that tickles, Farrah, and you know I can't be tickled."

As if listening with its little ferret ears, Farrah's tail relaxed on top of Dorian's right shoulder.

"Calm yourself, Dorian," Aunt Amelia said. "It's just pre-wedding jitters. With the Mystical Merfest opening this weekend, I think we have a clue as to why you're dreaming of mermaids. I'm sure as soon as Julian arrives, you'll feel much better. We must get on with the finalizing of the wedding and rehearsal dinner. Lizzy dear, please show Dorian the menu her son sent for tomorrow's dinner on *Queen of the Seas*."

"I don't think you understand what tripping down the aisle means for the bride. Per my daughter's book, I'll be an old maid for all time." Dorian reached in her bag and pulled out a large hardcover book titled, *Superstitions—Warnings from the Universe or Pure Bunk? You Decide. By Phoebe Starwood.* Pictured on the cover was a ladder leaning against a house, the chalk outline of a body under the ladder, and a black cat perched on the ladder's top rung with a Cheshire grin on its face.

Liz thought it prudent that Aunt Amelia only serve Dorian herbal, caffeine-free tea until the vows were exchanged. Trying to distract her, Liz handed over the menu, "I think your son's menu is fabulous, Ms. Starwood. Just look at those appetizers; pesto-stuffed cherry tomatoes, smoked salmon in dilled crepes and curry chicken phyllo bundles. Yum. I've been to his restaurant and had the best meal. Was it your idea to have free tarot card readings?" Dorian's son, Branson, was the owner of the restaurant The Soulful Sea in Vero Beach and would be supplying the food and beverages for the rehearsal dinner. The wedding food would be cooked by Chef Pierre and the Indialantic's housekeeper Greta.

"Please call me Dorian, Lizzy. I've known your great-aunt for ages, and you since you were five years old. We're family."

Aunt Amelia smiled, and Liz said, "Of course, Dorian." It had been eleven years since Liz had last seen Dorian Starwood. Ten of those years away she'd been living in Manhattan attending Columbia University, then pursuing her writing career. But when Liz was younger, she and her great-aunt would trek to Dorian's home in Palm Beach for readings, sometimes staying the night at her palatial mansion. Also, Dorian was no stranger to staying at the Indialantic, even once bringing her children, Branson and Phoebe.

"Yes, having Phoebe read the tarot at her brother's restaurant was my idea." Her smile quickly turned to a frown. "Phoebe's recently come back from France and seems a little lost since her father died. Cedric was my first husband. She's not a psychic per se, but she does know how to read the cards. I just wish she and her brother got on better. I know things will turn out all right for the pair in time. That's one vision that's very clear to me." She turned toward Liz. "Lizzy, I did try to testify on your behalf when Amelia told me about your defamation of character lawsuit last year. I had the jet waiting on the tarmac. Your lawyer wouldn't take my offer seriously, even after I showed him proof I'd helped the Palm Beach PD locate a couple of lost children and find a buried body or two. That reminds me. I brought a first edition of your novel, *Let the Wind Roar,* for you to autograph. I can't wait until *An American in Cornwall* comes out. I told your auntie many solstices ago, you'd be a prolific writer. Didn't I, Amelia?"

"Yes, you did, Dorian. I even wrote it in my journal."

"I appreciate your effort," Liz said. "It turned out okay in the end." She hadn't needed a celebrity psychic to help her; all she'd needed was the truth and her father by her side. He hadn't been her attorney because his license only encompassed Florida, not New York, but she couldn't have done it without him. Liz traced the scar on her right cheek. It was caused by a shard of broken glass from a bottle of scotch she'd fallen on after being shoved to the floor by her ex-boyfriend; a Pulitzer-prize-winning author who had a terrible drinking problem. He'd sued Liz in a defamation of character lawsuit because Liz had called 911, which in his mind alerted the media and supposedly ruined *his* good name. She'd won the case. After her stay in the hospital, Liz sold her Soho loft, packed up, and moved home to the bosom of her eclectic family at the Indialantic by the Sea Hotel and Emporium.

"You're correct, Lizzy. It's all behind us," Aunt Amelia said, blowing her great-niece a kiss. "Back to the rehearsal dinner. Remember, Dorian, if you need anything from our hotel chef or Pops at our emporium shop Deli-casies by the Sea, we're more than ready to help. Even Liz, who, as you know, was classically trained by Chef Pierre." She turned to Liz. "You wouldn't mind assisting, would you, dear?"

Between the upcoming Mystical Merfest and reviewing the galley proofs she'd just received for her second novel; this weekend was going to be a busy one. The Mystical Merfest was Melbourne Beach's celebration honoring Meribel the mermaid. Folklore said Meribel saved dozens of Spanish sailors by dragging them to shore after a hurricane destroyed their treasure-laden fleet. The 1715 shipwrecks were historical fact, as evidenced by the gold and silver still washing ashore today. Even if the story of Meribel was pure fantasy, everyone enjoyed dressing up once a year as mermaids, mermen, and pirates, tasting local island food, and visiting the town's quaint seaside shops.

"Sure, my pleasure. I'm here if you need me, Dorian," Liz answered her great-aunt with forced cheer. "No pro-blem-o."

Dorian gave Liz one of her penetrating stares. *Oops.* Liz forgot she was sitting with a psychic.

"Your second book will have as many accolades as your first, my dear." Dorian announced, then she waved her left hand in the air theatrically. On her ring finger was a huge peach-colored semitransparent stone. "No, it's not a raw diamond or gem." Dorian said to their questioning gazes. "Julian thought the best engagement stone for me would be a Himalayan salt rock. Wards off bad omens. Diamonds, I have plenty. The healing properties of salt are well proven." She turned to Aunt Amelia. "Don't you think it was such a kind and loving gesture?"

"Indeed," was all that Aunt Amelia could come up with, then looked away, stifling a grin.

Liz didn't need to be psychic to observe Dorian seemed to be talking herself into the merits of having a salty engagement ring. And why was she warding off anything? She wondered what would happen if Dorian got caught in the rain. Would it wash away? Would a deer come over to lick it?

With downcast eyes, Dorian mumbled, "As my fiancé has requested, it will be a small dinner and wedding. I'm sorry you can't bring Ziggy, Amelia. Julian tends to be overprotective. Especially after… You know if it was just us girls planning this wedding, it would be a no holds barred, bigger-than-life affair. Instead of using your hotel's sightseeing and ecotour boat we'd hire an entire Norwegian cruise liner for the rehearsal dinner."

"Totally understood, Dorian. And indeed, we would." Aunt Amelia's emerald eyes lit up with the possibilities. "Isn't it tradition to have the bride plan the wedding of her dreams?" Aunt Amelia fed a piece of kiwi to Barnacle Bob. A bribe to keep his beak shut.

Liz noticed that her great-aunt had missed the words, 'especially after…' that Dorian had just said then immediately segued into something else.

"It's not that. This isn't my first wedding, but it is Julian's." Her statement hung in the air for a few minutes.

"Even more of a reason to have a big wedding," Aunt Amelia said.

After hearing Dorian say she would like a larger-than-life party, it seemed it was Julian, the groom to be, who wanted to keep things on the down-low. Liz couldn't wait to meet him. "Even if it's small, rest assured, Auntie will make it wonderful."

Doubt clouded Dorian's eyes. "Maybe it's because of Julian's and my age difference? What if he's embarrassed to be twenty-five years younger than me?"

White warlock Julian Rhodes was only forty-five? Liz put her napkin to her mouth to hide her surprise. It seemed a little late for Dorian to be asking that question two days before her nuptials.

"Dorian, how long have you known Julian?" Liz asked, feeling protective of her great-aunt's friend.

"We've known each other for six months. Enough time to know our union was written in the stars. Plus, my son Branson is the one who introduced us. So that's enough for me. I know I'm being immature wishing we could have a larger celebration. It's just I never had a big wedding for my first marriage," Dorian explained. "My first was a quickie Paris affair. Orchestrated at the last minute because I had a brioche in the oven—my Branson." She laughed, and Liz and Aunt Amelia joined in out of politeness. "Plus, Julian wants to keep it as small as possible. Especially after what's been happening lately..." She clamped her hand over her mouth as if she'd said too much.

"What's been happening, dear?" Aunt Amelia asked.

"Oh, it's nothing. He tends to be overprotective."

"You're not in danger, are you?" Aunt Amelia's emerald eyes looked fierce. "You don't have to worry about anyone here or at the emporium. We're all like family."

Dorian relaxed her small shoulders and Aunt Amelia didn't question her further, just poured more of her Island Bliss tea into Dorian's cup.

The Starwood-Rhodes wedding was small. Small meant less work for everyone, but Liz had a prickly feeling at the back of her neck that things might not turn out as planned. Anonymity, per Aunt Amelia, had been the couple's top priority when choosing the Indialantic for their wedding. After Dorian's previous comments, Liz was dying to know why.

Snatching a cucumber, cream cheese, and cilantro finger sandwich from the pedestal dish, Aunt Amelia said, "Well, even if it's a small affair Dorian, I guarantee we'll make it as elegant as you deserve."

"Cheers, to that!" Liz said, raising her teacup in the air.

Dorian, Aunt Amelia, and Liz clinked their teacups together. Again, Liz thought how similar the two women were. Dorian with her glitter hair and Aunt Amelia with her trademarked baby-blue sparkly eyeshadow and thick black liner that extended two inches from the corner of her eyes, not to mention her auburn stenciled eyebrows. This afternoon, her great-aunt's long, bright red hair was coiled into soup-can-sized curls on top of her head.

"I know Julian's right," Dorian said, swiping a lemon-lime iced petit four from the platter in the center of the table. "As long as our stars are aligned, and I'm surrounded by loved ones, that's all that's required for a perfect karmic future."

Farrah woke up, made a little squealing noise, glanced at Barnacle Bob, then slithered into the tapestry carpetbag at Dorian's feet. The needlepointed design on the bag was of a white-bearded wizard holding up a wand, standing in front of a forest straight out of a King Arthur tale.

"Because I had a fitful night of sleep," Dorian said, "I'm afraid, so did my precious Farrah."

As if purposely trying to keep the ferret from napping, Barnacle Bob started ringing the bell on his cage and squawking in macaw.

"Behave yourself BB," Aunt Amelia admonished. Justly chastened, he sheepishly bent his head and tucked in his tail feathers. At least that's how it appeared to Aunt Amelia. As soon as she looked away, Liz saw BB turn around and shake those same feathers in Dorian's pet's direction, then began whistling the tune to "Pop Goes the Weasel."

Dorian said, "I am so sorry the two of you aren't invited on board for the rehearsal dinner. It was the only way I could get Julian to agree for us to leave the grounds before the wedding. It seems he thinks something might happen…"

"Tsk, tsk, not important," Aunt Amelia said. "Plus, you know I will be involved in the Mystical Merfest Regatta. But if you or your intended change your mind, I'll be there with bells on. Now on to the menu for the wedding brunch."

Dorian was glancing up at the bell tower, frown lines wrinkling her already wrinkled forehead. A cloud covered the sun and she shuddered.

Aunt Amelia clicked her fingers. "Dorian? What do you think? Are you happy with the menu?"

No response.

"We plan on serving *sea slugs* in aspic. What do you think Dorian?"

Dorian closed her eyes. With her head still looking upward she began to chant something under her breath. Then started rocking back and forth in her chair.

"Dorian!" Aunt Amelia shouted. "What do you think? Sea slugs? Yes or no?"

She opened her eyes, looked down, and murmured, "Sea slugs…fine. Do you think it will storm tomorrow?"

"No, the weather will be beautiful the entire weekend. Not to worry."

"I'm sorry, Amelia. I can't concentrate. I'll take the menus with me. I think I need a few moments alone in the enlightenment parlor. I feel a headache coming and I want to clear the cobwebs before Julian arrives. I keep trying to see a vision of our honeymoon in Bali but can't. Everything's so hazy." She got up, grabbed her bag with Farrah inside, and headed toward the open doorway leading to the interior of the hotel.

Susannah, the hotel's assistant manager came barreling through the doorway and into the courtyard. "Oh, Ms. Starwood. I'm so glad I caught you. I've brought my cousin Amy's book, and marked all the passages for the proper etiquette for small weddings. I think you'll find the passage on page fifty might help on what to do when you don't have a best man in the picture."

Dorian grabbed Susannah's arm. She closed her eyes and swayed from left to right. Susannah went to pull away, but the psychic held tight. "I see light, love, and peace in your future as soon as you vanish past hurts. Until then, you cannot find the happiness you deserve. You need to free your spirit, loosen your hold on preconceived conventions. Your cousin Amy wants you to know there is no reason to be so rigid in the twenty-first century. She regrets that because of her words you've lived a life full of convention and meaningless rules, instead of freedom and spontaneity." Dorian took the *Complete Book of Etiquette—a Guide to Gracious Living* from Susannah's other hand and held it to her chest. "I will keep this safe. Let us try, for the next couple days while I am here, to let go of the past and really live in the present. Namaste."

Susannah's mouth dropped as Dorian swished past her in her long cotton tie-dye dress, leaving behind the scent of patchouli as she went through the doorway leading to the hotel's lobby. Susannah glanced at Liz and Aunt Amelia, shrugged her shoulders, and turned, following behind Dorian. "Wait, Ms. Starwood...what does Namaste mean?"

After they left, Liz said, "Wow, could it be possible that Dorian will break Susannah's attachment to her distant cousin Amy Vanderbilt's rules for living?" Susannah claimed to be a distant relative to the first authority on etiquette, Amy Vanderbilt, who'd been a descendent of robber baron "Commodore" Cornelius Vanderbilt. It seemed Amy and Susannah shared a very diluted gene pool with American royalty, and she let everyone know it. Liz would bet that Susannah had memorized every word from her cousin's etiquette bible. The only problem with that was, the autographed, seven hundred page copy Susannah owned was from 1958. Susannah was in her late seventies. Liz knew the rules for etiquette would be completely different in a modern-day version of the tome. Between Aunt Amelia and her mid-century television shows, and Susannah with her mid-century etiquette book, Liz felt like she lived in a time warp.

Aunt Amelia shook her head. "Let's hope Dorian can get Susannah to leave all her rules behind. Maybe a good reading about a rosy future for Susannah might be the ticket. Although, I've seen such a change in her since your near-death experience last January. She dotes on you."

A little too much, Liz thought, especially now that Susannah's boyfriend was out of town. "I'm curious about the fact that Dorian's fiancé hasn't chosen a best man. Don't you think that's a little strange? And what did she mean when she said, 'after what happened'?"

"I'll have a chat with her. It's too bad I can't read her mind like she reads mine. I suppose Captain Netherton could fill in as best man?"

"Thought he got ordained online so he could perform the ceremony?"

"I forgot about that. Then your father would be perfect."

"How about Dorian's son? Branson? Wouldn't he be the logical choice? Dorian just said he introduced Julian to her. I think this whole wedding weekend might turn into one big fiasco."

"Reminds me of when I played a typist in Darren's advertising office for the pilot of *Bewitched*," Aunt Amelia glanced up at the sky, like she was looking into the past. "The episode where Samantha tells Darren she's a witch. Dick York and Elizabeth Montgomery were such consummate, giving actors. Agnes Moorehead was also charming, but I thought her look was a little over the top, even for the 1960s."

Liz nearly choked on her petit fours. In recent years, her great-aunt and the character Moorehead played, called Esmerelda, could have been twins; right down to their diaphanous jewel-toned caftans, beads, and bangles and hair color. She mused that Dorian's fiancé must have been *bewitched* into marrying a woman twenty five years his senior. Or vice versa. Dorian was a very wealthy woman. She'd started out in the '80s with a psychic talk line—a dollar a minute. Then when that went out of vogue, wrote bestselling books that sold in the millions. It was catty of Liz to question the white warlock's motives, but after what had been happening at the Indialantic in the past year, as in a few murders, okay four, her family didn't need any more bad press for the hotel and emporium.

Aunt Amelia was silent, staring at the bell tower like Dorian had done. It was rare that her great-aunt looked worried. Or was quiet. Liz didn't like it. She'd caused enough worry for her great-aunt and father in the past couple of years and was determined to pay back all the love and support she'd received from them both. "While you're at it, Auntie. Maybe you should ask Dorian why no one from her fiancé's coven is showing up.

From what you've told me, Julian's society is based out of Jacksonville. It would only be a three hour trip."

"I will, dear. I just hope, as their name says, the Sunshine Wiccan Society is full of sunshine and rainbows. I'm sure if there was anything evil going on, Dorian would sense it." She put her hand over her mouth, realizing that Dorian had sensed it—as in her dream—or nightmare. "I'd be lying if I didn't tell you I'm worried about her, Lizzy. Never thought a bad dream could affect someone so much." Aunt Amelia frowned, a rare facial expression, then removed the knitted cozy from the pot and poured more tea into her cup.

"You're right, Auntie. I can relate to the power of bad dreams." Occasionally, Liz had woken drenched in sweat, heart racing, and head pounding after a nightmare where she'd relived the night she'd been scarred. It was a blessing they'd been coming less frequently. It was thanks to all her family and loved ones at the Indialantic, including Ryan Stone. Time didn't heal all wounds, but it sure as heck made them sting less.

Blowing on her steaming cup of tea, Aunt Amelia said, "She'll be fine as soon as her fiancé arrives, but I'm worried about their future together."

The aroma of mint and orange wafted toward Liz. "Just hope whatever happens, it doesn't happen here."

Famous last words...

Chapter 2

An hour before the emporium closed its doors, Liz was in Deli-casies perusing the bounty of her and Ryan's work for tomorrow's Mystical Merfest. Tins of Aunt Amelia's now-trademarked Island Bliss Tea had been packed up and put on a rolling cart. They'd affixed labels to the glass jars of Pop's mango/jalapeno and guava/lime chutney and filled a basket holding brown paper bags of Deli-casies special blend coffees. Five tents corresponding to each of the emporium shops had already been erected in the emporium's parking lot.

The tents had been Aunt Amelia's idea to bring in extra revenue from the influx of tourists coming to the island for the festival. Besides Deli-casies by the Sea, there would be tents for Sirens by the Sea, a women's clothing and jewelry shop; Home Arts by the Sea, a women's lifestyle and arts collective; Zig's Surf Shop by the Sea, a surfboard and hang ten surfer's paradise; and Books & Browsery by the Sea, a used book and collectibles shop. Josie's flower truck would also have a space in the parking lot, along with the Island Eats food truck. When Dorian had booked her wedding venue, she'd also asked Aunt Amelia to have a tent set up for her to do psychic readings. All the proceeds would go toward the Sight Network, Dorian's favorite charity, where doctors traveled the world, restoring sight to people in underdeveloped countries. Seeing Julian Rhodes was so worried about Dorian's safety, Liz wondered what he thought of Dorian being exposed to the public on the same weekend as the wedding. Dorian's face was famous from years of being a guest on TV talk shows when she was touted 'Psychic to the Stars,' plus her distinctive look with her long violet hair graced all her book jackets, not to mention the time she helped the police find five-year-old Jordan Styles unharmed after being abducted from a Florida beach.

"I think we're all set, Bossy Pants," Ryan said, striding over, grabbing her and bending her backward, then swooping in with a satisfying kiss.

Once upright, Liz admonished, "It is important to line the crate holding the chutney jars with bubble wrap. I wasn't being bossy, Snoopy Pants. And speaking of bossy, I noticed you rechecking my labeling of the coffees."

"Touché," he replied with a roughish grin. A lank of glossy, almost black hair fell in front of his dark eyes, making him appear more vulnerable than usual. Liz had been smitten ever since he'd moved into the caretaker's cottage on the Indialantic's grounds. It was supposed to be a temporary arrangement until Ryan's grandfather got back on his feet following a knee operation. After the surgery, Ryan had planned on returning to Brooklyn where he was the lead FDNY arson investigator for his fire station. Fast-forward a year later, Ryan was now a permanent island resident, part-time worker in his grandfather's gourmet deli, and a licensed private investigator who assisted Liz's father, attorney Fenton Holt.

Ryan was also Liz's main squeeze, or should she say, only squeeze. They were in a committed relationship. She didn't need Dorian to foresee their future. She saw it right now in Ryan's smiling eyes. Earlier, she'd told him all about her tea with Dorian Starwood. Ryan had met Dorian the previous night for dinner at Squidly's Bar and Grill, a top rated seafood restaurant in walking distance of the Indialantic. Aunt Amelia and her new love interest Ziggy, owner of Zig's Surf Shop in the emporium, had also been at the restaurant, keeping Dorian busy with her prognostications of the elderly couple's rosy future. Aunt Amelia had giggled and blushed, saying, "Tell us more! Tell us more!" Sounding like her repetitive macaw, Barnacle Bob. Before Dorian had had a chance to move on to Liz and Ryan's future, one of Dorian's fans had recognized her and commandeered her over to a table of tourists from Michigan. Like TV character actress Amelia Eden Holt, Dorian seemed to love performing in front of crowd. Which made it sad that Dorian planned to have such a small wedding.

She took a sip of her macchiato, then set it on the barista counter. "I'm very curious to meet Dorian's fiancé, Julian Rhodes, leader of the Sunshine Wiccan Society."

"The what?" Ryan asked, arching his perfect brow. He held open one of the swinging doors while Liz passed through, pushing the cart packed with their choices for the Mystical Merfest tent.

"I know," Liz said, stopping the cart next to the restaurant grade stainless steel stove in Deli-casies kitchen. "I've never met a Wiccan, witch, or warlock before. He's supposed to be arriving soon, along with Dorian's children, and her financial advisor. I think it should be an interesting two days. I've already texted Betty his name and the society's name so she can do what she does best, cyber sleuthing from afar while visiting her granddaughter in Jacksonville." Indialantic resident Betty Lawson was an eighty-three-year-old teenage mystery writer who back in the late sixties to early seventies had written five Nancy Drew books under the pseudonym Carolyn Keene. Because of a nondisclosure agreement Betty wasn't even at liberty to tell Liz which books she'd written. Not that Liz hadn't tried. She remembered reading, *Mystery at the Moss Covered Mansion* and knew it took place in Cocoa Beach, just a couple towns over from the Indialantic. Liz had presented her theory to Betty, saying, "Ah Ha! Gotcha!" Betty had only answered with a sly smile. She was as good at writing and solving mysteries as keeping them.

"And here we go! Off to the races," Ryan said.

"What does that mean?"

"Getting involved in something you have no business getting involved with. And getting Betty involved too."

"Dorian isn't just Auntie's psychic but a close family friend. As a P.I., I thought you of all people would understand. The guy is twenty-five years younger than her, for gosh sakes!"

"I'm younger than you."

"By two months. Which makes me wiser and that's what Dorian should be when marrying someone who doesn't have any family or friends to vouch for him at their wedding. If he's the head of a whole society, where are his followers? Dorian said he's bringing his own altar. They've coordinated the wedding with the summer solstice and the Mystical Merfest. A marriage of two nontraditional spiritual beliefs, as Dorian put it."

"Hope the altar wasn't used for any sacrifices?"

She passed him a dirty look. "I'm serious. And why wouldn't they get married at his Wiccany place? Surrounded by all his followers?"

Ryan laughed. "Wiccany? Maybe he just doesn't want a big-hurrah blowout wedding. Most men don't. It might be a guy thing. Maybe if he's a witch or a warlock he's cast a spell on Ms. Starwood?"

"Exactly! I rest my case."

"Now, who's being a Snoopy pants?"

"I promise to keep out of it if you check into his background and find anything you can on him. I just want Dorian to be doing the right thing. Aunt Amelia counts her as a very close friend."

"Okay. If, as you say, you'll leave it to me?"

"And Betty."

"And Betty. Now what's his name again and the name of the witch group?" He took his phone from his pocket and tapped the screen, turned on the recorder, and held it up near Liz's mouth."

"Julian Rhodes. R-h-o-d-e-s. The Sunshine Wiccan Society. Jacksonville." He tapped the screen again and put his phone back in his pocket. "I'll do what I can, but you realize we only have two days until they marry. Not a lot of time."

She sidled up to him. "Not for the likes of you Mr. Private Eye, smartest guy I know, except maybe my dad."

He laughed and kissed her. "What do I have to do to get in the top slot over Fenton?"

"Hmm…it's getting close," she said. "I would say you're almost neck and neck."

"Is that so? Then listen to me for a change. Let me do the research, you don't worry your pretty little head about a thing."

She knew he was teasing when he said, "pretty little head," but before she could think of a comeback, Kate Fields came rushing into the kitchen holding a large sequined mermaid's tail the same color as Aunt Amelia's eyeshadow palette. Kate wasn't related to Liz's great-aunt, but had been part of their lives since she and her father came to live at the Indialantic when Liz was five. That was over twenty-three years ago. She considered Kate her sister from another mother.

Kate's face was flushed. She stopped, bent at the waist, and tried to catch her breath. When she stood, her long, shiny, chestnut ponytail swung from left to right. "You guys better get to the hotel pronto or you'll miss the fireworks. It seems not only has the wedding party arrived. But someone else! And I don't think Aunt Amelia knows what to do about it."

Chapter 3

A few minutes later, Liz, Ryan, and Kate entered the Indialantic's lobby through the revolving door to find a short man with his back facing them. He had light-brown hair and a ponytail almost as long as Kate's. He wore a white gauzy tunic top, tan drawstring pants, and brown sandals. He was addressing a wisp of a pale, waiflike, blonde haired woman dressed in a faded cotton print dress with white short socks and sandals. She looked like she was out of time and just got done milking a cow on her family's Amish farm. Liz knew she wasn't Dorian's daughter.

Phoebe and her brother Branson were sitting on one of the cushioned bamboo loveseats, looking like they were viewing a movie. Dorian stood next to them. They were focused on the couple in the center of the lobby. All they needed was a tub of popcorn and some Twizzlers.

Dorian's son Branson was tall, clean-shaven, and dressed in casual business attire. He had dark short hair. It was clear with his lean body and muscular torso that he visited a gym on a regular basis. The only thing that stopped him from being male model perfect was his protruding chin sporting a dimple so large you could lose a dime in it.

Phoebe was thirty, her brother thirty-three. She looked nothing like her mother. Her face was full, but unlined. Her dull brown hair was cut in a chin length bob. A white cotton shirt hung loosely over baggy khaki capris. Liz guessed she'd recently lost weight. Phoebe's eye color mirrored her older brother's dark gray, but that was where their similarity ended.

Aunt Amelia was behind the hotel's registration counter with Barnacle Bob perched on her right shoulder. Her gaze was also focused on the couple in the center of the room. Even BB seemed to be watching them.

Liz almost didn't notice a medium-sized man with tons of red hair tufting out from everywhere, except the top of his head, slouched in a bamboo chair behind a potted palm. His silky patterned shirt was unbuttoned. Hanging from a chain around his neck was an oversized gold nugget that nestled on top of red chest hair. He wore a sly smile, like he knew a secret the rest of people in the room didn't. Either that or he was really enjoying what was going on in front of him. She deduced the red haired man must be Garrett, Dorian's financial advisor. He was too old to be her fiancé, which left the ponytail man to be Julian Rhodes. But who was the young woman?

"Surprised I'm here, cousin Julian?"

"Yes, I am surprised you're here," Julian said to the unidentified woman. There was a definite edge to his voice. "How did you find my location, Wren?"

The woman's huge hazel eyes reminded Liz of those popular Keane paintings from the sixties of big eyed children. Aunt Amelia had been given one by the artist herself. She'd kept it on her sitting room wall until a young Liz made her take it down because she thought the child in the portrait's eyes were following her.

There was one difference between the paintings and the woman in front of them; there was no sense of innocence in her eyes when she said, "What does it matter, cousin Julian, I'm here and I want to share in your big day. Do you have a problem with that?" She wasn't angry, more like smug. "I missed you, cuz." She put both hands on her tiny hips. Her blonde almost white long hair was in pigtails, resembling the actress who played Laura Ingalls Wilder on TV's 1970s *Little House on the Prairie*.

Julian must have felt their stares from behind. He did an about face and raked his eyes over Liz, Kate, and Ryan. "Who are you? I told Dorian this was a bad idea. I was informed the hotel wasn't open to the public. Are you with the press?"

Aunt Amelia looked like a deer caught in the headlights as she stammered, "Mr. Rhodes, I'd like you meet my great-niece Liz, her best friend Kate, and her boyfriend Ryan."

As if a switch had been flipped, Julian smiled. His Caribbean-blue eyes seemed otherworldly in his tanned, angular face. He came over to them and took both of Liz's hands in his, then gazed into her eyes. After a few awkward seconds, she forced herself to blink, jerking her hands away like she'd been zapped with a Taser. Then she quickly slipped her arm through Ryan's. Julian pulled the same hypnotic routine on Kate. For once Kate was left speechless. Liz would ask Kate later if she'd felt the same reaction to Julian's touch.

Ryan gave Liz a questioning gaze, then said to Julian, "Congrats on your upcoming marriage." He extended his hand and they shook.

Julian didn't have time to respond, because Dorian asked, "Julian, love, don't you think we should move up to our suite? Your *cousin* should probably look for a nearby hotel to stay at."

The way Dorian said, *cousin*, was very clear. Chalk it up to her being a psychic, or woman's intuition, but Liz could tell Dorian didn't believe the woman was her fiancé's cousin. And neither did Liz.

Wren gave Dorian a piercing look before turning to Julian and saying, "Yes, cuz, it's been a long day of travel. My bag is outside on the pavement. I've already checked in town. Everything is booked because of some mermaid festival."

Dorian stepped to the center of the lobby and stood under the Lalique chandelier. "I'm sure there's something in Vero Beach."

Aunt Amelia came from behind the counter and stood next to Dorian. Barnacle Bob rode her shoulder like a pro. Addressing Julian, she said, "If you'll give me a little time to get another suite cleaned out, there shouldn't be a problem having your cousin stay here." Then she turned to Wren. "I'll have some finagling to do but rest assured things will be straightened out shortly."

It was obvious Aunt Amelia had missed Dorian's message of not wanting Wren to stay at the Indialantic. The hotel suites had been cleaned and aired out for the guests; which included Dorian, her fiancé Julian, Dorian's financial adviser Garrett, and Dorian's children. Julian wanted a small wedding and he was going to get one. The guest list hadn't included anyone from Julian's side of the family. She was just happy Aunt Amelia was starting small in her quest to turn the Indialantic into a destination venue. The last event at the hotel, the Literary New Year's Eve Masquerade Ball had been a success, with a slight glitch, as in a murder. Now, with the wedding, and the extra money brought in from the Mystical Merfest, along with the rent from the emporium shops, the Indialantic would continue to keep its head above water. The hotel's five permanent residents also paid rent. Most were on social security with small pensions. Kindhearted Aunt Amelia only charged them what was within their means. Liz's attorney father, Fenton, also lived and worked at the Indialantic in a four room apartment at the rear of the hotel, which included an office with a separate entrance. He took on small legal cases, sometimes being paid in grouper or sea bass instead of cash. He was as altruistic as his paternal aunt and that was one of things Liz loved most about the pair.

Barnacle Bob remained unerringly quiet. Something was up. Liz glanced around for Dorian's ferret, but didn't see Farrah.

"In the meantime," Aunt Amelia said to Wren, "Why don't you have a seat in the courtyard? Someone will bring you iced tea or Pierre's lemon limeade."

Smiling, Wren said, "I would prefer something stronger. A shot of tequila or one of those umbrella type tropical drinks you guys are known for down here, if not, a margarita will do."

Barnacle Bob, who'd so far had been on his best behavior, leaned forward, his sharp beak close to Wren's small, pert nose. In his TV announcer's voice, he said, "How about a punch? A Hawaiian Punch? Bam!" The macaw was referencing an old fruit drink commercial, Hawaiian Punch being one of her great-aunt's go to beverages. Liz thought the drink's sugar content was enough to make a type 2 diabetic out of a vegan.

Wren laughed. "You're a nasty bird, aren't you? I like nasty."

She was no Laura Ingalls Wilder.

Dorian whizzed by her, giving the young woman an almost imperceptible elbow jab on her way to her fiancé's side. "Julian, darling, Amelia's assigned us the Oceania Suite. Wait until you see it. The terrace has a magnificent view of the ocean. And I've been down to the beach. It will be perfect for tonight's blessing and ritual of prophecy, protection, divination, and love under a full magnificent moon."

Not wanting to have to take control of the awkward scene, Liz breathed a sigh of relief when assistant manager Susannah entered the lobby. She looked around, assessed the situation and went to stand next to Aunt Amelia like she was ready for battle. For all the skirmishes she and Aunt Amelia had been in when it came to snagging prime parts at the Melbourne Beach Theatre Company, the two could still surprise everyone by acting like they were besties.

"Susannah, just in time," Aunt Amelia said. "I need to get the Swaying Palms Suite aired out. Can you deliver some towels and clean linens to me when you have a chance?"

"Of course, Amelia." Something was up, Susannah wasn't usually so agreeable. Susannah looked at Liz and pointed to the nonexistent watch on her wrist, then mouthed, "I need to talk to you."

Liz made sure no one was looking, then gave her a thumbs up.

As Aunt Amelia led Wren to the open doorway leading to the courtyard, Liz thought she saw Wren wink in Julian's direction. He didn't return it, only scowled.

The red haired man cleared his throat and Dorian said, "I'm sorry. This is Garrett McGee, my financial advisor and friend." She gave him a warm smile.

"Friend first," he added, giving Dorian a huge grin. He got out of his chair and came to where Susannah, Liz, Ryan, and Kate were standing. Then he exuberantly shook their hands. His grip was firm, and his green eyes matched his easygoing grin. "Crazy thing. A wedding and a mermaid festival all rolled into one."

"Garrett, don't forget the summer solstice," Dorian said. "It will be the perfect merging of my spiritualism and astrological views and Julian's Wiccan beliefs.

"Sounds complicated," Garrett replied, shooting a distrustful glance at Julian. It was obvious there was no love lost there.

"Yes, Garrett," Dorian answered, obviously not seeing the animosity in his eyes when he looked at her fiancé, "A Mystical Merfest and the summer solstice are perfect for our union. The Gemini twins are snug in their house and the full moon will be on hand in the next couple days. Right, dear?"

Julian remained mute, so Dorian explained. "The Sunshine Wiccan Society is different from other sects. They do use the pentagram, the only traditional symbol most people think about when they think of witchcraft. Other than that, it's as the name suggests. Julian's society is all about light and spiritual blessings. Pagan, but not archaic and dark. Spells are only performed for good, never evil. Right, dear?"

He shrugged his shoulders and looked like he would rather be anywhere but where he was.

"We best get you unpacked," she added.

"Susannah, do you know what suites Auntie has assigned our wedding guests?" Liz asked, wanting to break up the not-so-cozy scene.

Her straight stance and in control, no nonsense demeanor took over. "Yes of course. Mr. Starwood you're in the Golden Sands Suite…"

"My last name is Arnaud not Starwood," Branson said.

"My apologies, and your sister, Ms…"

"She goes by Starwood, even though it's mother's maiden name. Helps her sell that ridiculous book of hers."

Susannah seemed to have had enough. Acting like a subservient servant wasn't in her wheelhouse. She snapped, "Whatever name she goes by, she will be in the Island Breeze Suite." Realizing everyone was staring at her, including Dorian, she continued in a softer tone, "Mr. McGee, you've been assigned the Indian River Suite. Everyone can leave their luggage here, and someone will bring it up to you."

"Thank you. It's no problem. I can get mine," Garrett answered, making it clear he wouldn't be carrying anyone else's.

She looked toward Ryan. He smiled and gave Susannah a salute. "I'll bring everyone's luggage up." It wasn't his job, but Liz appreciated him helping out, especially by the looks of Phoebe's two huge suitcases.

Dorian grabbed Julian's wrist. "Now that that's settled." She led him to the bottom of the lobby's spiral staircase, and they started up the staircase.

"Mama. Dorian," Phoebe called out, "aren't you going to introduce me to your fiancé?" She had a very slight French accent, not as strong as Pierre's, the Indialantic's eighty-one-year-old chef and Liz's surrogate grandfather.

Branson slapped his sister on the arm. "He already introduced himself to you before Mother came in, dweeb. And what's with that fake French accent. You were only in Paris for three weeks."

Phoebe shot her brother a dirty look. "Just because you're old pals with our future stepdaddy..."

Liz saw Julian wince at her words.

She continued, "Doesn't mean he and I can't do some bonding in the next couple of days."

It seemed Phoebe had never met Julian before.

Branson made a fist and tapped her upper arm.

"Mama, he slapped me."

It wasn't forceful, and it wasn't a slap.

Halfway up the staircase, Dorian turned to look down at them.

"For heaven's sake, Mama! You know it's bad luck to turn on a staircase. Thought you read my book? At least you listened to me and are getting married in June." In a singsong voice she added, "Married in the month of roses—June. Life will be one long honeymoon."

Branson added his two cents. "Why would anyone read a book on superstitions? Only to have more things to worry about. You know you only wrote it as a publicity ploy, taking advantage of the Dorian Starwood franchise. A bunch of bull. Just like your tarot reading at my restaurant. You're no intuitive. If I could only tell you how many complaints we've gotten about your doom-and-gloom prognostications."

"It's not *your* restaurant. Mama bought it for you after she pulled you out of that hellhole you were living in. You want me to just make crap up? I read 'em as I see 'em. Mama taught me how to weave the cards together to create a story that supports my intuitive abilities. Right, Mama?"

"Branson!" Dorian admonished.

Her son's face was redder than BB's chest feathers. He closed his eyes and slipped into some kind of meditative state for about the count of ten, then opened them. "Sorry, Mother."

Dorian looked toward Liz, Kate, and Ryan. "No worries. I know how things turn out. Soon they'll be best friends." Then Dorian and Julian continued up the staircase.

Liz couldn't wait until the wedding was over. Come Monday she could get back to her editing and start collecting ideas for a third book. It was funny, when she first came back to the Indialantic after the trauma she'd been through, she couldn't write a word. Now, she couldn't wait to get started.

Ryan must have been on the same wavelength as he whispered to her, "If the whining doesn't stop, I might be the first one to throw a punch as Barnacle Bob alluded to. Looks like this small wedding's going to pack a big wallop."

Now who was the psychic?

Chapter 4

Friday night when dinner rolled around, Liz had no problem filling in as server for the Indialantic's housekeeper Greta. Aunt Amelia was at rehearsals for Melbourne Beach Theatre's production of *The Sea Witch,* where she had the leading role. Liz had promised to make sure everything went smoothly and was thrilled she wasn't invited to dine with the motley crew, who, as she glanced around, looked more like a group of mourners than wedding celebrants. Glancing to the other side of the dining room, she saw Dorian and Julian seated at a table for two near French doors opening to a moonlit ocean view.

The hotel's original dining room had been double what it was now, but it was still big enough to seat sixty people. There were fifteen square tables topped with white Irish linen tablecloths dating from the hotel's opening, personally ironed by Aunt Amelia, who thought ironing was a therapeutic activity when rehearsing lines for her latest play. Liz had helped prep the meal after finding the menu on Pierre's desk in the butler's pantry. The dish was one of Liz's favorites, lemony salmon and spiced chickpeas with arugula. The lemon came from one of the Indialantic's trees and the arugula and herbs from Pierre's kitchen garden. Greta had stayed in the kitchen with Pierre assisting him with the cleanup. Even though the chef's memory was improving with his new medication, Greta and Liz tended to hover over him.

Minutes before dinner, Susannah, Aunt Amelia's sometime assistant manager, depending of the workload, had conveniently gotten one of her migraines. Her myriad of ailments appeared whenever grunt work was involved or there wasn't anyone around important enough to praise her expertise and poise. However, she was always on the ready to give her "expert" advice on any situation. After what had happened last January, she and Susannah had grown closer. But that didn't mean Susannah had changed when it came to her sense of entitlement. Liz was happy that after the scene in the lobby and Susannah's cryptic need to see her, she'd immediately sought her out.

What Susannah had told her still echoed in her head. The only thing was, Liz didn't know what to do about it. Susannah was sure she'd seen some unidentified figure in dark clothing and a baseball hat creeping around the grounds. More specifically, in Aunt Amelia's cutting garden, the future site of the Rhodes-Starwood wedding, lurking near the altar that Julian Rhodes had brought from his Wiccan society.

"Are you sure it wasn't a gardener?" Liz had asked her.

She had put both hands on her hips. "Do you know who you're talking to? Every person who works on the Indialantic's grounds has to come through me. I deliver their checks. But only after I'm sure they did an exceptional job." Susannah hadn't known if it was a man or a woman that she'd seen, but she knew one thing, they didn't belong on the grounds bordering the south side of the hotel. Liz decided to store the information away. Likely, it was just someone from the emporium who wanted to view the Indialantic's gardens; a stop every year on the barrier island's garden and orchid tour.

Glancing toward Dorian and Julian's table, Liz was happy to see that their water glasses needed filling. It would be the perfect opportunity for a little eavesdropping, as she was curious as to why the pair were sitting so solemnly with nary a grin on their faces. She tucked an errant section of long, wavy strawberry-blonde hair behind her ear, then went to the sideboard where she grabbed a Baccarat crystal pitcher filled with water and floating lemon slices. She advanced toward Dorian and Julian's table, thinking by the looks on their faces, they might as well have been sitting next to the dumpster in the hotel's back parking lot instead of a million-dollar view. Could it be a case of cold tootsies on Dorian's part? Had she found out that Wren wasn't Julian's cousin?

Halfway to their table, Liz heard Julian say under his breath in a throaty growl, "What's the meaning of this!" He looked straight at her. "First the hotel staff brings out seafood, after I specifically said on our preference sheet that I am seafood allergic, then they come to serve bacteria filled tap water, when I said we specifically only drink the bottled artisanal water from SWS."

Liz knew there was no such thing as a preference sheet. Unless Chef Pierre had received it and forgotten to tell anyone. Dorian seemed mortified by his outburst and Liz's hand shook, causing water to spill on the Spanish tile. There was something commanding about Julian Rhodes. For his small stature, he sure could get your attention with just a few words and his piercing stare. She wondered if his hypnotic ice-blue eyes ever warmed. She didn't fancy getting on his bad side.

When she reached their table, she said, "I overheard you say you're seafood allergic. Let me whip up something for you in the kitchen." Julian seemed mollified after she asked how he liked his steak prepared. She left the dining room before he could demand anything else.

In the kitchen, she found Pierre with his feet up on a chair, his chef's toque askew as usual, and the new e-reader Liz had bought him on his lap. At first, he'd protested at the thought of an e-reader, not wanting to give up his beloved books, but after she'd set the type to a large font and told him he could even read in the sun, along with the amount of trees he'd be saving—he was off to the races, finishing a book, usually a mystery, in two days tops.

"Grand-Pierre, did anyone give you a paper saying that Mr. Rhodes was allergic to seafood?"

He twirled one end of his Hercule Poirot mustache and looked pensively toward his desk in the butler's pantry. "I don't believe so, *ma cherie*."

Liz went into the pantry. There was nothing on Pierre's desk. Under the window in the corner of the room were stacked cases of bottled water. She opened the top case and pulled out a cobalt-blue bottle. Pictured on the label was a sun in front of a pentagram with "SWS Artisanal Water" printed beneath, and in even smaller print, "sweetened with organic orange juice, bottled at the source and consecrated." Dorian had explained to Liz and Aunt Amelia that each bottle was filled with water from a bubbling mineral spring on Julian's Jacksonville property, then infused with juice from his own trees. She'd also explained, that after the bottling process, some kind of pagan ritual was performed where the entire Sunshine Wiccan Society blessed the bottles at the exact moment the sun rose up from the Atlantic. Dorian had gone on about the water's numerous benefits, which must have been the reason why there were five cases of the stuff.

She took a bottle with her and stepped out of the pantry at the same time Greta came into the kitchen from the back hallway that led to her father's law office and apartment. "Hey, Greta." She put the bottle in the fridge, then asked Greta about the supposed preference sheet.

"Never saw anything of the kind." Greta was tall and thin, in her late seventies with long white hair she wore in a French braid. When Liz had first met Greta, she'd looked fifteen years older than the woman who stood before her now. "Ms. Starwood is the only one who's come into the kitchen and she never mentioned anything, only talked about the wedding cake. Right, Chef?" Greta went and stood next to Pierre.

"Yes, Uhm, sounds familiar."

"I'm going to make Mr. Rhodes a filet. Not the end of the world," Liz said, wanting to banish the confused look in Pierre's eyes. She grabbed a tenderloin from the fridge, cut off a good-sized piece and dusted it with the chef's special spice rub mix, then cooked it in an iron skillet where she'd added a generous amount of butter and minced garlic. In the pantry she grabbed one of the hotel's plates and put it in the oven. When the filet passed the touch test, she removed it and put it on the warmed plate, pouring the pan's juices over the top. The aroma wafting off the top reminded her she hadn't eaten dinner, and neither had her kitten Bronte. Before leaving the kitchen, Liz added a few sprigs of fresh rosemary. Who said the Indialantic couldn't be accommodating?

Back in the dining room she stood at Julian and Dorian's table, and asked, "Mr. Rhodes, would you like me to pick out your side dish from the buffet or would you prefer to get them yourself?"

Dorian took a furtive glance at her fiancé then shot up from her chair. "I'll get them, I know what my Julian likes." She said it more like a mother would to her son, instead of a lover to her betrothed. "And please call him Julian, Lizzy. I've told him that you, your great-aunt and father are like family to me."

He didn't look at Liz, instead addressed his fiancée, "No starchy carbs, Dearest."

Liz handed Dorian the plate and Dorian scurried to the sideboard.

After checking everyone had what they needed and wanting to keep in earshot of the future bride and groom, Liz turned around and grabbed the water pitcher from the buffet. She sidled up to Wren and Garrett's table. "Water, anyone?"

"Not for me," Wren chirped. "I already have my drink." More like drinks, plural, Liz thought, as the girl raised her glass in the air for proof. Wren was on her third umbrella drink, looking bored, occasionally glancing over to Dorian and smiling with a twisted grin when Dorian caught her eye. Her grin was like the one Liz imagined Barnacle Bob having after he played one of his dirty tricks. An example being the time BB kept meowing when Ryan's pup Blackbeard was visiting, causing the dog to chase Betty's innocent feline Caro through the hotel until she climbed the thirty foot palm in the hotel's interior courtyard. Ryan had to get an extension ladder to get her down in true firefighter style.

Garrett smiled politely but said in a serious voice, "When hell freezes over, I'll drink that witchcraft H20."

Liz explained that it wasn't the Sunshine Wiccan Society's bottled water. "In that case," Garrett said, "fill her up!" He held out his glass.

Earlier, when everyone had met for drinks in the lobby, Garrett, who Dorian had explained was not only her accountant but also a quasi-agent, seemed gregarious and outgoing. Now that he was seated with Wren, he nervously fingered the gold nugget at his neck. Perhaps he thought of the charm as a lucky rabbit's foot as he glanced in Dorian's direction with lovesick cow eyes. It seemed obvious he was smitten.

After filling his glass, Liz lingered near the busboy—or in this case—bus*girl* station, stacking dirty dishes, wanting to overhear any conversation between Garrett and Wren. She hoped to get a handle on Wren's true relationship with Dorian's fiancé. However, Wren remained quiet, her gaze glued to Julian's back. No titillating conversation to overhear. Which was just as well seeing Liz should have learned long ago to "mind her own beeswax," an expression Aunt Amelia always used when gossiping about someone.

At the end of the meal, Phoebe pulled a chair next to her mother's and Julian's table and sat, her lower lip in a pout. "Why can't I be your maid of honor and Branson Julian's best man?" She put her hand on Julian's wrist, and matched his glowering stare. "I don't understand, it's not like you have any of your best friends or followers here to fill the spot. If you really cared for my mother..." Phoebe's droning voice reached a crescendo, "you would let her have a bigger wedding."

Julian took her hand off his wrist and dropped it like it had been infected with the plague. "Enough of you and your whining! You're upsetting your mother."

Dorian didn't look upset, it seemed she also wanted an answer.

Phoebe only paused for a second, not about to give up, she said, "Why, Stepdaddy Julian? Why can't Branson be your best man? He told me he introduced you to Mama. Aren't you old pals?"

Julian snapped, "For God's sake, Dorian. I thought you explained things to her?"

Branson sat alone and seemed amused by Phoebe's behavior.

"Phoebe!" Dorian chastised. "What's wrong with you? Ever since coming home from Paris, you've seemed changed."

"Well, losing a father changes you. But I guess it didn't affect Branson, he didn't even bother coming for the funeral."

"That's enough," Dorian told her daughter, firmly. "The restaurant had just opened. Your father was okay with it. They saw each other over the holidays. Please, can we just get along?"

Two tables over, Branson shifted uncomfortably in his chair, glancing at Wren, like he was embarrassed by his sister's behavior.

Wren returned his gaze and smiled.

"You're an idiot, Phoebe," Branson said. "Will you ever learn to think before you speak?"

When Dorian turned her attention back to Julian, Phoebe stuck her tongue out at Branson. He responded with the middle finger. Liz saw Wren smile and give Branson a thumbs-up.

It seemed they had a long weekend ahead. Liz couldn't wait until it was over. Heck, she couldn't wait until this meal was over. She turned to go back to the kitchen where she knew everything was safe and cozy. No witches or warlocks allowed. When she went to push one side of the swinging doors open, something scampered by, then shot like a rocket to the dining room's sideboard. Dorian's ferret leapt on top, grabbed a crab claw from a slab of ice, and took off toward the open doorway into the hallway leading to the lobby.

"Farrah, come back with that!" Dorian chastised, her lips upturned in a smile.

Her smile faded when Julian said softly, but sternly, "What have I told you, Dorian?"

She slunk back down in her chair.

Liz came to her rescue. "I'll try to find her for you."

But she didn't have to because Captain Netherton came trotting in from the kitchen followed by Killer, his huge Great Dane, whose temperament was the opposite of what his name inferred. Killer would probably lick the ferret to death before anything else. The elderly, distinguished captain paused for a second, "That little thief stole one of my U.S. Coast Guard gold cufflinks I got at my retirement. Come Killer, just sniff her out for me." He sped past them with a slight limp.

Dorian called after him, "Her cage is in the Oceana Suite, I'm positive I secured the latch."

Julian gave her another chastising look.

"I did, I remember. I wouldn't put it past one of my darling children to let her out as a prank. In fact, I think I'm sensing which one. Over the years, they've always been jealous of my precious ferrets. You know, darling, without my ermines, I would lose half of my psychic powers when it comes to channeling the dead. Just like your sect with their cats and owls. Farrah doesn't assist me in reading the tarot or someone's palm, but for some reason when one of my pet ferrets is in the room, it's easier to connect with those that have passed to the other side. Plus, they're snuggly companions, just like you my darling. Did you know Cleopatra was buried with her ferret? Wish you'd give Farrah another chance. She did find your father's tiepin that he gave you. She deserves kudos for that."

Julian snorted. "You're stereotyping witches again, Dory. What have I told you? Our new millennium ways are quite different from everyone's vision of witchcraft in seventeenth-century Salem."

Dorian once again looked beaten. She didn't seem the same person Liz had known over the years. Her great-aunt's psychic friend had always seemed upbeat—if anything—too upbeat.

Having had enough drama, for the time being, Liz left the dining room for the sanctity of the Indialantic's kitchen. The same place she ran to as a child when she had a boo-boo and needed Grand-Pierre to apply one of his magic, herbal poultices. She believed in the power of nature's alchemy, so why was it so hard for her to believe white witch Julian Rhodes was all he professed to be? She'd try to be more open-minded. "Try" being the key word. The verdict was still out.

Chapter 5

Later that night, Liz stepped onto her deck, drinking in the tangy salt air, wishing she had enough energy to work on her galleys for *An American in Cornwall*. She was a morning and early afternoon writer, saving the late afternoons and evenings for editing and reading her favorite authors. A tip one of her instructors passed on when Liz decided to become a novelist was to read everything she could, especially from the genre she'd planned on writing. However, she was too beat to think of reading a thing—hers or someone else's. Her home, formerly the hotel's old bathing pavilion, had been converted to a beach house and was in walking distance of the Indialantic. On days when the weather was too foul to write in the hotel's bell tower, her cozy domicile with 180-degree ocean views afforded her the privacy and solitude she needed to write, and at the same time she was only a hug away from her eclectic family.

One thing she wasn't going to miss tonight was her late-night ritual of walking the shoreline. She took the steps down to the ocean. When she reached the sand, she kicked off her sandals, glancing up at the huge moon that reflected saffron like threads of yellow on top of gently rolling waves. Like Dorian had informed them during dinner, the moon was a waxing gibbous with ninety-nine percent illumination. Tomorrow's moon would be full, strategically coordinated with the summer solstice and Julian and Dorian's nuptials on Sunday. Evidently, suns and moons were a big deal to both psychics and witches. Liz was quite partial to them herself.

June was the beginning of the sea turtle nesting season and she knew not to bring a flashlight on nights there wasn't a moon. At the end of the season the hatchlings would make their slow crawl to the sea under a full moon. Looking toward a placid Atlantic, she thought back to the awkward evening meal at the hotel and started her walk north. It was low tide and she saw ahead that a bonfire blazed on the beach fronting the hotel. Bonfires were only allowed by special permit and never during turtle nesting season. She saw two figures. Julian Rhodes and Wren. She crept closer and saw that Wren was holding a folder and pressing it to Julian's chest. She was shouting at him, but Liz couldn't make out her words. Julian was laughing at her, his teeth reflecting moonlight. Then Wren said something and his smile disappeared.

"*Julian. Julian-n-n-n!*," Dorian's voice came loud and strong from above, drowning out the gentle crash of the waves. She stood on the hotel's boardwalk, her head turned to the south. Wren looked up and bolted toward the stairs leading up to the boardwalk. Once there she hid underneath, lost in the shadows.

Liz followed Wren's example. She moved as close to the dune as she could without being noticed, and secreted herself from view.

Soon, she saw Dorian galloping toward Julian, her voice carrying on the breeze, "I was so worried when I saw you weren't on the sofa in the sitting room. Is it because I insisted we don't stay in the same bed before our wedding? It's just after that dream—or nightmare—I don't want to take any chances of Sunday not going smoothly. Are you terribly upset with me, darling?"

He kissed her on the forehead. "Of course not, Dory. I just wanted to clear my head. I'm doing the cleansing ceremony to assure our blissful future and getting ready the items we need for the solstice and our wedding day."

"What would I do without you?

"I was charging the water with moon energy," Julian said. He raised something cupped in his hands up to the moon, then closed his eyes.

"How long have you been down here? Does it take long to charge? And what spell are you performing?"

Liz felt something crawl across her bare left foot. She stifled a scream, hoping it was just a small sand crab not a huge land crab that only came to the shore to lay its eggs. Their pincers were strong enough to snap off a toe. Or two. She relaxed when she realized it was June. Next month was when they laid their eggs.

She saw Julian grab Dorian's hand and they stepped closer to the stairs. "It's been long enough to charge the water, Dory. Let's go up. After we're married, I will protect you with my physical presence, instead of just wellness spells."

Liz waited to come out of hiding until after she saw Wren slink up the steps. Wanting to make sure the fire had been completely snuffed out, she made her way over to where they'd been standing. It hadn't. She used her foot to kick sand over the glowing embers.

Before heading to her beach house, Liz took a second to breathe in the salt air. It was as if she was the only person on the planet and the universe had bestowed upon her a moonlit seascape for her eyes only. Or, hopefully soon, for her and Ryan's eyes only. *Two days*, she told herself. Then she was free to get back to her blissful island life. She turned to follow the shoreline south and had a feeling that she was being watched. Glancing up to her right, she thought she saw movement behind a palm near the Indialantic's boardwalk. She glimpsed a figure in black wearing a baseball cap. Just as Susannah had told her about earlier. Feeling angry and vulnerable at the same time, she called up. "Who's there? Show yourself! This is private property." There was a flash of black, then, whoever it was, disappeared from view.

A few minutes later as she climbed the steps to her beach house, she mused about all the crazy things going on since the Wiccan leader and his cousin arrived. Even though psychic Dorian didn't seem to be trusting hers, Liz trusted her intuition that Julian wasn't a good match for Dorian. Had Dorian known that Wren and Julian had been on the beach together? Was that why she'd been so frantic after he'd disappeared from their suite? And who was the baseball capped figure she'd seen up on the boardwalk?

For now, Liz decided to let Dorian deal with her errant fiancé.

Liz had a kitten to feed.

Chapter 6

On Saturday, the Mystical Merfest kept everyone at the Indialantic busy. They were almost sold out of Aunt Amelia's tea, and the other emporium shop owners seemed quite pleased with the amount of traffic visiting their tents. Aunt Amelia had supplied Dorian with her own tent. Even the hundred-dollar fee for a fifteen-minute reading hadn't dissuaded anyone from waiting in the long line snaking its way from the tent and ending at the hotel's old motorcar garage. The garage butted up to the lagoon and at one time you might find a couple of 1930s Rolls Royces inside, or Al Capone's 1928 Cadillac V-8 Town Sedan protected by three thousand pounds of steel, sporting bulletproof windows. Not that it was advertised, especially not in the 1930s, but Capone had been a visitor to the Indialantic by the Sea and Aunt Amelia had the hotel register to prove it.

The garage now housed Pierre's vintage motorcycle with attached sidecar. The rest of the space was used for storage when they had to batten down the hatches due to a forecasted hurricane. The motorcycle was in working order, polished and maintained weekly by the hotel's chef. She had the best memories of sitting in the sidecar when she was around age ten. She and Grand-Pierre would hit the nearby Jungle Trail off Highway 510 for a close-up view of the island's natural flora and fauna. With the recent issues with Pierre's memory, Ryan, a motorcycle buff himself, had volunteered once a week to take Pierre around the island in the sidecar. Ryan's kindness to the man Liz thought of as a grandfather was one of the reasons she'd fallen in love with him. She'd learned his sometimes dark brooding good looks hid a heart of gold. They'd both grown in the past months since deciding to be in a committed relationship. However, she couldn't help but be wary. One thing Ryan never talked about was his past relationships in New York. She really didn't want to know. Or did she? Ryan knew every nuance of her relationship with Pulitzer Prize winning author Travis Osterman because it had been all over the national news.

She stuck her chin out and blocked any thoughts of Travis from her mind, then smiled at a passing stroller with a merchild inside. The small girl flapped her glittery tail at Liz in hello. She wore a huge smile, her face smeared with powdered sugar, no doubt from Chief Pierre's French version of funnel cake that Pops was selling in the Deli-casies tent.

Around one, Aunt Amelia sent Liz to check on Dorian and bring her and her fiancé sustenance. The Island Eats food truck was parked in the Indialantic's parking lot. Pops, the owner of the emporium shop, Deli-casies by the Sea, and Sam, the owner of the Island Eats food truck, were old friends and shared a long list of local suppliers, including Chef Pierre, who on his good days supplied amazing French desserts and bread products. Like Aunt Amelia, Ryan's grandfather was a huge supporter of local commerce and never thought of his buddy's food truck as competition. That's the way things were done on the small barrier island.

"Hi Sam, can I please have two of your Cuban sandwich plates with Cajun sweet potatoes fries?" The best item to order were Sam's crab cakes, but she knew to avoid shellfish when it came to Julian. After last night's dinner, Dorian had pulled Liz aside and apologized for the scene in the dining room, explaining that her fiancé was allergic to shellfish, not fish, and he'd asked her to apologize for him. *Doubtful*, Liz had thought. She just hoped Dorian knew what she was getting into. Maybe she did, as in her nightmare. Liz wondered if Dorian was having other ominous premonitions about her intended that she was keeping to herself, letting her heart lead the way instead of trusting her psychic powers. Though not a medium, Liz had done the same thing with her ex, Travis. And look where that had gotten her.

"Coming right up, Liz." At the word Liz, Sam expelled a whistle through the gap between his two front teeth. Sam reminded her of Aunt Amelia's Howdy Doody ventriloquist doll replica that Kate had found on one her antiquing excursions. Kate had given it to Aunt Amelia, knowing that her first foray into television acting was in 1960 on the final episode of the *Howdy Doody Show*. In Liz's opinion, it wasn't exactly an acting debut, because her great-aunt's job had been to hold the strings for the show's Flub-A-Dub puppet.

As Aunt Amelia had explained to Kate and Liz, Flub-A-Dub was a mixture of eight animals. It had a cocker spaniel's ears, a raccoon's tail, a dachshund's body, a duck's head, a giraffe's neck, a seal's flippers and a cat's whiskers. Kate had said, "That's only seven animals." Aunt Amelia had answered, "I almost forgot, and an elephant's memory." Then she'd pulled out a photo of herself holding Flub-A-Dub, autographed by Buffalo Bob Smith, the actor who did all the puppet's voices.

At the thought of *Bobs*, Liz remembered the irritating fact that whenever Barnacle Bob heard the words, Howdy Doody, he'd start repeating, "Say, kids, what time is it? It's Howdy Doody.... Time," then he'd break into a macaw's version of the show's theme song, "It's Howdy Doody time, it's Howdy Doody time..." ad nauseum. And instead of chastising the dirty bird, Aunt Amelia would always roar with laughter. Liz smiled at the memory.

Sam's son came back to the window and handed Liz two paper plates of food. He was an exact replica of his father, with the same red hair, wide nose covered in freckles and large ears, along with the same space between his teeth. Only in his case, his mouth was filled with braces and a retainer. She took the plates then held them up to him. He leaned out the window holding a plastic squeeze bottle filled with a spicy, pale peach mango ketchup and drizzled it over the sweet potato fries. "Dad said the food's on the house because your father did such a great job getting his permits cleared with the town."

"Tell him I said thank you." Her father had struck again, always helping the locals. Sometimes his clients would pay it forward in produce, seafood, and free repairs when things needed fixing at the almost hundred-year-old hotel—an almost constant occurrence.

On her way to Dorian's tent, she saw Julian standing in the shadow of an oak tree. Hanging moss hid the person he was talking to, or more succinctly, yelling at. Julian's face was controlled but his hands were clenched in fists. There was something attractive about Julian's long light brown hair that today fell to his shoulders. Even from a distance his arctic-blue eyes drew you to his handsome face.

Balancing a plate in each hand she took a detour behind the tents to get closer to the action. When she reached the back of Sirens by the Sea's tent, she inched up to a nearby palm and hid behind it. She spotted Garrett, Dorian's financial advisor. He must be the person that had Julian so riled up.

Garrett took a step toward Julian, clutching a piece of paper in his hand. "All you have to do is sign, buddy boy. Show that you really care and you're not marrying her for her money. I've been looking into your financial affairs at the SWS and things look pretty sketchy. Especially when it comes to your Sunshine miracle water. I'll keep those details to myself if you sign. Dorian and her children won't hear a peep from me."

"I'm not your 'buddy boy,' and I certainly won't be blackmailed by you."
Julian raised his closed fist and brought it up to Garrett's chin.

Garrett had to be about five inches taller and probably weighed at least
fifty pounds more. He was solid like the oak he stood next to.

Julian continued in a calmer voice, "Dorian and I love each other. Do
what you will, but I also have something to parley back at you. It seems
Dorian and I have discussed her future and things are looking promising
that I might take over your lackluster role as financial advisor and agent.
I've had my own accountant looking into last year's financials. The numbers
just don't seem to jive, buddy boy."

"That's ridiculous!" Garrett shouted, "I've never mismanaged a penny.
I've been with her for almost thirty years and she's had more than enough
money to spend as she wishes."

"I suppose you okayed the money to open her loser son's restaurant.
If that's your idea of a good investment, you better get with the times."

"Oh, I see where you're going with this. You want Dorian to sink more
money into that hocus-pocus medicine man water you're peddling. You
don't give your fiancée enough credit, Mr. Warlock. Oh, I forgot you're a
white witch not a warlock. Same evil practices I'm sure. Just white washing
your title doesn't change the things I've heard about your little operation.
Whatever spell you've put on Dorian, it didn't work when it came to the
water, did it? She has good business sense and nixed your expansion plans.
Dorian told me you're a self-made man with only a high school diploma.
Maybe you should sign up for junior college, take a few business classes.
Of course, it would be years before you could earn an MBA like I have,
not to mention passing your CPA exams."

Liz watched Julian's face turn from rosy pink to burning red. He didn't
even budge when Garrett bent down and gave him a light push on the
shoulder.

"Don't you touch me!" Julian put both hands on Garrett's wide chest
and pushed. Nothing happened.

Garrett laughed. Even though he was decades older than Julian, his
red hair and solid body reminded Liz of a Viking ready for battle. "You'll
have to do better than that, buddy boy," he spat.

It was then that Ryan's dog, Blackbeard came barreling toward her. As
if in slow motion, she watched the huge mutt stop dead center in front
of her, bark, then jump up and grab one of the plates from her hand and
carry it off between his teeth. "Come back with that, you little scamp!"
she shouted. Both men turned toward her as she watched Blackbeard drop

the plate and almost inhale the sandwich and fries in under five seconds. Julian scowled and Garrett grinned.

She had no choice but to lie as she walked up to them, holding the remaining plate in front of her. "Mr. Rhodes, Dorian sent me to deliver you some lunch. Cuban sandwiches." Then she chattered on about the Mystical Mermaid Festival and the story of Meribel, until both men looked bored. At least she'd diffused the situation.

Finally, Julian said, more like demanded, "Bring my food to Dorian's tent. We'll eat together. I have something important to discuss with her that won't wait." Then he fixed his gaze on Garrett, "Don't forget to pay this bill that Dorian signed off on. He reached in the pocket of his pants and fished out a folded piece of paper, then stuffed it into Garrett's free hand. Garrett's other hand held what Liz assumed was a prenuptial agreement.

Through gritted teeth, Garrett said, "I think I'll ask her myself. I wouldn't put it past you to forge her signature." Realizing he had an audience, Garrett turned to Liz. "I'd love to get some local food. Point me in the right direction."

"Island Eats food truck. It's across from Dorian's tent. Tell him Liz sent you."

"Thank you, Liz."

She watched him walk in the direction she pointed to. When she turned back, Julian strode up to her. He was so close she could smell his minty breath. "About that tent you set up for Dorian. Whose idea was it? Hers or your aunt's? Trying to use the poor woman to make an extra buck for your crumbling hotel? I am totally against the whole idea. It's too much exposure."

Reining in what she really wanted to say, something along the line of *You're a pompous ass, Dorian deserves better*, she said, "Aunt Amelia's my *great*-aunt. I'm pretty sure the tent was Dorian's idea, not Auntie's. One of the reasons Dorian planned your wedding at our hotel was because it was the same weekend as this fabulous festival." She spread her arms to encompass the parking lot. She didn't see one unhappy face in the boisterous crowd.

"That's not what Dorian told me. She said it was your *auntie's* idea. I'll be sure to have a talk with her. It's time people stopped trying to take advantage of her because of her advanced age."

Who did he think he was marrying? His grandmother? His words, "poor woman" and "advanced age" didn't fit the dynamic Dorian Starwood Liz knew. "I assure you, Mr. Rhodes, no one at the Indialantic, including Aunt Amelia, would ever take advantage of Dorian. Our family has known her for years." She wanted to ask how long he'd known his fiancée, but she kept quiet for Dorian's sake.

"Bring the food to her *circus* tent and we'll lunch together. That way I can keep an eye on her."

Heard you the first time. She wanted to give him a military salute and click her sandals together. Instead, she bit the inside of her cheek and chirped, "Will do, Mr. Rhodes."

He didn't respond but his ice-blue gaze showed triumph. Then he turned and walked away.

After she picked up the abandoned plate that Blackbeard left behind, she realized she had to place another order of food for Dorian. Not in the mood to get in line behind Garrett, she ran up to Aunt Amelia's boyfriend, Ziggy and enlisted his help in getting two more orders of food, then she found a table in the open dining tent and sat. Even though she'd already shared an order of sea scallop kabobs with Ryan, she had no problem cleaning the remaining plate of food in about the same time as Ryan's dog. Even cold, the sandwich and the sweet potato fries were delicious. Wiping her mouth with a napkin, she glanced toward the Indian River Lagoon. Rosie, the Indialantic's mascot rosette tern, was on her favorite piling. Calm and unbothered by all the commotion around her. Liz wished she could say she was unbothered after the little fracas she'd just witnessed between Dorian's fiancé and financial advisor. She pondered what business it was of hers. *None.* Dorian was a mature adult with a good head on her shoulders. Then she remembered how Dorian had carried on about her nightmare, and the fact she'd mentioned something cryptic when she'd said, "After what happened…" What *had* happened? Then there was the subservient way Dorian had acted last night at dinner.

Gathering her plate, fork and napkin, she headed for the nearest trash receptacle, wishing she had some of Pierre's thirst quenching lemon-limeade before she met Ziggy for the hand off of Dorian and Julian's food. As she took a step toward her and Ziggy's designated meeting place, a piece of paper flitted toward her like a moth to a flame and flattened itself to her right leg. She bent and picked it up, then quickly glanced at it. It wasn't a prenup. Instead, it was the folded piece of paper Julian had just handed Garrett—a four-hundred-thousand-dollar invoice for a water filtration system.

She knew from reading the label on the Sunshine Wiccan Society's water yesterday that the water was bottled at the source of the SWS's grounds in Jacksonville. The invoice for the filtration system had a delivery address in Ocala. Maybe the society planned on moving? She stowed the invoice away, thinking how she would get it to Garrett without him knowing she'd been listening to his and Julian's conversation. She wished the Indialantic's resident teenage mystery writer, Betty, were here as a sounding board. Ryan would listen, but he would tell her that not everything was a conundrum to be sorted out, or some Machiavellian plot.

One thing was for sure; there were a lot of interesting dynamics going on with the players in the Starwood-Rhodes wedding weekend.

After Ziggy passed her the two hot plates, he went in search of Aunt Amelia. Liz headed in the direction of Dorian's tent. Out of the corner of her eye she saw Garrett next to Rosie's flower truck talking to a man wearing a black baseball cap. As soon as Garrett noticed her, he waved in her direction. He said something to the man and he disappeared into a throng of festival goers. Was that the figure she'd seen last night on the boardwalk? The same person Susannah spied in the Indialantic's garden? Or just someone wearing a black baseball cap? If this was the mystery person, she knew one thing for sure, he was male.

Chapter 7

Liz parted the beads to Dorian's tent and felt like she was stepping into Jeannie's bottle from the mid-century television show Aunt Amelia had a few guest parts in, *I Dream of Jeannie*. Velvet cushions and pillows in jewel tones trimmed with gold tassels were scattered on the floor. New age music played and there was smoke and the scent of sandalwood escaping from four brass incense holders in each corner of the tent. Dorian sat with a blonde haired woman wearing a cheery watermelon print sundress at a round table and was in the process of scooping up a bunch of tarot cards. She looked up and gave Liz a weak smile, then placed the deck of cards next to her crystal ball. Also in front of her was an empty teacup, an indigo china teapot decorated with a crescent moon and stars, along with a Ouija type board. No letters were on the board only hieroglyphic type symbols. Above the board, pointing down from a chain, was a crystal in the shape of a Native American arrowhead. Liz knew from her great-aunt's readings in the past, nothing on Dorian's table were mere props. Dorian believed in choosing whatever conduit seemed most natural to befit the person she was having a session with.

The woman in the sundress stood. "Thank you, Madame Starwood. It was such a blessing to meet you in person. I understand completely what you're saying about my brother. You've given me such peace and closure." She smiled as she passed Liz on the way to the exit. "Best hundred dollars I've spent. You don't even have to tell her why you're here. She knows." She clutched Dorian's latest book in her hand, pushed aside the beads, and walked out into the sunlight. A definite lightness to her step.

"Another satisfied customer, I see." Liz went to the table and placed the two plates of food on top. "Auntie insists that you break for a late lunch. I also ran into your intended. He said he'll come here so you can eat together. You look a little peaked as Auntie says. Why don't you start without him while the food's still hot?"

Dorian looked the opposite of the young woman who'd just left. She had major bags under her eyes that she'd tried to cover with makeup, only causing her wrinkles to stand out more sharply. She looked every bit her seventy years. "I'll wait."

How did Liz know she'd say that? She sat in the vacated chair and leaned in to meet Dorian's downcast eyes. "You must be excited about the rehearsal dinner on board *Queen of the Seas*. The whole ship is at your disposal. I told you the weather would be beautiful."

She didn't answer.

"Are you okay, Dorian? No cold feet, I hope."

That didn't seem to be the right thing to say, because Dorian burst into tears. Through her tears she gave Liz a knowing look, like she was cognizant of what Liz was thinking when it came to Julian Rhodes. Something was squirrelly about her intended. Then she remembered all the people who'd tried to get her to see her ex-boyfriend Travis for who he was. Maybe if she had listened, a murder might not have taken place.

"I've had another premonition," Dorian said. "Only this time it was when I was wide awake. It had something to do with water. And a warning from my dead ex-husband to watch my back. I haven't seen Cedric for years. Have to admit he looked quite handsome." She smiled and there was a mischievous twinkle in her eye. That was the Dorian Starwood Liz knew over the years. Joking, kind, and modest. Dorian smiled. "I'm being silly. Yes, the cruise tonight will be splendid." She leaned in closer and whispered, "I am so sorry that even Amelia can't be on board for the rehearsal dinner. I had to make a pact with Julian that if Garrett was invited no one else except family would be."

Placing her hand on Dorian's, Liz said, "No worries. Auntie will be busy anyway because of the Mermaid Regatta, but she'll be front and center for your wedding tomorrow morning. As will Dad and I."

"I have to ask you a favor."

"Sure."

Dorian cast her gaze to the floor. "I told Julian the tent was Amelia's idea. He doesn't understand how much I love getting back to my roots and also the money will go to my favorite charity. I'm sorry I told a fib, but I've found sometimes it's easier."

"Uhm, sure. But there might be a little problem. He already confronted me about it and I told him I thought it was your idea. I'm so sorry, Dorian. If he asks me again, I'll say it was Auntie's idea."

"No worries, my dear. I need to stand up for myself but sometimes it's easier to tell a fib. Julian is so worried about me, I think sometimes it borders on the obsessive."

"How long have you two known each other?"

"It will be six months to the day, tomorrow."

"Did you meet at the Sunshine Wiccan Society?"

"Oh, no. I've never been there. The coven's temple is getting a renovation. Julian wants to wait until it is finished to present it to me. It's part of my wedding present."

That and the salt-rock engagement ring, Liz thought. "Have you met any of the society's members?"

"No. We've been busy traveling the world. Just the two of us. It was my son who introduced us when Julian came into his restaurant. A serendipitous meeting. Thank you, Liz. I feel better already just talking to you and remembering how lucky I am."

"There you are Dory!" Julian strode in and stood behind Liz. She swore she could feel the hairs on the back of her neck stand on end, or maybe it was the fan blowing a cloud of incense her way.

He looked down at a stack of Phoebe's glossy hardcover superstition books, opened the top one and sneered. "I see your daughter's been here. Dropped the books you coerced your publisher to print, then she disappeared to spend more of your money."

Dorian turned her gaze to Liz in embarrassment. Liz, who had scurried to the corner of the tent when he'd walked in, pretended to be looking at a display of Dorian's books. She smiled back at Dorian and nodded her head, *it's all good.*

When Julian saw Liz, he said, "Good. The food's here." Then, almost grudgingly, he added, "Thank you…"

"Liz," Dorian said to refresh her fiancé's memory, then Dorian got up from her chair and went toward him.

He gave her a kiss on the lips. Definitely not one you would give your mother or grandmother. "Let me get you some water, love." He went to a silver tub set on a small table. Crowning from the ice were the necks of cobalt glass bottles of SWS mineral water. He grabbed one, untwisted the cap and handed the bottle to Dorian.

Then he offered one to Liz, adding, "I notice you have a brisk business in your deli at the emporium. I guarantee if you carried some of our SWS water you'd make a tidy profit."

"What a great idea," Dorian said.

"I'll pass that on to Pops. And thanks, I'd love to try a bottle." She walked over and reached for the bottle in his hand, curious about its magic powers. When her fingers touched his, she felt once again his otherworldly magnetism and heat flushed her cheeks. "Well, you guys better eat before it gets cold. Oh, and I asked if their fries were cooked in the same oil as their clams and shrimp and they said they weren't."

A rare smile bloomed on Julian's face. He said in his rich velvety voice, "Thank you, Liz."

Taken aback by his change of attitude she made an excuse to exit the tent. As soon as she stepped outside, she heard Dorian say in a strained voice, "Your cousin was here, Darling. She insisted I give her a reading for free. Seeing as you're family, I did it for you. But I don't understand why she's here and why you never mentioned her before?"

An elderly person passed by Liz, then stepped into the tent. Liz heard Julian say, "She's closed. There will be no more readings today."

What a jerk, Liz thought as she walked toward Deli-casies' tent. She'd almost convinced herself that perhaps Julian did have Dorian's welfare at heart.

Almost.

Chapter 8

It was five o'clock. Liz and Ryan were seated on a white cushioned bench in the stern of *Serendipity*, her father's vintage Chris-Craft cabin cruiser. They'd dropped anchor a couple of hundred feet from the Indialantic's dock and waited alongside a dozen of other boats for the Mystical Merfest Regatta Boat Parade to pass by, wanting to cheer Kate and Aunt Amelia on. Kate had been chosen as the parade's mermaid princess, Meribel. Soon, she and her sweetie merman prince, Alex, would be approaching; flapping their tails, waving at onlookers, and tossing hibiscus flowers at spectators moored on the Indian River Lagoon. Aunt Amelia would be traveling on the second boat, representing the Melbourne Beach Theatre Players. Ever since its inception, she'd been given one part or another. Always stealing the show. Francie, expert seamstress and part owner of the Indialantic's emporium shop Home Arts by the Sea, had designed both Kate's, Alex's, and Aunt Amelia's mermaid tails.

Aunt Amelia would be dressed in the costume for her next play, *The Sea Witch*. Naturally, she had the lead role as the Sea Witch. If Liz knew her great-aunt, her costume would be something spectacular and no doubt she would use items from her arsenal of clothing and accessories stored in her room sized closet. Her closet and half of the hotel's old luggage room were packed with swag given to her from costume and set designers from her glory days as a mid-century television actress.

"About time!" Liz joked, as her father stepped up from *Serendipity's* cabin bearing a tray topped with a couple of bottles of local craft beer and two glasses of rosé. Behind him, his fiancée, Charlotte, followed with a fruit and cheese platter. Her father and Agent Charlotte Pearson, lead detective for the Brevard County Sheriff's Department, had gotten engaged under the mistletoe on Christmas Eve. It was rare that Charlotte wasn't out on a call, and Liz looked forward to spending the evening with her.

When Liz first met Charlotte, she'd come across as cold and reserved. After her engagement to Liz's father, she'd let down her guard, and became more approachable. Charlotte even had a sense of humor, a very dry one, and Liz now counted her as a friend.

"What you guys reading?" Fenton asked.

Liz and Ryan had been looking at an old book Kate had loaned them about the island's history, including a tale about the island's merfolk who saved most of the crew from a shipwreck near the Indialantic's beach. "You're just in time. We were about to read a passage Kate bookmarked about a legend I'd never heard before."

Fenton laughed. "You mean the fable about the sirens, merpeople, and the 1715 Spanish Plate Fleet shipwreck? How the mermaid Meribel helped lead the survivors to shore and then guarded the sunken treasure until she was outsmarted by an evil siren, almost drowned in a hurricane conjured up by said siren until her merman savior rescued her?"

"No. Not that one, Dad," Liz said, laughing. "This is a different mermaid story but same island. This one takes place much later. It's from a book called, *Island Folklore of Central East Coast Florida*. It has a date of 1938. This particular story…"

"Legend," her father corrected.

"Semantics. This passage was transcribed from a local woman's diary and given a chapter in the book by the author."

Her father handed them their drinks and sat across from them. "I'm not putting down these mystical mermaid tales. In fact, I remember my great-grandmother telling it to me as we sat on the hotel's veranda. It's just two mermaid tales on one island seems a little coincidental, don't you think? I know Katie believes everything she reads in books, fiction or nonfiction, has some magical power."

"And you don't?" Liz asked, incredulously. Her father was the biggest bibliophile she knew, having access to both the hotel's mammoth library and his own packed shelves in his apartment.

"You mean the way Kate talks to the them like they're living, breathing creatures?" Charlotte grinned, placed the cheese platter on the table, and took a seat. "I've almost gotten used to Kate's antics and have to catch myself when I'm reading, trying not to talk back to a character I'm unhappy with." She turned and looked at her fiancé. "Fenton, you're so unromantic. I don't think there's anything wrong with believing the fantasy that mermaids exist."

He gave her a surprised look. "Did you ever hear of the Feejee Mermaid?"
They shook their heads in the negative.

"I think it was in the 1840s, P. T. Barnum put on a display of a mermaid
under glass. People paying to see it must have been disappointed, expecting
the beautiful mermaids in the legends we know about."

"What did they see?" Ryan asked.

"They saw a dead monkey's head, arms and torso attached to the bottom
part of a fish."

"Eww, creepy," Liz said, feeling queasy. Not knowing if it was from
disgust at the thought of Barnum's grotesque sideshow hoax, or the rocking
of the waves caused by the wake of a passing boat. She remembered trips
as a child to Ripley's Believe it or Not museum in Orlando and knew the
shrunken heads she'd seen were authentic.

"Fenton," Charlotte chastised, "let us believe the fantasy, after all this
is our Mystical Merfest Weekend and you just caused a mermaid to lose
her scales with that story."

"Like an angel loses its wings in *It's a Wonderful Life*?" her father
said, laughing. He made his hand into fist like it was a judge's gavel, then
tapped it on the table. "Hear ye, hear ye. Quiet in the court. 'Just the facts.'
Pragmatic, Agent Charlotte Odette Pearson, just used the word *fantasy*?"

"Odette," Liz repeated. "From the ballet *Swan Lake*? Charlotte, were
you a dancer?"

"No, my mother was, and she'll never let me forget I didn't follow in
her footsteps. More like stumbled in them with my size ten feet. I was way
too tall to be a ballerina. Although, my proper straight-edged mother tried
to make me one. After years of dance instruction, she finally gave up. It
had been a waste of money. I would have rather been out riding one of
our horses. Why are parents so intent on living vicariously through their
children? That's why I never planned on having any."

Her father was in his mid-fifties and Charlotte in her mid-forties. Liz
grinned. "I always wanted a little brother or sister."

Charlotte laughed.

"You have Kate," her father answered, almost spitting out his beer.

The boat rocked again from a powerboat's wake and Charlotte grabbed
her fiancé's arm. "What about your *fantasy* football games, Fenton? A
little fantasy goes a long way in life." Instead of sticking to the cold, hard
facts, Agent Pearson was channeling her inner child.

"Hear! Hear!" Ryan said, with a grin. "Always wondered what the
difference was between a siren and a mermaid. Are sirens like the
emporium's Brittany Poole at Sirens by the Sea?"

Ryan knew how to rile Liz by bringing up the subject of Brittany. Brittany had been Liz's arch nemesis all through her school days. While Liz had been away in New York, Aunt Amelia, lover of all people and pets, had rented the space to Brittany and now the woman seemed intent on following Ryan around like a sick puppy even though she knew Liz and Ryan were in a committed relationship. However, she did have to give Brittany credit for having a beautiful assortment of women's clothing and accessories in the emporium.

"Sirens lure poor lost sailors to the rocks with their high-pitched singing, then watch them sink, aiding pirates to their booty. Brittany lures men, then watches them crash and burn, like she almost did to Kate's brother Skylar."

"Now, now. Lizzy, that's old news," her father admonished. He was also the type to see the best in everyone. Defender of the innocent until proven guilty.

"Kate wants to donate the book to the Barrier Island Historical Society," Liz said. "This is our only window to read it."

"Fenton can't wait to hear it. Right, darling?" Charlotte fed him a grape before he could protest. "In honor of the Mystical Merfest, I think we should listen to your daughter read the passage."

"Fine. And I'll keep my eyes peeled for any mermaids." Fenton grabbed a piece of artisan truffled cheese from the tray.

Liz elbowed Ryan. "How come you never feed me grapes?"

"Uh, because it's something done in one of your romantic comedies. Or your auntie's. 'Oh Gidget, oh Moondoggie,' I'm too macho for that." He plucked a grape and fed it to her.

He was referring to the old movie *Gidget* starring Sandra Dee and James Darren. Liz would never let on that *Gidget* was also in her top ten of romcoms.

Aunt Amelia always told Liz she had an old soul. Probably, due to all the old television and films her great-aunt had exposed her to over the years. "That's more like it, buster. Hey, look over there," she said, pointing. A bunch of bald dark-gray heads were swimming in their direction. Liz said, "Speaking of legends, many old sightings of merfolk were found out later to be manatees or sea cows. It's because of the shape of their round heads and fingerlike flippers."

Ryan leaned over to pat one of the manatees. "They're so friendly, like dolphins."

"Very loving," Liz added. "They travel in packs, keeping their young in the center. And if one of them is wounded, they all try to save it." Ever since moving to the island at age five, Liz had been schooled in the many attributes of the gentle sea creatures. "So, shall I read about the newer mermaid legend?"

"You know, I've been teasing you daughter. I'd love to hear it," Fenton said, "but first clue me in on the wedding party and how things are going with Auntie's grand scheme to turn the Indialantic into a destination venue?"

"As we speak, everyone is on *Queen of the Seas* for the rehearsal dinner." Liz glanced behind at the empty slip at the end of the Indialantic's dock. "They plan to end the cruise near the inlet and catch the tail end of the boat parade. I, for one, am happy I wasn't invited to the rehearsal dinner, even if the dinner menu looked fabulous."

"After everything I witnessed yesterday, I'll second that." Ryan took a swig of his beer. "Good choice, Fenton." He tipped the bottle in Fenton's direction.

Fenton clanked his bottle against Ryan's. "This one came from a new microbrewery in Sebastian. Just a hint of orange. I know you like those craft beers. I'm still trying to get used to them. But I'm all for supporting local businesses."

Liz filled her father and Charlotte in on what went down yesterday with the surprise addition of Julian Rhodes's supposed cousin, Wren, the weird dinner hour, followed by the scene on the beach, and the person in the baseball cap. "I don't know about Aunt Amelia, but I can't wait until Monday morning rolls along."

"Wren is such an unusual name," Charlotte said, popping a chocolate covered almond in her mouth. "Did she get invited on the boat for the rehearsal dinner?"

"She certainly did," Liz answered. "Susannah said she'd insisted. Also, Greta told me there was quite a scene last night when Julian found out Susannah would be serving the food for the dinner on *Queen of the Seas* and that Ashley would be taking photos."

Charlotte looked at Ryan. "Ashley, your part time barista at Deli-casies?"

"She just graduated high school. She'll only be with us until August when she goes to college, majoring in fine arts. Quite a talented photographer and barista. We're gonna miss her."

"There's something shady about this Julian Rhodes," Liz said. "He's twenty-five years younger than Dorian and he's obsessed with privacy and seems very controlling."

Ryan laughed, "Not to mention he's a warlock."

"He told Auntie he's officially a white male witch, not a warlock. Supposedly, no one uses the term warlock anymore. Guess it goes against the 'sunshine' part of the Sunshine Wiccan Society tableau." Liz saw her father and Charlotte exchange peaked eyebrows. "What's up, you two? Spill."

"Well..." Her father glanced at Charlotte and she nodded in assent. "There've been a few threatening letters dropped off at Dorian's home in Palm Beach."

Charlotte took a sip of wine, then put her glass in the swinging drink holder bolted to the edge of the table, a handy thing in case the boat got hit with a huge wave. "Before arriving on the island, Ms. Starwood's financial advisor contacted the Sheriff's department about the incident and sent us copies of the letters."

"What did the letters say?" Liz knew what was coming.

"I'm not at liberty to tell you. Just want you to know the situation in case you see anyone lurking around."

Liz thought about the guy in the baseball cap. "Were they death threats?"

No answer.

Chapter 9

The boat swayed in the gentle evening breeze and for a moment they all took advantage of the perfect evening. The sun was setting, the sky rosy with promises of a sailor's delight. In the far distance, Liz heard music. The Mystical Merfest Regatta Boat Parade was fast approaching.

"Okay, enough about psychics and witches, who wants to hear about mermaids?" Even though the sun was lower in the early evening sky, she pulled her wide brimmed straw hat down to protect her scar. It would always be visible, no matter how many surgeries she had, and she'd made peace with it. Things could have turned out way worse, and almost had.

She didn't wait for their consent and began to read a short passage.

"Wow," Charlotte said as Liz closed the book. "That was certainly apropos for today's festivities. What did you think, Fenton?"

Her father winked at Ryan, "A fanciful tale that's for sure. I'd like to hear a man's version of it. The way Ernest Hemingway would tell it."

Ryan raised his beer and said, "Something like this…The storm came in. The ship capsized. A big fish saved the drowning sailors."

Fenton laughed.

"A lot of people put down Hemingway's simple style," Liz said, "but he was a master of dialog. His dialog was what told the story. There were times when he never gave any description of the surroundings or what his characters looked like, just revealed their true nature through dialog. I also read that for all of Hemingway's simple sounding prose, he revised his stories and novels so many times it became an obsession. He was quoted as saying, 'A writer's words should be simple and vigorous.' I believe good writing is a combination of both, and if this was written by a child, I think she did a darn good job. Not girly or fanciful as you're implying, Dad."

"Hemingway was a chauvinist," Charlotte said, simply. "But he also told a darn good yarn, just like your mermaid storyteller."

"That was a simple analysis," Liz said, laughing, "but I like it."

Before they went on to discussing different authors writing styles, they heard the sound of steel drums and calypso music filter toward them from the north.

"Here they come," Ryan said, standing.

The rest of them stood, balancing on their sea legs as the boat swayed and waited until the lead forty-three-foot sailboat came into view. Kate sat on the bow, facing them, while Alex's back faced the mainland to the west. Kate's mermaid tail was exquisite, its jewel-toned sequins reflecting the waning sun in dazzling splendor. She was very much the mermaid Meribel, her gold crown studded with colored rhinestones over her long brown shiny hair. Waving with both her hand and her tail, Kate shouted, "Isn't this a blast! Meet you at Ryckman Park in an hour. The skipper said he'd drop us."

They all waved back. Fenton blasted the foghorn and when the boat came nearer, Charlotte shouted to Kate, "Magnificent mermaid's tail!" Then she snapped a dozen photos with her phone.

Kate tossed a few hibiscus flower heads onto the *Serendipity* and the sailboat continued south toward the Sebastian Inlet where the *Queen of the Seas* would be moored and waiting for the tail end of the Mystical Merfest Boat Regatta. Something Aunt Amelia had commandeered for the rehearsal dinner guests' viewing pleasure.

As Kate's sailboat pulled away, Aunt Amelia's boat came into view. On the side of the boat was a banner. Centered inside the graphic of a mermaid's tail was the tagline: *The Melbourne Beach Theatre presents Sea Witch—not your typical Fairy Tail.* The word "tail" purposely used instead of tale. Liz wasn't sure it worked, but it was fun all the same. And no doubt her great-aunt's idea. Aunt Amelia was smiling and waving. Instead of hibiscus heads, she was throwing gray rubber fish. At least, Liz thought they were rubber. Her great-aunt's face and body were painted a glossy blue-green and she wore a long red wig with a single braid that fell over her left shoulder and hit below her waistline. Around her neck was a scarf of seaweed. Liz also hoped that wasn't real.

Fenton laughed. "I see Auntie's drab, army green and black mermaid's tail. But what the heck is she wearing on top?"

"What's she supposed to be?" Ryan asked. "Don't tell me she's playing the Little Mermaid? She's not little and…Why do I bother, I should know by now, there is no part she can't play."

"Just go with it and blow her a kiss. All will be revealed next Saturday. Opening night." Liz raised both hands in the air and waved frantically, calling out, "Brava! Brava!"

Aunt Amelia spotted them and lifted what looked like the pitchfork from the famous painting "American Gothic." Liz guessed it was meant to be a trident. For her bikini top, she must have gotten inspiration from years ago being on the set of *Gilligan's Island*. She'd taken a coconut from one the Indialantic's trees, cracked it in half, then glued one to either side of a bikini swimsuit top. All in all, Aunt Amelia made quite the voluptuous Sea Witch, perfect for her part in the theater's upcoming production about a misunderstood sea witch, *loosely* based on Hans Christian Andersen's 1836 story, *The Little Mermaid*. The script from the play had been written by her great-aunt with a little, okay, a lot, of tweaking from Liz.

"Hope she doesn't fall and break something in that getup," Fenton said, "you know how excited she gets when she's 'in character'."

"She seems confident she won't," Liz answered, "and assures me that after watching Carolyn Jones wiggling around in her formfitting black spider skirt on the set of TV's *The Addams Family,* she'd learned a few tricks." Liz hadn't asked what they were, but Aunt Amelia had passed on two anyway. "Don't drink any liquids in case you have to go the restroom and use Vaseline on your legs to get the tail on and off. Just like you do when putting on leather pants."

Leather pants! Aunt Amelia? Luckily, that was one thing Liz had never witnessed her wearing.

Charlotte laughed. "So that's why she brought me to her viewing room to show me her cameo as Uncle Foster's love interest in the old sitcom."

"It's Uncle Fester not Foster," Fenton added, joining in the laughter.

Fenton said, "Hopefully when *Queen of the Seas* pulls into port, everyone will make it an early night, and be refreshed for the wedding, Auntie included. In less than twenty-four hours she'll be able to rest her dogs."

"Her barking dogs. Although I've never known Auntie to rest anything," Liz added. Did she have to worry about both Aunt Amelia's health and Grand-Pierre's? Both eighty and both precious to her. Without them she didn't know how she'd go on. She didn't have time to think about it because the hotel's eco-tour sightseeing ship, *Queen of the Seas* came out of nowhere, heading toward them at full throttle, its horn blaring in SOS beats.

"Dad, Look!"

Fenton stood, immediately went to the wheel, and started the engine. The regatta spectator boats next to them also started their engines. Captain

Netherton was at the wheel. As the ship came closer, she heard his voice over the loudspeaker, "Clear the end of the dock. We have an emergency!"

There wasn't any billowing smoke or flames shooting from the portholes of the engine room, but Liz did see Ashley, Phoebe, Branson, Garrett, and Wren standing stiffly at the ship's guardrail.

Where were Dorian, Julian, and Susannah?

Had they fallen overboard?

Or something much worse?

Chapter 10

On a scale of one to a million, what had transpired on *Queen of the Seas* was close to a 999,999. An extra point taken away because there was some good news—with the exception of one person—everyone was alive.

When the *Queen of the Seas* docked, Liz tried to run on board. "Oh no you don't, Liz." Charlotte morphed into her official role of detective Agent Pearson. "You know you aren't allowed on the boat until I check it out." Then she turned to her fiancé. "Fenton, when my team arrives, please send them and the paramedics inside. I trust you'll make sure no one leaves or comes on board."

"Okay, we'll make sure," Liz answered for her father. Before Charlotte could correct her pronoun usage, she continued, "Don't you think Ryan would be an asset until the ambulance arrives? He's had emergency training from being on the FDNY."

Charlotte hesitated, then said, "Okay, Ryan, come along."

Liz and her father stood sentry at the foot of the gangplank. Liz felt awkward and kept her gaze toward shore, avoiding the quizzical eyes of those above them on the ship.

Garrett called down, "What's going on? Why can't we get off?"

Fenton called up, "Please be patient, sir. Agent Pearson is on board checking on the situation."

When Fenton asked his daughter who the man was, Liz quickly explained. She also pointed out who *cousin* Wren was.

Only a few minutes passed until they heard sirens. Just as the ambulances and sheriff's cars pulled up, Liz saw Charlotte and Ryan coming down the gangway with Dorian. Each holding an arm. Captain Netherton followed behind the trio. In one hand he held what looked like a white linen tablecloth turned into a knapsack and in the other, Farrah's cage. The ferret's black raisin eyes peered out from beyond the mesh screen. Too bad ferrets couldn't talk like macaws, Farrah might tell them a thing or two.

Dorian wore a long, gossamer, full-length gown with flowing sleeves in a kaleidoscope of jewel-toned colors. Liz noticed her salt-rock engagement ring was missing. Dorian stumbled on the dock's uneven planks, and like a curtain, her long violet hair covered her face. When she flipped back her head, purple rivulets of mascara ran down her tear streaked cheeks. "I had a premonition," she mumbled, "I'm to blame. There was a curse I should've learned how to reverse." Liz darted over to Dorian, wanting to take her into an embrace.

Charlotte motioned her back. "Better give her some breathing room." What Agent Charlotte Pearson really meant was, *don't compromise evidence, until we know what's going on.*

"He's dead. My Julian's dead." Dorian murmured, incredulously.

Paramedics scurried toward them with two gurneys, followed by four agents from the sheriff's department. One pair of paramedics stopped near Dorian and the other pair hesitated.

Captain Netherton looked at Charlotte. "Should I show them where to go?"

"Please, Clyde, that would be great."

"If it's something he ate," Captain Netherton said, "I thought using the tablecloth to wrap up Mr. Rhodes's dishes would be the quickest way to preserve any contaminated food. We left everything as it was in the stateroom from when Susannah called us in. It only happened a short time ago. I immediately called the coast guard and they told me not to move him, that I should pull into the dock, and wait for the sheriff's department. Of course, I attempted CPR, but it was too late."

Charlotte nodded. "You did good, Captain."

He passed her the tablecloth knapsack just as a coast guard cruiser pulled up next to *Queen of the Seas.* Then, for some reason the captain handed Liz the ferret's cage. She was about to protest, thinking about her kitten Bronte waiting at home and how the two of them would interact. Then she glanced at Dorian's forlorn face and took the cage. "Hey, little guy, I mean gal," Liz said in a soothing tone. Aunt Amelia always taught her to be sensitive to a pet's feelings. However, this particular pet wasn't in her wheelhouse.

Charlotte motioned to an approaching officer. "Tell the coast guard that the Brevard County Sheriff's Department will take over. I'll contact them as soon as I get back to my office."

"Want me to take that tablecloth to one of your officers?" Liz asked. Charlotte gave her a suspicious look. And based on the past, rightly so. "No." She handed the tablecloth and its contents to a young officer who'd been shyly standing away from the action. "Get the food analyzed as soon as possible. We have to know what we're dealing with."

Surprise showed on the young officer's freckled face. She pulled back her shoulders and stood straighter. "You can count on me, Agent Pearson." Then the officer took off down the dock, taking slow steps and swaddling the sack like it contained a delicate robin's egg.

Turning to a sobbing Dorian, Charlotte said in a soothing voice, "I think you should take a trip to the hospital Ms. Starwood, and let them check to make sure you're okay. I'll have your family meet you there."

"Dorian let out another sob and glanced at Liz who was holding Farrah's cage. "Please take care of my baby. She's all I have left. And she will be my only conduit to Julian from this point forward."

Ignoring Charlotte's admonitions about not touching Dorian, Liz squeezed her hand. "Have no worries Dorian, I'll take care of her. But soon you'll be back to be with her. I'll tell Auntie about what happened as soon as she returns from the Merfest Regatta."

"Thanks, Lizzy," Dorian said, tears still streaming down her cheeks. One of the attendants went to help Dorian onto the stretcher. "Just give me your arm, young man. I don't need that thing." She put her arm through his and they walked down the dock toward the waiting ambulance.

After the ambulance left the parking lot, Liz glanced up at *Queen of the Seas* and saw that Susannah had joined the others on the upper deck.

"What's going on?" Phoebe screamed down at them. "Where is Mother going? What's with the ambulances and where's future stepdaddy?"

Charlotte looked up. "Please remain where you are until one of my officers can get a statement. Soon you can follow your mother to Melbourne Hospital."

Branson pulled his sister back from the railing and whispered something in her ear that seemed to calm her. In fact, she actually smiled. Had big brother told her that something must have happened to Julian because he was the only one missing?

Charlotte went back up the gangplank, followed by new members of her team. She told Fenton, "When Keisha arrives please send her in. You might as well go back to the hotel. I don't think anyone here is going anywhere until we find out how Mr. Rhodes died."

It was only a few minutes later that the medical examiner arrived. When she passed, she nodded her head toward them. Keisha Jones knew

Liz's father from his days as lead public defender for Brevard County, and Liz and Ryan from the last couple of murders at the Indialantic. Liz hoped she'd rule that Julian died from natural causes. However, glancing at Ryan's face, she had a feeling there was nothing natural about how the future groom died.

"Wow," Liz whispered to her father, "Glad we didn't cook the food for the rehearsal dinner. And I'm thrilled Auntie hasn't arrived back from the regatta yet. I can't believe Julian Rhodes is dead. Wasn't Dorian the one who was getting threatening letters? Do you think it's related? If they ate or drank the same thing and were poisoned it might prove she'd been the target, and someone just took Julian along for the ride."

"Poison, daughter? We know nothing of the kind. Pull in the reins until we know more. Where did Ryan disappear to? He was just here."

Liz knew exactly where he'd gone. After Charlotte had boarded *Queen of the Seas* with her second team, Ryan followed unnoticed. Liz was proud of her P.I. boyfriend and wished she could have done the same.

Twenty minutes went by until they saw the stretcher with Julian's body travel down the gangplank. Following behind the body were Keisha and two CSIs. As the body passed Liz and Fenton, a section of the sheet covering the body slipped off. Before the attendant could cover him, Liz got a quick glimpse of Julian's contorted face. Even though long released from it, his pale blue eyes still held pain. His face seemed frozen in a combination of shock and horror. White foam covered his lips and chin like shaving cream. The image was something that would take Liz years to forget and reminded her of another face she'd viewed six months ago wearing death's mask.

Keisha passed, giving Fenton a look that Liz deciphered to mean, *this is no natural death.* Whether by accident, or on purpose, it would soon be determined. One of the CSI's held a plastic bag with a half filled bottle of SWS water. Had Liz been right? Had Julian been poisoned? Is that what Keisha and Charlotte thought? And what about Dorian? Had she ingested the same substance? Liz prayed she'd be okay.

As the gurney with Julian's body traveled down the dock, it made slow repetitive thumping sounds over the uneven planks of wood. To Liz, it sounded like a funeral dirge. She and her father stood silent for a few minutes either out of respect or shock. Or a combination of both. "Dad, I'm going to try to get Susannah aside. Seeing she was the one who found him, and of everyone here, she seems the most upset." They glanced up at the main deck, at Susannah's ghostly, tear stained face. "Dorian's kids look almost gleeful and Wren, well Wren looks like Wren, can't put my finger on her part in all this."

"All this? Let's not jump to conclusions. This could have been a simple case of unintentional food poisoning or maybe he had a heart attack."

Not many people who had a heart attack foamed at the mouth. "He was shellfish allergic." Liz thought back to last night's dinner. "What if someone had stowed aboard the *Queen of the Seas*?" Her first thought was the figure dressed in a baseball cap and dark clothing.

"One thing at a time. It's Auntie I'm worried about," he said.

Liz put her hand on her father's arm. "I'll wait on the dock for her to get dropped off. Kate and Alex have an event at Ryckman Park. Ryan and I were supposed to meet them there. I'll text her our apologizes but I won't tell Kate what happened until later. She deserves to enjoy her time in the spotlight."

"Agreed. Your great-aunt will want to be at the hospital with her friend. I'll drive her. Just have her come to my office." His office was at the rear of the Indialantic, only five hundred feet away. "I'm going to head there now. I don't want to be in the way of Charlotte's investigation and I also don't want to witness how soon it will be before the vultures descend." He was referring to the media. "Come by if you need to talk or need the comfort of these old arms."

Keeping things light, she said, "You're not old. Fifty five's the new thirty."

"I rest my case. Your twenty-eight would be the new ten. And I'm always worried. Especially with what happened last New Year's Eve."

"Dad, I'm fully recovered. At least there's no connection between me and Julian Rhodes if this does turn out to be foul play. No worries."

"I won't worry, if you won't."

"Have I told you lately, I love you?"

"Yes. But I never get tired of it." He bent down and kissed her on her brow. "Stay out of trouble."

She kissed him back on his smooth cheek and waited for Aunt Amelia to show up, trying to find the right words to tell her what had happened.

Unfortunately, there weren't any.

It appeared that instead of a wedding, they would soon be planning a funeral.

Chapter 11

After everyone on *Queen of the Seas* was released, they trudged down the ramp with heads down, shuffling as they walked like in a chain gang from an old black-and-white movie. The only one not appropriately sad looking was Garrett. Liz had thought she'd seen a grin on his face and a sparkle in his green eyes. Charlotte had been tightlipped as she'd passed Liz. When Liz had stopped Susannah to ask her to meet up later she'd refused, explaining she was too distraught. But after Liz added a second "pretty please, it will be quick, promise." Susannah agreed.

Back at the Indialantic Liz had given Chef Pierre and Greta a heads up that the wedding was canceled and passed on that Charlotte wanted everyone to bunker down at the hotel until the cause of death could be determined. It seemed Liz's family run hotel would once again become a holding tank for possible murder suspects. Knowing she had an hour until meeting Susannah, she left Farrah's cage in the butler's pantry, much to Barnacle Bob's delight, and took the service elevator up to the second floor. She crept down the hallway to the Oceana Suite, Julian and Dorian's suite. As she passed the Golden Sands Suite, she heard voices from inside and paused at the door.

"You can't get money from a will if there's no money to get," she heard Phoebe say. "She got the villa in Tuscany, and father had been renting the apartment in Paris, most of his money went to nursing staff over the past couple years. At least that's what *she* told me."

"What about the Degas?" Branson asked. "He said it would be ours."

"His solicitors came after he passed and when they read the will, it was listed as ours to share, but there was only one problem. The statue had gone missing. The wife said she hadn't noticed because they'd only used the bottom floor of the apartment. The statue was supposedly in father's study. The Matisse was there. But of course, that belongs to Madeline now. I wouldn't put it past her to have taken the Degas and hidden it. I know she resents Mama and us. You must let it go. Now, tell me the truth, did you kill future-stepdaddy?"

"Don't deflect, Phoebe. You seem way too happy about getting nothing from our father's estate. Maybe you gave Julian shellfish so he would croak? He wasn't so keen on supporting your lavish lifestyle. I'll be honest though, I'm not exactly unhappy about his passing. Just worried about mother."

"Oh, she'll be fine." Phoebe answered. "Barely knew the guy. I read Mother's cards yesterday and saw it coming. I think she saw it too. And what's that country bumpkin doing here? Wren? What kind of a name is that? And what were you and she talking about on the boat? Hope you're not interested in her. She probably fed Julian shellfish."

"Nice change of subject, sister. Don't think I'm letting Father's Frenchie wife get away with stealing the Degas. How easy would it be to stick that little statue in Stepmonster's handbag? I asked Garrett to hire someone in Paris to look into its disappearance."

"You did what!" Phoebe screeched. "Does Mama know? I wanted to keep her out of it."

"No. Of course not Phoebe. Just Garrett. He's going to give me an update Monday morning."

Liz heard Branson's footsteps moving toward the door. She shot into the next suite, which was unlocked, and took a minute collecting her breath and her thoughts.

The Oceana Suite, Dorian and Julian's suite, was her favorite. Even after what had happened in it a year ago. The Baccarat chandelier illuminated a room decorated in rattan Bombay style furniture with blue and white décor. Chinese ginger jars sprouted white orchids. Over the sofa was a large piece of art covering almost the entire wall. It was made by Home Arts by the Sea's mixed-media artist, Minna Presley. The down cushions on the white sofa in the sitting room showed the imprint of a body. Based on Friday night's conversation on the beach between Dorian and her fiancé, the imprint must have been from Julian Rhodes's prone body. Sadness enveloped her. No matter how Julian had died and how big of a jerk he might have been, his death was undeserved. Was any death deserved?

Suddenly, she felt like a voyeur. She'd only wanted to see the suite in case there was a sign of a something Julian could have eaten that sent him into anaphylactic shock. Squidly's next door was known to deliver to the hotel. Maybe they'd ordered a lobster or clam roll for a snack? But there wasn't any half eaten food. She even checked the trash can.

Peeking in the bedroom, she saw Dorian's colorful wardrobe hanging in the closet next to Julian's natural fabric drawstring pants and tunics. All were in either shades of white or off-white. Susannah's book on etiquette was open on the nightstand as if Dorian had been reading it and wishing her wedding could be more lavish. Poor Dorian. She must be devastated. Liz sent up a silent prayer that she would be fine.

She went back into the sitting room and looked around. There was nothing in the Oceana Suite to point to Julian's presence. A closed suitcase; no witchcraft paraphernalia. His wallet was on the credenza. Should she look inside? No. There had to be a line. And this wasn't the time to cross it. Next to the wallet was a blue bottle of Sunshine Wiccan Society Water. She picked it up and read the back again with the address in Jacksonville. She wasn't sure if using the word Wiccan on a bottle of water was a selling point. But obviously she was wrong, if Julian had planned on investing in a new filtration system like she'd seen on the bill he had handed Garrett earlier, business must be good. She put the unopened bottle down and quickly left the suite.

At the door to Branson's suite, she paused. As she put her ear to the door, it inched open at the same time something flashed by her feet. A furry weasel nosed her way inside. "Farrah! How did you get out of your cage? Barnacle Bob, I'd bet. Darned bird! Farrah get back here."

She had no choice but to go inside and get her. Right?

"The suite was on the messy side. Through the open doorway to the bedroom, Liz saw Branson's suitcase open on the luggage stand, clothes spilling onto the sisal bedroom rug. Next to her on the counter that divided the sitting room from a small kitchenette, was a nearly empty bottle of Patrón tequila, two shot glasses and a half of an unwrapped lime. Someone had been partying. She smelled the floral scent of perfume. Phoebe's, she assumed, seeing she'd just overheard, okay, eavesdropped, on their conversation minutes ago.

"Farrah! Come out this instant." She thought she saw the tip of the ferret's tail under the bed. She went in the room, worried that Branson might return and think she was snooping. Quickly, she got down on all fours and looked under the bed. There she was. And she was holding something between her teeth. "What is that? Give it to Liz. Come on, Farrah, I'm in charge of you until your mommy comes back from the hospital. Hand it over. The ferret took a step toward Liz's hand then backed off. "You little, rascal! Okay, I'll lock you in here. No treats." At the word *treats* she turned her little head. The word seemed a universal bribe no matter what kind of domesticated animals. Farrah inched forward and finally Liz grabbed her by the scruff of her neck, at least she thought it was her neck. She carefully got up, then wrapped her around her shoulders like she'd seen Dorian do. "Hand over the gum." It was an unwrapped piece of Extra mint flavored gum. "I'll take that, missy."

Not knowing if it was Branson's gum or some previous guest's, she threw it in the trash next to the nightstand, and perused Branson's reading material. A magazine for restaurant owners and a book on the artist Degas.

When she came back into Branson's sitting room, Dorian's financial advisor, Garrett, was standing just outside the open doorway. He smiled when he saw her, then quickly asked, "Any news about Dorian?"

Farrah nuzzled under Liz's chin at the name Dorian. "That tickles, Farrah. No, sorry Mr. McGee…"

"Garrett."

"Garrett. I haven't heard anything."

"Thank you. Do you know what happened to him, I mean Julian, uh, Mr. Rhodes?"

"No, I don't. I was going to ask you the same thing," she said.

"It is such a tragedy." He said the words, but his eyes almost looked gleeful. He must have realized it and said in a somber tone, "Branson told me to meet him here so we can go to the hospital and check on his mother. Have you seen him?"

"No, I haven't," she answered, "the door was open, Farrah ran in and hid under the bed. The little scamp." She didn't know why she was explaining. For once she had a real alibi to her snooping.

"Okay. I'll go check in the lobby for Branson. Must have gotten our wires crossed." He reached over and gave the ferret a satisfying scratch behind the ears. They seemed old friends. Aunt Amelia's motto that being kind to an animal was a true measure of a man, seemed to fit in Garrett's case.

As Garret walked away, Liz couldn't help liking him for it.

Chapter 12

It had only been three hours since the *Queen of the Seas* had pulled into the Indialantic's dock. Susannah and Liz sat in Aunt Amelia's cutting garden, gazing ahead at the vista of a full moon shinning on a tranquil sea, the scent of night jasmine drifting toward them. The bench they sat on and the flowers planted in front of them were dedicated to her great-aunt's numerous fur babies who'd passed over the rainbow bridge. They sat silently for a few minutes. The only sounds were a few crickets, the occasional hoot of an owl, and the steady sound of the waves lapping the shore. The sun had set, but between the full moon and the lamppost lit garden paths, there was no need for a flashlight.

Beyond the garden, in view of the Atlantic, was the wedding altar Julian had brought from the Sunshine Wiccan Society's sanctuary. It stood under a white latticed arbor with pale peach flowering vines intertwined with fairy lights. The altar waited for a union that would never happen. Liz felt a tear swell, then course slowly down her right cheek. In the past, following a good cry, the salty tears would sting her scar. But now that the wound had healed, she felt no pain. The four-inch crevice would always remain, but she'd made peace with it. If only she could make peace with the memory of the man who'd caused it.

Liz's tears were for Dorian and Julian's family. If he had any. No matter what kind of a person Julian Rhodes had been, it was clear Dorian had loved him. Liz had never heard of him or his society before Dorian came to the Indialantic. Last night she'd done some cyber sleuthing and hadn't found one item mentioned about him or his sect. She'd eventually given up and sent a text to Betty who was visiting her granddaughter in Jacksonville, giving her full rein to investigate. Knowing if there was anything to find, she would dig it up. She'd also followed up a little while ago with a text, telling Betty about Julian's death. It seemed more important now than ever to find out who he was.

What Liz had unearthed on Dorian's son, Branson, was a different story. There was a plethora of information. Good and bad. His arrest record came up immediately under a public court search in Broward County, along with an article in a local Palm Beach paper. The story went that in Branson's senior year of high school he sold psychotropic mushrooms to a ninth grader. He'd been eighteen at the time, so he was tried as an adult. But he got off with a light sentence. After graduation, the judge allowed him to go to a camp for troubled kids and slapped him with tons of community service. Liz wondered if his mother, the famous psychic, had anything to do with him not getting jail time. If Branson had introduced his mother to Julian, then what was the reason Julian didn't choose him as best man? From what she'd seen, they'd barely exchanged two words in the last couple of days. Did they have a falling out?

A strange noise broke into Liz and Susannah's momentary peace, a sort of clicking or clucking sound. As far as Liz knew Aunt Amelia hadn't bought any pet chickens. Though she wouldn't put it past her. Then she remembered what she just read while waiting for Susannah to disembark from the boat.

"What's that noise?" Susannah jumped up and wrapped her arms around herself as if it were a chilly, fall night, instead of a balmy seventy-five degrees.

"It's Farrah the ferret," Liz told her.

Susannah sat back down.

"They call it dooking. It means the ferret's in a good mood." After Liz had met Aunt Amelia and walked her to her father's office, she'd waited with Farrah at the end of the dock for Charlotte to release everyone from the doomed voyage. Trying to pass some time, she looked up on her phone the proper care of ferrets. After reading, the first thing she'd done was to make sure Farrah's cage was securely latched, especially after learning that "ferret" is Latin for *furittus*, meaning "little thief." The rascals had a penchant for secreting away small things. They also liked to eat high-end cat food, of which Liz had plenty in her cupboard because of her kitten Bronte. Hopefully, Dorian would be returning home soon with a clean bill of health and reunited with her pet and children.

"That darned weasel. You have to be careful," Susannah said. "She's very sly. Amelia told me she somehow got into her rooms and stole a pair of gold hoop earrings. Dorian Starwood's daughter found them in her shoes."

Liz laughed. The timing seemed as good as ever to broach the subject of what Susannah witnessed on *Queen of the Seas*. Before now, Susannah hadn't said a word from when she'd joined her in the garden. Liz reached over and squeezed the long fingers on her right hand. "You should be a pianist."

Looking off toward the Atlantic, Susannah said, "I used to play. Went to Julliard. But I wasn't good enough, so I turned to entertaining my husband's clients, going by the..."

"Book, as in etiquette book," Liz finished for her. "Was that rewarding?"

"Nothing was rewarding after we lost..."

"Sorry. Didn't mean to bring you to that place again." In a weak moment last January, Susannah had confided in Liz that her stiff, unbending, old-fashioned adherence to the rules of etiquette had to do with a tragedy early in her marriage when a baby she and her husband had adopted was claimed by its birth mother. The mother took the child to Canada, refusing to let Susannah and her husband ever see or correspond with her. Susannah and her husband divorced soon after.

"When you feel ready," Liz said gently, "why don't you just tell me what you know about what happened to Julian Rhodes?"

She turned to Liz, her face with that pinched, I-just-gnawed-on-a-lemon look that only disappeared on rare occasions. This wasn't one of them. Liz always thought if Susannah released her dark brown hair from the tight librarian bun she wore twenty-four-seven, it might soften her sharp facial features and make her more approachable. She guessed her stiff countenance was a façade—armor so she wouldn't have to go to the dark side of her painful past—keep inside the lines of her paint by numbers life so she couldn't get hurt again. Liz knew all about that.

Susannah narrowed her eyes. "I'm not sure Agent Pearson wants me to take you into my confidence, Elizabeth. Also, it was a scene I'd rather forget. I don't want you to have any nightmares thinking about it."

Liz was about to protest that she could handle it but didn't need to. She'd forgotten, for all her proper manners and rules, Susannah was basically a gossip and a busy body. In the past, her nosiness helped them catch a murderer.

Leaning closer, Susannah looked around them to make sure no one was listening. The only living things in hearing distance were a pair of Sandhill cranes, pecking at the ground near the gazebo. Liz never saw them out after dark. Maybe it had something to do with the huge moon that shed a radiant light mimicking daylight. She'd have to look inside Phoebe's book on superstitions and find the meaning of the cranes' presence.

"It was a violent death," Susannah whispered. "He was still alive when I walked in. Barely alive. I never saw such agony. It will be a long while before I forget the image of his twisted body. The foam around his mouth. His eyes beseeching me to help. But I couldn't. It was as if he was being burned from the inside out. I'm allergic to bees and I knew about his shellfish allergy, so I gave him an EpiPen injection. It didn't do a thing. He tried to speak, I leaned in, put my ear to his lips, he said, 'Tell Dory I'm sorry,' There was a whooshing sound. His last breath. I screamed for the captain. He came immediately and tried to revive him but couldn't."

"Could he have choked on something?"

"There wasn't any food in the room. I did notice a weird smell on his breath."

"Like almonds?" Liz had read enough Agatha Christies, given to her by Chef Pierre, to know that the scent of almonds was closely related to someone who'd swallowed arsenic.

"No. It wasn't almonds, but it did smell sweet."

"Was Dorian with him?"

"No. She came in after me. Hysterical. It wasn't a pretty sight. He didn't go peacefully. Captain Netherton left to call 911, and I stayed with Ms. Starwood. We had nowhere to look, both our gazes falling on the body. Then Ms. Starwood threw herself on top of her fiancé, sobbing. I opened the bulkhead and found a tarp. I pulled her away and covered him with it. Gave her some of that blue bottled water he insisted we have on board. It seemed to calm her down, but she kept repeating, 'He was so beautiful. It's all my fault. I take full responsibility.' It was awful."

"How about during dinner? Did Julian seem well?"

"Didn't notice him being unwell. He and Ms. Starwood were seated at their own table. Something was strange about that, too. They didn't seem to be a happy, till-death-do-us-part, blissful couple." Susannah realized what she'd said and covered her mouth with her hand. "Ms. Starwood's son had set up the food, buffet style. He insisted Ashley and I plate and serve Mr. Rhodes and Ms. Starwood's plate from the galley, knowing Mr. Rhodes was allergic to shellfish."

"The shellfish main course was on the menu for everyone else, right?" Liz thought back to when she wanted to go over the menu with Dorian yesterday and how distraught she'd been from her dream.

"Yes. Shrimp. Key West pinks in a coconut milk broth. Mr. Rhodes got a gingered citrus chicken over orange grits. I tasted it myself. Delicious. But he never tasted it because when we brought up the main dishes to his and Ms. Starwood's table, he wasn't there. The first course didn't include shellfish, just salmon, and he didn't seem to have a problem with it when we served him. He even told me it was only shellfish he'd reacted to in the past. Ashley served Ms. Starwood, and I served Mr. Rhodes."

"I read once that someone allergic to nuts kissed their fiancée right after she'd had a peanut butter sandwich and then he died."

"He wasn't on deck for the shrimp course, no matter who he kissed. So that can't be what happened. Plus, I'm sure my EpiPen would have worked if it was a shellfish allergy. He wasn't really complaining he couldn't breathe, he…I really think, I need to lay down. I feel one of my migraines coming on." She reached into her pocket and handed Liz a copy of the printed menu.

Liz had a copy of the menu from yesterday but took it from her shaky hand. "Of course. I'll check on you in a little while. Have Greta bring some of your Lipton tea to your rooms. Just one last question. Do you have any idea why Julian Rhodes was in the stateroom, not upstairs with his fiancée and guests?"

"I have no idea. After I left his dinner plate with Dorian, she sent me to look for him. That was when I found him." She stood. "By the way, Ashley from Deli-casies deserves a raise. She not only took photos of the dinner but helped clear the dishes and plate Ms. Starwood's and Mr. Rhodes meal. She even promised to shoot some comp-card headshots for my acting portfolio. I think it's time for me to look for another theater company. Maybe the Vero Beach Players. Your great-aunt seems to have cornered the market on the leading roles at the Melbourne Beach Theatre Company. And I'm sure it has nothing to do with her boyfriend Ziggy owning the theater."

"Now, now, Susannah. If memory serves, you've had the last two leads."

"She always upstages me."

There it was. She was back to her old self. Instead of being irritated, Liz was happy Susannah's mind had so easily switched from Julian Rhodes's gruesome death to everyday things like her and Aunt Amelia's competitive nature when it came to their acting careers.

"Thought your role was a fairly large one? You're playing Auntie's sister, right?"

Susannah laughed, "A sea witch's sister? I've counted. I only have thirty lines. Not enough to be considered a main player. I know you helped write the script. Maybe…"

"I'll see what I can do. I'm sure Auntie will be accommodating." *Like she always is when it comes to you Susannah Shay*, Liz thought. Aunt

Amelia had written the play with her usual flair for the dramatic. Her ideas, per usual, had needed honing. Lots of honing.

"Aren't you coming with me?" Susannah asked, standing up.

"In a little. It's so peaceful."

"I assume all the festivities for the Mystical Merfest will continue tomorrow."

"I don't see why not? The tents will be open from noon to four. They were timed not to interfere with the wedding ceremony and brunch. Then the wrap-up will be at Ponce De Leon Beach Park. There was a change of plans, after"—Liz hesitated—"what happened to Julian Rhodes. They're going to move the emporium's Mystical Merfest tents to Squidly's parking lot. Charlotte informed Aunt Amelia that the emporium shops will be closed till further notice, until they get results from the sheriff's department on cause of death. Though it seems doubtful they'll find anything. As far as I know, Julian Rhodes never set foot in the emporium."

"That's not true," Susannah said, "I saw him and his fiancée inside the emporium yesterday afternoon. They were in Kate's shop, buying some hocus-pocus books. And I saw that Wren creature also. It looked like she was stalking them. She's a weird one. When Charlotte was questioning everyone on board *Queen of the Seas*, Ms. Wagner told her that before dinner was served, Dorian had abruptly gotten up and disappeared for a good ten minutes. I don't know why she had to proffer that information. It was very spiteful. Don't stay out too long. If you think foul play was involved, better safe than sorry. By the way, where's Ryan? He should stay close to you until we know what's happened."

Ryan! She'd almost forgotten that when everyone disembarked from *Queen of the Seas*, he was noticeably missing. She hoped he'd unearthed some good intel. "I'm a big girl, Susannah. I'm going to see Ryan in a few minutes, I just want to digest everything. And I'm sorry about what you went through today. Call anytime if you need to talk."

"It should be the other way around," Susannah said, giving Liz a small pat on the head. "I'm old enough to be your grandmother. I've lived through a lot in my life and I'm here if you need me. This is just one more hurdle to overcome. You've had your own tragedies. Losing your mother at such an early age and the scar you'll wear as a brand for the rest of your days because of that man Travis. At least that part's finished. Let's pray Mr. Rhodes's death was from natural causes and we can all move on."

Liz heard the doubt in her voice and said, "I'm sure you're right." They were both pretty good actresses.

"I'll tell Amelia where you are. I'll also tell her you've agreed to rewrite the script for *The Sea Witch*." There it was, again. Her sense of entitlement. "I never said I would help..." But she was already gone.

Liz realized Susannah had left her with more questions than answers.

Chapter 13

She sat for a few minutes, then took out her phone and texted Ryan. *Where are you? I'll meet you at your cottage in ten. Wine and sustenance would be much appreciated. Skipped dinner. LY XOXO.* After stowing her phone in her pocket, Liz placed the cage with Farrah inside on the bench. The Sandhill cranes had disappeared. "Just you and me, kid," Liz whispered. She could barely make out the ferret's dark sable body, the only thing that stood out was the white mask on her face and the glint in her tiny eyes from the bulb in the lamppost. "I'm sure your mom is okay. In the meantime, we'll make the best of it. I know Aunt Amelia would love to take you under her wing, but then there's Barnacle Bob. You want to stay away from that scoundrel."

Farrah let out a tiny chirp. It seemed she agreed.

Taking in a gulp of salty jasmine infused air, Liz let out a long exhale, *ohhm-m-m,* like she'd learned in yoga. She mused about who would be running the society now the Wiccan leader was gone. Or, would it no longer continue without its founder? Last night, she'd talked to Kate about Julian Rhodes's magnetic personality. Even though she and Kate were in relationships, they'd felt the same attraction to the dead man. They'd agreed when his hypnotic *Paul-Newman-blue-eyes* took you in, as Aunt Amelia called them, their intensity was like an electrical current sending shock waves to your toes. Liz understood Dorian's attraction to him, but she also saw how his female followers might feel the same way.

And what had been the deal with him and Wren? What was in that folder she was pushing at him and why was she so angry?

Perhaps one of Dorian's children killed him. Phoebe and her brother both had a reason for wanting Julian dead. If Julian had married Dorian and became their warlock stepdaddy, then when their mother passed, they wouldn't inherit her fortune. Or at least the lion's share of it. Or was Dorian the target? She'd received threatening letters. Now that she thought about it, Branson and Phoebe also had a motive for killing their mother before she wedded Julian. They would inherit, and Julian wouldn't. But Liz couldn't go there. It was too calculating. Too cold a scenario, and against all the laws of nature.

Then the niggling devil on her right shoulder whispered, *It's done all the time. Natural or not.*

Might Garrett have killed Julian, not wanting him to squander Dorian's fortune?

Liz was getting ahead of herself. It might take days for the medical examiner to come back with any results of cause of death. She knew one thing; Agent Charlotte Pearson would treat the case as a suspicious death based solely on the threatening letters that Dorian had received.

Suddenly, at the same time as a wispy cloud covered the moon, she heard voices.

A female voice said, "It has nothing to do with me. I don't think you understand. It was probably a curse someone put on him."

"Phoebe, I don't believe in curses. I might believe the validity of your mother's readings because they've been proven time and time again. But whatever happened to him is good for us. You can tell me the truth. I won't tell anyone. We both wanted him out of her life. Now he is. I would rather know now if it was you. Because if it wasn't you, then your mother might be in danger. Remember the letters she received." Garrett stepped under a lamppost by the gazebo. Taking both of Phoebe's hands, he looked down at her. But she pulled away.

"Don't you play all innocent with me, *monsieur*. I had nothing to do with the warlock's death. Did you? How long would it be before he got rid of you and took over all of Mother's finances? And you're not fooling anyone, it's obvious you're in love with Mama."

"If it turns out to be…ah…"

"Murder," she said. Phoebe's voice changed. It was softer, more agreeable. "You're right, Uncle Garrett, Mama's well-being should be our only concern. Instead of arguing, we should be toasting our champagne flutes that Julian Rhodes is no longer one of the living."

Liz missed Garrett's response because Farrah started making strange noises. Not the happy dooking, expressing her glee; more like a whiny, whimpering sound. Whatever it meant, Liz had no time to look it up on her phone. Grabbing the cage, she whispered to the ferret to put a lid on it. Thankful another cloud covered the moon, she crept away in the direction of the caretaker's cottage. She tripped over a palm frond and let out a little squeak, which turned Farrah into a chatterbox.

"Who's there?" Garrett demanded in a deep voice.

Liz broke out in a run, feeling Farrah sliding from one side of her cage to the other. Veering off the curved flower lined paths, she sprinted into a small grove of orange and lemon trees. Garrett's voice faded into the sounds of the night. Ahead she saw a light in the caretaker's cottage and thanked her lucky stars Ryan was home. Lately, the word "home" had two meanings. Ryan was becoming her home, a cozy port in a storm when she needed it.

She stumbled on the seashell path and for a moment her old anxiety about being in a committed relationship crept in, along with memories of last New Year's Eve. Farrah started her dooking, no doubt thinking her roller-coaster ride in the cage was all great fun. When she reached Ryan's door, Farrah's clucking was soon met with Blackbeard's deep bark.

This should be an interesting meeting she thought, as she turned the knob and charged inside.

What was that old saying, fools rush in? Liz was no fool, but the last thing she expected was to find petite waifish Wren dressed in one of her prairie dresses encased in Ryan's buff ex-firefighter arms.

The surprise on Liz's face mirrored Wren's.

"What's she doing here? And why does she have that awful thing with her?" Wren asked between sniffles, pointing at the cage.

Liz assumed she meant Farrah, who was now hissing in fear as she set her on the floor.

Blackbeard had no problem jumping on Liz in welcome, giving her a few dozen kisses on her cheek and nose. Liz scratched behind his furry ears; tufts of hair, some long, some short, stood out from his unpuppy like body. He was technically under a year old but couldn't get much larger. His coloring was that of a calico cat; caramel, black, and tan. His long, pointed goatee was solid black; the reason Ryan christened him with the name of a bearded pirate.

While Blackbeard was thrilled to see Liz, Ryan on the other hand took his sweet time getting up from the loveseat. When he reached her, he stumbled over his words, "Liz, uh, I was, uh, getting worried about you. This is Wren Wagner, Julian's cousin."

Duh, Liz thought, *I was with you in the lobby the first time we met her.* She arched her brow and turned her full attention to Wren, who reached over and grabbed Ryan's bottle of beer, taking a long swig.

Feeling her face heat, Liz asked, "What kind of host are you? You didn't offer the girl her own beer?" Even though she called Wren a girl, she looked to be in her early thirties. Her pale, delicate features and physique made her look young and vulnerable. Liz had a feeling she'd been playing damsel in distress for Ryan's benefit. Then again, if Julian had really been her cousin, she couldn't fault Wren for mourning a family member. But they couldn't have been that close because when they'd first met Julian and Wren in the Indialantic's lobby it was clear Julian wasn't happy to see her and hadn't wanted Wren staying at the hotel. Neither had his fiancée, Dorian. And then there was the scene on the beach.

"He did offer," Wren said between sniffles. Her nose was pink, either from a sunburn or she'd been crying. There was a pile of tissues on the side table, so Liz guessed the later. Wren scooched her thin frame to the edge of the leather loveseat and looked up at them with a wan, tearstained face. "I better get back to the others and see if there's any more news about Julian." She dramatically, at least in Liz's opinion, swiped at the corner of her eye to catch a single tear, then stood and came to where Ryan and Liz were standing. Awkwardly standing, at this point.

The top of her head only reached the middle of Ryan's chest. He blew Liz an air kiss that Wren didn't see, and Liz relaxed. Ryan was obviously just pumping Wren for information about what happened on *Queen of the Seas.*

Wren put her hand on Ryan's bicep, stroking the tanned, muscled flesh while Liz bit the inside of her cheek to distract herself from pushing Wren out the door or siccing Blackbeard on her.

"Please don't share anything I've told you," Wren said softly to Ryan, her eyes saucer like and pleading. "I'm distraught and no doubt misconstrued the entire thing. Whatever I told you, stays in this room. Pinky swear!" She glanced at Liz, giving her a weak grin and raised her right hand in Ryan's direction, her pinky finger extended.

Embarrassment flushed his face as he entwined his pinky with hers and said, "Swear."

Liz wasn't the only one jealous about their exchange. Blackbeard jumped up on Wren, nearly knocking her to the floor. His large front paws on both of her shoulders, slow dance style. Then the pup let out a low menacing growl that caused Farrah to start bouncing off the walls of her wire cage, emitting high-pitched ferret screams.

"Blackbeard! Down!" So, Ryan did have a voice. Blackbeard listened to his master and came to Liz. He knew which side his dog treat was buttered.

Ryan removed Wren's hand from his arm and said, "Do you need me to walk you back to the Indialantic?"

"No, thank you. I can handle it," Wren answered.

Chapter 14

After Wren left, Liz collapsed on the loveseat, looking up at Ryan's dark, unreadable eyes.

He quickly averted her gaze. "Need anything?"

He strode to the kitchen, now remodeled with all new top-shelf appliances, countertops and cupboards. It was a chef's kitchen. And they'd had many cook-offs, taking turns at his place, then hers. At one time, the caretaker's cottage had been Liz and her father's home when they'd moved from New York until she went away to Columbia University at age eighteen. Ryan rented the cottage from Aunt Amelia. Liz's former frilly pink daisy wallpapered bedroom was now his. No traces of daisies anywhere, after he'd put his masculine stamp on the five room cottage. The only splash of color was the art on the walls, along with a few teal throw pillows and hand thrown pottery Liz had given him to "soften things up."

"No, I'm good," Liz said in answer to his query.

"I'll be right there. I want to grab paper and a pen and write some things down that Wren told me."

"You do know Julian Rhodes could have died from natural causes and your undercover work might've been for naught," she said.

"I just heard from your father about Mr. Rhodes. He told me his death was no accident. Got the call when Wren was here, so I don't know many details," he said.

"I knew it! How?" He came back to the loveseat and sat next to her. After a dramatic Aunt Amelia type pause, he said, "Julian Rhodes was poisoned."

"Snap! With what?"

"Antifreeze."

"Where would someone find antifreeze in Central Florida?"

"That's not the real question. The real question is, who poisoned him and why. They sell antifreeze in Florida, especially for the snowbirds making trips back and forth to visit relatives in the North. Also, we do have freezing temperatures on the island. Last February for example."

"Point taken. How about Dorian? Is she okay? Did she also have antifreeze in her system?"

"No. She's back from the hospital. They didn't find anything. You have been out of the loop. Charlotte's over at the Indialantic, now. She's talking to Dorian. Where've you been?"

"With Susannah. She's the one who found Julian in the stateroom. And I just overheard a little meeting between Dorian's daughter Phoebe, and Garrett, Dorian's accountant/manager." She told Ryan what she'd heard. "They both seemed pretty pleased Julian was dead. Murdered or not."

"What about Susannah? What did she tell you?" Ryan's dark, intense eyes looked at her. "Was he alive when she found him? I couldn't ask her when we were onboard. Charlotte was with me the whole time."

"He was barely alive, per Susannah."

He started writing on the notepad. Pausing, he asked, "Did he say anything?"

"Yes, he said, 'Tell Dory I'm sorry.'"

"Anything else Susannah could tell you?"

"Not really. Just that she was traumatized by the whole scene. Now that we know he was murdered we should probably ask Susannah more questions. She did say that during the rehearsal dinner Dorian and Julian didn't seem to be getting along at their table for two. Even that's strange. When I've attended rehearsal dinners in the past, everyone sits at the same table. It's not like there's a large group. Far from it."

"Nothing about this planned wedding has been what I consider normal," he said. "Including a medium and a witch marrying."

"True." She kissed him on his perfect nose, which was peeling from being sunburned. He'd recently started playing golf with her father, even though she knew it wasn't his first choice when it came to leisure sports. Too much leisure, he'd told her. He liked more active sports like softball, kayaking, and hiking. She said, "I have a question for you. What did Wren tell you that was so confidential? And why the heck isn't everyone who was on *Queen of the Seas* under house arrest? Not allowed to go moseying all over the grounds. That little avian Wren needs to be caged like poor Farrah here. There's something not right about her." She tried to decipher his expression. All she came up with was that he thought she was amusing. "You're enjoying this aren't you?"

He gave her a wry smile. "Uh-hm, Indeed, I am. I'm sure once Charlotte delivers the news to Dorian, she'll have to share it with the public."

It suddenly hit Liz, that this wasn't an Agatha Christie murder to solve. This was real life. And one of the people on *Queen of the Seas* was a murderer. Dorian would be devastated. Thank God she had Aunt Amelia nearby to comfort her."

Ryan wiped away a tear from her cheek, then in a soft tone he said, "Charlotte isn't telling anyone, including the media, that it was antifreeze that did him in, only that he'd ingested poison."

"Dorian won't even know it was antifreeze?"

"Especially not Dorian. You do realize she'll be the sheriff department's top suspect. Husband and wives are always the primary suspects in a murder investigation."

"Good one Sherlock. But you're forgetting they weren't married yet. How would she benefit from his death?" It wasn't like her to be so snarky. She felt protective of Aunt Amelia's friend, and didn't believe for a second that Dorian had killed her fiancé. It just wasn't in her. Liz thought back to all the times they trekked down to Palm Beach and had overnights in Dorian's large home, Villa Luna. She'd named her little palace after the moon, because during a full moon the moon shone over the Intracoastal Waterway on one side, and the ocean on the other.

"Sorry," she said, "I just don't believe Dorian would kill him." Her hand instinctively went to her cheek where she traced her scar with her finger.

Ryan noticed and pulled her to him. Once in his arms, she told him everything Susannah had told her. After, she said, "You know what? Do you mind if I grab a glass of rosé, I think I need one?"

"Sure. I think there's an open bottle in the fridge."

"Need anything? Another beer that doesn't have cooties?" Then she winked as she looked over at the bottle that Wren had been drinking from.

"Ha, no, I'm good."

She got up and went to the kitchen, got down a handblown turquoise wineglass, took out the bottle from the refrigerator, and filled the glass an inch to the brim. She wasn't a big drinker for many reasons, but sometimes the occasion called for it. This was one of those occasions. She could hear her therapist's words echoing in her head: *Only drink when you're happy, not when you're sad.* She wasn't sure what she was. Surely not happy Julian Rhodes the Wiccan leader was dead. But she was relieved that if the killer was really targeting Dorian, he'd died instead of her. Did that make her a bad person? She supposed so.

After she sat on the loveseat and took a sip of wine, she said, "Seriously, what would be Dorian's motive? If he was poisoned with antifreeze, that's premeditated."

"Jealousy. Maybe the guy cheated on her. That might be enough of a reason for Dorian to poison him. As you pointed out, there was quite an age difference. Or, like you've also brought up, he was marrying her for her money, and she found out."

"No. I'm not buying Dorian as his murderer. I think it's more feasible that Dorian was the target. Charlotte should have no problem narrowing it down to our fantastic four; Phoebe, Branson, Wren, and Garrett. Someone on the boat gave it to him."

"You mean fantastic five. You can't leave out Dorian. I'm not trying to nullify your gut feelings about this, but if it's one thing we've learned from watching some of your auntie's favorite cop shows," he said, adding a wink, "All we want are the facts, ma'am."

"Yes, I suppose you're right, Sgt. Joe Friday." Ryan was referring to the old TV crime drama *Dragnet* starring Jack Webb. Aunt Amelia had played a dead gangster's blonde, floozy girlfriend. She had a three word part as she addressed Sgt. Joe Friday with a cigarette dangling between her bubblegum pink lips, "Gotta light, Sergeant?"

Liz took a gulp of her wine and stared at the liquid inside before saying, "Also, until we know in what form he ingested the antifreeze, we need to be circumspect. It could've been added to his food or even that fancy water beforehand."

Ryan jotted something else down on the pad.

"And that guy in the baseball cap could be involved." She reminded him about the sightings.

Blackbeard had taken the prone position in front of Farrah's cage. Maybe there was a chance they could be friends. The person Blackbeard hadn't seemed to be happy with was Wren Wagner. She smiled and blew the big mutt a kiss. "Okay, spill. Your turn to share what Wren told you. And I wouldn't mind hearing what you found when you went on board *Queen of the Seas?*"

"The first time I went in, I just confirmed Mr. Rhodes was dead. After checking Dorian's pulse, Charlotte sent me and Susannah out of the room. Susannah went up to the top deck with the others and I followed Charlotte and Captain Netherton out."

Liz raised her right eyebrow. "And the second time?"

"The second time I just snooped around, trying to avoid Charlotte and everyone else. Captain Netherton saw me but didn't let on. On my way off the ship, he whispered that he did see a guy in the parking lot taking pictures of license plates with a cellphone."

"Let me guess, he wore black?"

"No, navy T-shirt and jeans."

"Same thing."

"Not really."

Liz glanced at Ryan's navy T-shirt and smiled. He always dressed in dark clothing like he had back in New York City. Island life didn't change his mind about his style. But soon the summer heat would start, and she was sure white would be the color of most of his days.

"I saw a bottle of water brought off as evidence. Do you think that's where the antifreeze was added? Do you know where the bottle came from?"

"Actually, when I was leaning in to examine the body, I saw it peeking out from under the sofa. I grabbed a tissue and rolled the bottle in sight, leaving it for the sheriff's department to find it."

"Okay, back to Wren," Liz said, giving him a small pinch on his knee.

He put the pen down and looked at her. "You heard me. I pinky swore not to tell."

Her mouth gaped open. He was enjoying this.

Serious once again, he said, "Wren claims to have caught Dorian and her financial advisor Garrett coming out of a room on *Queen of the Seas* during the rehearsal dinner."

"So, that's no big deal."

"Wren said he took her into his arms and that Dorian had been crying."

"They're friends," Liz said, not convinced it was more than that. At least on Dorian's part. "Garrett's been her financial advisor for years. Maybe he found out some dirt on Julian and told her about it. It would explain about how Dorian seemed so distant during last night's dinner. What part of the evening was it?"

"I was about to ask her when you came barreling in with both guns blazing and a caged ferret."

"Darn. I still don't believe Dorian killed him. Garrett could have. He's in love with Dorian for sure." She reached into her shorts pocket and showed him the crumpled bill for the water filtration system that Garrett must have thrown away after Julian handed it to him. "There was definitely no love lost between Julian and Garrett." She said reflectively, "We should pass everything on to Charlotte and the sheriff's department."

"Well…remember yesterday you wanted me to look into Julian Rhodes past? I did find a few things that were interesting, and a half hour ago, I had a little chat with our octogenarian cyber sleuth Betty in Jacksonville. By the sounds of her screaming great-grandchildren, I think she'll be happy to come home to the Indialantic."

"Tell me. Tell me."

"The Sunshine Wiccan Society isn't listed as a religious group, but The Sunshine Wiccan Society Water Company, Ltd. was registered within the last year by Julian Rhodes. The only other thing I could find on Mr. Rhodes was that fifteen years ago he had a business called Sunshine Serenity Springs. It had the same address as where the SWS water company is."

"And why is Betty talking to you, not me? No wonder she's not answering my texts except the one I sent saying Julian was dead."

He raised an eyebrow, amused once again, crinkling the laugh lines by his dark brown eyes. "Because earlier…you said you would stay out of it and let me do the research on the guy. I told Betty to keep it between the two of us."

Letting out a breath she didn't know she was holding, she said, "So, what does it all mean? Did Betty go to the physical location?"

"Yes. There's nothing there that looks the slightest bit witch or warlock like. There is a natural spring and a warehouse that was locked tight. And lots of land. Before she could check-in or break-in which is more her MO, Betty was chased off by a pair of Rottweilers."

Liz covered her mouth. "Oh my! Is she okay?"

"Betty said it was the best time of her life. Instead of writing a scene from a mystery, she was living one. She made it to her car, no problem."

"That's even more scary," Liz said with a laugh. "Have you ever been in the car when she was driving? She doesn't even have a license, that's why I have her Blue Bomber and act as her chauffeur."

"She's fine," he said. "But I do agree with you that you *and* Betty should stay out of this from now on. We aren't dealing with a background check. We're dealing with murder."

"Maybe there is no Wiccan Society?"

"Or they could be located somewhere else. Too early to jump to conclusions."

"I bet he was just with Dorian for the money," she said, taking another sip of wine. "Just like that whopper of a bill I just told you about that Julian gave Garrett for the new bottling plant in Ocala."

Liz shot up from the sofa. "I better go check on Auntie and Dorian. Aren't you glad I had you dig into Julian Rhodes? At least we have something to go on. Have you told Charlotte everything?"

"Briefly. She wants me to write up a report and send her everything I know. As of an hour ago, I am on the payroll of the Brevard County Sherriff's Department."

"That's wonderful. Now we'll be sure to be in the loop for a change. Make sure to send me a copy of your report, too."

"I don't think Charlotte would say that was okay. I don't want to jeopardize my first case."

"Okay. As long as you include me in the intelligence loop. I am concerned Dorian might be next," she said, walking to the door.

As she put her hand on the knob, he said, "Oh, and by the way, Wren also confessed to something else. I guess she figured everyone would find out eventually…"

She turned toward him. "Let me take a stab at it. Wren is not Julian's cousin."

"Bingo!" he said. "She said her mother and Julian's were best friends and she called Julian's mother, 'Aunt.' She's known him for years."

Liz laughed. "Wren probably figured Charlotte would find out soon enough that she and Julian weren't related. Watch your step with that one Mr. P.I."

"Will do. Aren't you forgetting something?"

She went back to the sofa and gave him a kiss.

"I'll take the kiss," he said, "but I meant the ferret."

"Oops."

Chapter 15

After leaving Ryan, she made a beeline for where she suspected Aunt Amelia might be hiding out. The place her great-aunt always escaped when needing a break from modern-day reality, her screening room.

Julian Rhodes murder was one of those realities.

Liz opened the door to semi-darkness, the only light came from the TV screen on the stage. Last month the old projection screen had been upgraded to a huge theater size smart TV enabling her great-aunt to watch all her favorite mid-century television shows via streaming channels, YouTube, DVD, or recorded to a DVR.

Up ahead, third row center, Liz recognized Aunt Amelia's updo hairstyle silhouetted against the screen. Barnacle Bob was perched on the back of the stadium seat next to her. At the sight of the macaw, she left Farrah's cage by the door.

Careful not to bump into the framed photos on the wall of her great-aunt arm-in-arm with famous stars from Aunt Amelia's glory years as a character actress, she crept down the aisle, then slipped into a seat on the other side of Aunt Amelia, away from Barnacle Bob. Depending on when he'd been last fed, the brat was known to take a nip at an earlobe, or worse.

"Thought I'd find you here, Auntie." She took Aunt Amelia's soft veined hand in hers and they sat silently for a few minutes staring at the screen. Her great-aunt had a tendency to tune out, by tuning in to old television shows. Liz didn't recognize what was playing. And that said a lot.

Since an early age, Liz and Aunt Amelia had spent numerous hours in the hotel's screening room, usually watching episodes her great-aunt had a part in. Some roles were small, some large. But always, her radiance overshadowed those around her. Liz had once asked if she'd ever tried out for any lead roles, and she'd responded, "No, not really, Lizzy. I never wanted to be pigeonholed into being a leading lady. When I played one of the maids on *Dark Shadows* it afforded me time to do other television projects. I even snuck in a few parts in musicals and dramas at the Pasadena Playhouse. *The Fantasticks* for one." Amelia Eden Holt's voice was best heard on stage. Even at eighty, she knew how to belt out a show tune even Barbra Streisand would have trouble competing with. "And, think of all the people I've met in the business by playing a bit part," she'd told her. Once, Liz found Aunt Amelia's rolodex in a drawer in her sitting room and was amazed by the famous names that filled it. Including Alfred Hitchcock. Liz knew he had a reputation for being a womanizer.

Leaning close to Aunt Amelia's ear, Liz whispered, "Thought you'd be in bed. What ya watching?"

Aunt Amelia aimed the remote at the screen and pressed pause.

"Ugh, Auntie, what's that smell!" Instead of her usual L'Air du Temps perfume, she reeked of garlic, and it was coming from around her neck.

"Ring around the collar. Ring around the collar,'" Barnacle Bob squawked. Referring to an old 1960s laundry commercial featuring an obnoxious parrot chastising his female owner for not getting the stains out of her husband's shirt collar. For Christmas, Liz's father had given his aunt a DVD collection of popular commercials from the sixties and early seventies, knowing several of the commercials Amelia Eden Holt had starred in. Sometimes she showed just a hand, like in the Palmolive commercial with Madge the manicurist, or even a pair of arms like in the Morris the Cat nine-lives commercial.

"This is no ring around the collar, BB." Liz turned on the flashlight function of her phone and shined it on her great-aunt. Replacing Aunt Amelia's usual collection of multicolored beaded necklaces was a wreath of garlic.

"Thanks, BB. Now, I'll never get that jingle out of my head," Liz said.

Aunt Amelia smiled at her bald headed pet. He could do no wrong in her great-aunt's book. But in this case, Liz was happy see her great-aunt smile after what had happened to Julian Rhodes. Her great-aunt never saw half of Barnacle Bob's pranks and never heard him cuss like a drunken sailor right after she left a room. Liz had to hand it to him. It seemed Barnacle Bob's parroting was always en pointe. Liz suspected his brain size was bigger than most macaw's. Though she'd never let on she thought so. The thirty-year-old loudmouth had been in Liz's life for twenty-five years. Seeing Liz had no siblings, she almost thought of BB as an irritating older brother. *Almost.*

"Don't worry, I'm wearing it on Dorian's suggestion," Aunt Amelia said. "It will ward off..."

"Barnabas Collins from *Dark Shadows* or any other vampires roaming the Indialantic's grounds. Or, for that matter, your great-niece!"

Even though she wore a grin, she said, "This isn't funny, Lizzy. Dorian certainly doesn't think so. She says wearing garlic will protect me and everyone at the Indialantic from any evil spells from witches or warlocks. She's convinced someone put a spell on her and that's why Julian died because of an allergic reaction to shellfish. She even told me they still use garlic in the West Indies as a protection from evil sorcerer's spells. And once, one of the writers on *my show* told me that people in Malaysia smear garlic on the forehead of their children to protect them from vampires. After what happened to Mr. Rhodes, it can't hurt to use a little precaution. Dorian suspects Julian's cousin. She says the girl is not a cousin at all and purposely added some shellfish into his food."

So, she hadn't heard Julian had been poisoned. And not by shellfish. Liz didn't think garlic would help anyone who'd ingested antifreeze. "You've taught me garlic's a good insect repellent. Let's leave it at that. It might also keep your boyfriend Ziggy away."

She was trying to keep things light. She knew soon enough everyone would know what happened to white witch Julian Rhodes. Ryan had told her that Charlotte said they were keeping the type of poison he'd ingested out of the press and with so small a suspect pool, Liz agreed with the decision. Not even Aunt Amelia should know the details of his death. She'd do something rash, like she'd done in the past, and perhaps become the killer's next victim. "Have you seen Dorian since she came back from the hospital?"

"Yes."

"Did they find anything wrong with her?"

"No, but she said she was definitely ill from something. They pumped her stomach just in case. I think she should have stayed the night. She doesn't look well enough to be released. I didn't want to tell Dorian this, but before I left for the Mystical Merfest Regatta I found an angry Mr. Rhodes holding an envelope addressed to Dorian. He demanded that I tell him where it had come from. Apparently, it was just lying on the hotel registration counter. He flashed it in my face in a very rude manner and I saw it only had Dorian's first name on it."

"Was it typed? Or handwritten?"

"Handwritten. Printed. Childish almost. I explained to him that I knew nothing about it. I could tell he wasn't buying my explanation. He said not to mention anything to Dorian, he would tell her himself."

"Did you?"

"Did I what, darling?"

"Mention it to Dorian."

"No, he said he would. Did I do something wrong by not telling her?"

"Of course not, Auntie."

Liz stored away the information about the letter. If it was another threatening letter, it would seem that the person threatening Dorian had either followed her to the Indialantic or was a wedding guest. Or wedding crasher, as in Wren. She gave her great-aunt's hand a squeeze and said, "So, whatcha watching? And before you answer, I insist you take off your garlic necklace. I've never known you to be superstitious."

"I'm not. I did it for Dorian. I don't think if I take it off now, she'll find out. She was on some kind of heavy tranquilizers. I'm sure she'll sleep through the night." She took off the strand of garlic and handed it to Liz. "Be a dear and hang it on the doorknob by the exit. This is a terrible thing to befall my dear friend."

Liz got up and gave her a kiss on the cheek, then took the odorous necklace away. When she came back, she sat and asked, "So, what's on the screen?"

"*Voyage to the Bottom of the Sea.*"

"Never heard of it."

"Not surprising," Aunt Amelia said with a slight smile. "It was a sci-fi series from the mid-sixties about a subatomic submarine and the captain's and crews' strange encounters undersea. Aliens were the least of their problems. The main cast was basically all male, so I never had a role on the show. I did have a huge crush on David Hedison, the lead actor who played Commander Lee Crane. He reminds me of your Ryan, don't you think?" She pressed the play button, then froze it on an actor with dark Hollywood looks.

"Yeah. If Ryan cut his hair, was clean shaven, and shorter. Actually, your commander reminds me more of Dad."

"Whoever he reminds us of, to my young self, he sure was dreamy. I managed to get on the set of this particular episode by promising one of the cameramen I'd go on a date with him. I'd been right next door on the Twentieth Century Fox soundstage filming an episode of *Batman*. The Riddler was the bad guy and I played one of his crew, dressed in a green leotard with question marks printed all over it. No lines but I did manage to get front and center in every scene."

Liz laughed. "Not surprising, Auntie. And I've seen that episode."

"Golly, I just remembered, *Batman* was where I met Joan Collins. She played the Siren. And now I'm playing a siren of sorts in our play, *The Sea Witch*."

"Never saw an episode with Joan Collins. You'll have to find it and we'll watch together for inspiration. Only let's save it for tomorrow. It's been a long day." Liz didn't like the dark circles under her great-aunt's eyes that stood out even in the dim light. Aunt Amelia had taken over the role of mother after her mother passed away twenty five years ago and would never let Liz see her cry. Now that she thought about it, her great-aunt had never cried in front of her, while Liz, on the other hand, couldn't count the times.

"I'm near the end, only a minute or two left." She pressed the play button on the remote. "They filmed the underwater scenes by working in a water tank surrounded by cyclorama..."

"Cyclorama?"

"Kind of like IMAX, where they use a circular diorama around the water tank. Quite advanced for the sixties. Anyway, it was an excellent experience. But not as exciting as when I had a walk-on role with David Hedison when he was the guest star in an episode of *Love, American Style*. It was right before I came back to the Indialantic after my father, your great-grandfather's passing."

Liz remembered watching a snippet of the episode her great-aunt had mentioned because she'd fallen asleep and had to be prodded awake in time for Aunt Amelia's cameo. Some vintage television shows didn't carry over to the twenty-first century very well. In her opinion, *Love, American Style* and *Fantasy Island* were good examples if you were looking for a snooze fest. Kate, on the other hand, had loved both syrupy-sweet shows because she was a hopeless romantic. Not every love story turned out with all rainbows and butterflies, as evidenced by the scar on Liz's face.

They remained quiet for a few minutes watching Commander Crane fight off a foreign agent who wanted to blow up a peacetime ship using the *Seaview's* nuclear torpedoes. She was surprised by how much she enjoyed the episode, never guessing the twist as to who the undercover-murdering spy was. There were similarities between what transpired on the submarine *Seaview* and what had just happened on the *Queen of the Seas*—A killer in a small pool of suspects and a twist ending on who the murderer was, just like last January at the Indialantic. "I bet Pierre would love this series. It's actually a whodunit, like in an Agatha Christie book."

As if reading her mind, Aunt Amelia said, "I plan on having a talk with Charlotte. I don't think Dorian's fiancé died of natural causes. For one thing he was too young. For the other thing, that young Wren creature seems suspicious to me. Dorian sure thinks so, too. When I asked Wren questions about her cousin, she didn't have any good answers, and she wasn't very distraught over his death. But maybe I'm just imagining everything. I know a shellfish allergy can be life threatening, but I also know that Branson knew about it and wouldn't serve anything with shellfish. I've been trying to talk to Captain Netherton, but he keeps evading me. I'm not some old lady ready to be sent out to pasture. Didn't I help you with that horrible business last January?"

"Yes, you did more than help. And you're not old. And no one's putting you out to pasture. Let's just remain calm until we get more information."

"You're right. I need to check on Dorian." As the credits rolled, she continued, "I've decided to give back Dorian all the money she put down for the weekend, including whatever cost the dinner was to her son Branson."

"Are you sure? It wasn't anyone at the Indialantic's fault?"

"I've made up my mind."

"That's kind of you." She knew Dorian was a very wealthy woman, but she also knew her great-aunt would always do the right thing.

Aunt Amelia yawned, and Barnacle Bob added, "Sleep tight. Don't let the bedbugs bite." Something her great-aunt said when Liz was a child after reading her and Barnacle Bob a bedtime story. "No one's worried about bedbugs, BB. Just earlobes and fingers," Liz said. "Come, Auntie. Let's get you tucked in. You need your beauty sleep."

"I need more than sleep to help this wrinkled face."

"You're not wrinkled or old!" Liz repeated for the umpteenth time. "For gosh sakes, you still surf."

"Sharing Ziggy's board, not getting up on my own. There was a day…"

"You take kickboxing lessons, you spend hours rehearsing for your plays."

"Speaking about plays. Susannah just told me, you promised we would rework the *The Sea Witch* script and give her more lines."

"Is that all Susannah told you?" Liz asked, worried Susannah had given Aunt Amelia the same blow-by-blow description of Julian Rhodes's gruesome final minutes, like she'd just done to Liz.

"She had one of her headaches, so we couldn't talk further about what happened on the boat. Wonder if the headache's another one of her phony-baloney excuses."

"I saw her earlier. She looked to be in real pain."

"My bologna has a first name, it's..." Barnacle Bob crooned, jumping onto Aunt Amelia's shoulder."

"Can it!" Liz told him before he sang the entire Oscar Meyer bologna television commercial jingle. If she didn't stop him, it would repeat in her head and keep her awake all through the night, along with ring-around-the-collar, ring-around-the-collar. "Those midcentury advertising geniuses sure knew how to write a jingle. Now, celebrity endorsements or talking lizards seem the norm."

"Sad, isn't it?" Aunt Amelia said.

Liz wasn't so sure.

A few minutes later, holding Farrah's cage, she followed Aunt Amelia and Barnacle Bob up the lobby's circular stairway to the second floor. As she passed Wren's suite, she had a thought. *Tomorrow, I'll clean Wren's suite, and see what I can find.*

What, she had no clue.

She followed her great-aunt into her sitting room. Aunt Amelia turned toward Liz and put a finger to her lips, then pointed to the cushioned lounge that held a sleeping Dorian. She whispered, "Poor dear."

Even though she'd been released from the hospital, Dorian didn't look well. Her violet hair cast pale shadows on her face making her appear to have been drained of blood. She belonged in one of Aunt Amelia's *Dark Shadows* episodes. Liz watched Aunt Amelia cover Dorian with one of Betty's crocheted throws, she placed Farrah's cage on the chair next to Dorian, then blew her great-aunt a kiss and silently left the room.

An hour later, Liz walked out the lobby's revolving door, finally heading for home. A few minutes ago, she'd caught her father and Charlotte just as they were leaving the hotel. The only info she gleaned was that so far there wasn't any concrete proof that someone in the wedding crew had killed the Wiccan leader. Charlotte had been short in her answers to Liz's probing. She let it go and could only imagine the pressure from the sheriff's department about finding Julian's killer. Especially seeing once again the Indialantic was involved. Her father had told her another unsavory fact—Charlotte planned on having a news conference—hello paparazzi! Thankfully, he'd also told her that after some pressure from the mayor, Charlotte was waiting until tomorrow, after the closing ceremonies of the Mystical Merfest.

A trio of sheriff's cars were parked in the hotel's circular drive. Once again, they were besieged with law enforcement. She went up to one of the cars and tapped the window. The window lowered. "Hi, Agent Pike, how's Mom?" She knew the elderly officer was only weeks from retirement.

"Doing well, Liz. Thanks for asking."

"There's coffee and one of Pierre's chocolate orange truffle tarts in the kitchen. Make sure you take some."

"You don't have to twist my arm. Need an escort home?"

"Not as long as everyone who was on the boat, with the exception of Ashley, Captain Netherton, and Susannah, are inside the Indialantic."

Agent Pike didn't answer, just said, "Take it easy. We've got it handled."

She hoped they did.

It was a moonlit night, a full moonlit night. The same moon meant to guarantee Dorian and Julian a blissful wedding day. She followed the front drive, glancing over at Aunt Amelia's cutting garden. The moon reflected off something that glowed silver. Realizing it was the altar from the Sunshine Wiccan Society, she went closer.

The base of the altar was constructed of interwoven reeds and branches, its top made from three rough-hewn planks of wood. Loose yellow and orange flower heads were scattered on top; along with seashells, two strawberries, a peacock feather surrounded by a circle of crystals or salt rocks like on Dorian's engagement ring. There was a brass symbol of some kind that had three spirals forming a triangle shape. That must've been the item that she'd seen reflecting the moonlight. Lastly, a ladder type thingy was draped over all the items on top of the altar. Its rungs looked like they were made from fish bones, held together with string. Tied to the bottom rung were two rooster feathers. If Liz had to guess it was some kind of dreamcatcher or wind chime. Not the items used in a pagan sacrifice or dark magic as Liz had feared, just nice sunshiny items to celebrate the summer solstice and a wedding between a psychic and a white witch/warlock.

It was funny how prejudices of other people's beliefs could cause fear and anxiety. To each his own was her philosophy; as long as "do no harm" was indoctrinated into a person's spiritual beliefs, she was all for it.

She heard the hoot of a barred owl. In the far distance she thought she saw a glow like a firefly's next to the summerhouse. Liz had never seen a firefly on the island. In New York City's Central Park, yes. But not here.

Spooked she took a step back from the altar. On a single shelf tucked under the top of the altar, she saw a jar. Could it be the same jar of charged water that Julian had showed Dorian Friday night on the beach? She bent and reached for it, then held it up to the moonlight.

This wasn't a jar of water. Inside was an amber liquid and floating in the liquid were straight edge razor blades, pieces of barbed wire and rusty nails. There was also a penknife missing its hilt.

Her hand trembled as she quickly set the jar back on the shelf. So much for the "do no harm" part of whoever made the jar. Wren? Julian? She knew it wasn't Dorian's handiwork. Or did she? Things were getting weirder by the second. But, then again, what wasn't weird about this whole weekend, even if you excluded the murder?

She tentatively took a step toward home, almost turning around and reconsidering Agent Pike's offer of an escort. Instead, she soldiered on until she reached the seashell and gravel path that led to her cozy beach house. Soothing her nerves were the familiar cacophony of nature sounds; owls, frogs, and crickets making their presence known. Soothing, but not enough to keep her from quickening her pace. There was a killer on the loose. But were they really on the loose, or relaxing in one of the Indialantic's luxury suites? She'd never felt any danger walking alone in the sweet scented night, but the jar of sharp objects floating in liquid that she'd just held made her walk faster. She had no ties to Julian Rhodes and had to remember things were much different with this murder.

Hard to believe she could actually separate her murders into their own category.

A loud crunch of shoes on shell and gravel came from behind her. *What was that!* Whipping around, she searched the shadows. Nothing.

To her left was a thicket of palmettos and behind the palmettos, a lush palm tree. Suddenly, a flurry of bats flew out from the canopy of the palm leaves. She laughed. They must have caused a small coconut to fall on the path behind her. Bats were no rare occurrence on the grounds of the Indialantic. In fact, ever since she was a child, she'd learned to embrace them as part of island life and an important part of the island's ecosystem. Bats were nature's friends and ate tons of mosquitoes.

She heard the crunch again, only closer. That was no falling coconut. She took off in a gallop, her chest heaving as she went. She stumbled once, and when she was on all fours, took a nanosecond to look behind her. Someone was coming up the path, walking at an even pace. She couldn't see who it was because a cloud covered the moon.

Realizing this was no time to wait and see, she got up, her knees raw from the seashells and gravel, then sprinted the last hundred feet to the steps to her oceanfront deck. She leapt up the steps, two at a time. *Almost there*, she thought.

She'd left the French doors unlocked and slipped inside.

With shaky fingers, she set the alarm code to her mother's birthday, then bent to catch her breath, her lungs burning like she'd inhaled a lit match. Up until this evening there'd been no reason to set the alarm.

She stood in the darkness, peering out between a crack in the blinds. Something rubbed against her shins. She jumped and almost bit her tongue in half. Bronte uttered a soft meow.

"No worries, kitty. No one is there," she said, more to herself than the cat.

She thought of calling Charlotte or her father. But no, they had enough on their plates. It would wait till morning. If the person wanted to accost her, he'd had plenty of time.

On second thought, she decided to call Charlotte.

"Liz, you okay?"

When Charlotte answered the phone Liz could tell she was surprised. In fact, Liz had never called her on her private number, except when needing help on what to get her father for Christmas or his birthday. She was pleased that her father's fiancée and chief detective for the Brevard Sheriff's Department sounded concerned. After Liz had told her about the man, Charlotte promised to send over a car to watch the beach house. She also promised not to tell her father about it until the morning. Liz thanked her. She didn't need her daddy sleeping on her sofa. Charlotte, like Liz, didn't think there was any danger, especially when Liz explained about how slowly the person had followed her.

She and Bronte slept soundly. The only things waking her were the painful cuts and scrapes on her knees when she turned over in bed and the vision of Julian Rhodes's face when the sheet fell off his body.

Chapter 16

When Liz passed Aunt Amelia's meditation garden early Sunday morning, she saw a stoic Wren sitting on a mat in the full lotus position. Wren seemed as still as the cement Buddha that faced her on the smooth stones. Liz gazed straight ahead as she passed, not wanting to disturb her. That was before she noticed a Cattleya Trianae Alba orchid behind Wren's right ear.

Aunt Amelia had been growing the rare, white, ruffle edged orchid, whose common name was Nieve Blanca, for over thirty years. It was her great-aunt who got Liz involved in growing orchids. They were both members of the AOS, the American Orchid Society. Since she was an adolescent, Liz had been following Aunt Amelia around the orchid house, learning the Latin names and inhaling the delicate aroma of the most fragrant and rare varieties.

The small greenhouse sat on the southwest corner of the Indialantic's property and was built shortly after her great-great-grandmother Maeve came to Melbourne Beach. Maeve had wanted to embrace the island's native flora and fauna, which were so different from her formal gardens at Castle Isle Tor in Cornwall. Aunt Amelia had followed in her grandmother's footsteps. In her great-aunt's mind, her Florida orchids were almost as cherished as her pets. Sadly, her great-aunt had told her that in modern times orchid species were becoming extinct faster than they could be described and classified. All Wren had to do was go to Aunt Amelia's cutting garden and snip to her heart's delight.

Liz's face heated as she marched on. She should box Wren's ears for decapitating the delicate orchid. The flowers were meant to bloom on their plant, not be cut down in their prime. She prayed the plant itself was still intact. More importantly, what was Wren doing in the orchid house in the first place? The doors were padlocked shut because of the value inside and only Liz, Pierre and Aunt Amelia had the keys.

Instead of confronting her, Liz continued toward the hotel. It would be the perfect opportunity to do her own snooping—in Wren's natural habitat—the Swaying Palms Suite. She spied three sheriff's cars parked in the drive, but unbelievably, not a single news van. The hotel had enough bad press in the past year. The same year that coincided with Liz's move home. After Charlotte had her news conference, she knew they wouldn't be so lucky. Her heart broke for Aunt Amelia who'd banked on the first wedding at the Indialantic to be a success.

Passing the cutting garden, Liz paused and looked at the spot where the wedding was supposed to have taken place. The arbor was still there, but the altar Julian had brought from the grounds of the SWS was missing. Where had it gone and who had moved it? She shrugged her shoulders, happy it and the jar of disturbing objects she'd seen last night were gone. She continued to the side door leading into the hotel's kitchen. At the door, she pressed in the security code, then walked inside.

After greeting Pierre and Greta, she grabbed a star fruit pastry from under a glass domed plate on the counter and sat at the long wooden farm table. Greta was at the sink putting the breakfast dishes in the one of two industrial dishwashers. Pierre was feeding lemons and limes into a juicer. The smell of citrus was as comforting as the scent of pine at Christmas, "How far did you and Greta get on the wedding brunch preparations?" she asked.

Wiping his hands on his apron, his toque pitched to one side, Pierre answered, "The cake still has to be assembled, but the food has all been prepped. *Bonjour, mon amie.* Did you hear the wedding has been canceled and the young groom lost at sea?"

That wasn't exactly how things went down, but with Pierre's fragile mental state, she would let him believe it. "Yes, very tragic."

Greta turned to Liz. "Your auntie wants to serve a small memorial brunch in the courtyard at eleven. Right now, she's talking to Charlotte and your father."

"Cracker! Polly wants a freakin' cracker, blast it!" reverberated from the butler's pantry.

"Watch your mouth Barnacle Bob!" Greta said, "Or I'll wash it out with soap." Greta was the only one at the hotel besides Aunt Amelia who the macaw would listen to.

Barnacle Bob knew not to bite the hand that fed him his kiwi and closed his beak.

Liz tried to sound nonchalant. "Do you know what room Dad and Charlotte are in? I'd love to get an update?"

"The library." Greta gave her a knowing look, also clicked her tongue in warning and glanced at Pierre. Liz liked that Greta was overprotective of her friend, wanting to keep him from any kind of worry. "I'm sure if you want to attend the brunch Liz," Greta said, drying her hands with a hand towel, "there's more than enough food."

"No thanks, Greta, I think I'll pass on the brunch." Then on second thought, she said, "But I'll help you and chef set up and give Auntie a break. That way she can stay by Dorian's side. Afterward, I'll have to run out because I promised Kate I'd be at Ponce De Leon Park to see her perform her closing mermaid schtick. It's the last day of the Mystical Merfest. They've got rides and food and Kate's playing our island's mermaid princess from the legend. You remember the legend, don't you Grand-Pierre?"

"Of course, I do, *ma petite.*"

Liz glanced over at Greta. "You guys should come along."

"Sounds like an excellent idea," Pierre said as he poured the lemon and lime juice into a huge pitcher. He added a couple of heaping scoops of confectioner's sugar, then stirred. Though he was a Cordon Bleu chef, he believed simple was best and was not a fan of molecular cooking or any tricks with dry ice. He put the pitcher in the refrigerator, then joined Liz at the table.

Greta came over and sat next to her. "Sounds like fun. We all know the legend. We watched the Mystical Merfest Boat Regatta from the bell tower. Kate makes a perfect mermaid princess."

Pierre laughed. "I heard your auntie is elaborating on the legends of mermaids by playing the part of the Sea Witch from the story *Little Mermaid.* I have yet to read her script. You do know that Hans Christian Andersen's version of the *Little Mermaid* is a lot different than the Disney cartoon you used to watch, Lizzy. There's no happy ending between the Little Mermaid and the Prince."

"I'm much older and wiser than to believe in fairy tales, Grand-Pierre. But you can't blame a child for hoping to find their prince or princess."

He raised a furry eyebrow. "Are you saying Ryan isn't your prince? He's such a nice young man."

"Could be," she said, then winked. "I better go. I'll meet you back here at nine thirty." She stood, then bent and gave him a kiss on the end of his nose, the smell of Old Spice aftershave as calming as the ocean waves that lapped onto her beach.

Hustling out of the kitchen, she headed for the back hallway, her mind on fairy tales. She and her ex, Travis, didn't have a happy ending either. It was comical that everyone in Manhattan's literary world had thought they were the perfect power couple. Instead of tracing the scar on her cheek, her usual reaction to thoughts of Travis, she forced out a cheery whistle. The past was past, and she smiled inwardly at the chance that Ryan was indeed her prince. And she, his Little Mermaid. Theirs would be a different ending than Hans Christian Andersen's.

She'd planned on meeting Ryan at the park for the closing ceremonies of the Mystical Merfest. Right now, he was busy getting the Deli-casies tent ready over at Squidly's, which was good because she had some sleuthing to do and didn't want him to talk her out of it.

While Wren was still outdoors in the mediation garden, Liz planned to check out her suite, hoping the girl was busy asking the universe for forgiveness and atoning her for her crimes. The orchid being the least of them.

As she stepped into the back corridor, she heard Greta calling after her, "Liz wait up."

Liz stopped.

Greta stepped in close and whispered, "I wanted to talk to you without Pierre overhearing." She went on to tell Liz that she'd seen something disturbing when Greta and Pierre were up in the bell tower before the *Queen of the Seas* left port for the rehearsal dinner cruise.

"What did you see?"

Greta looked behind her to make sure Pierre couldn't overhear. There was no need to worry because he was busily humming one of his favorite French tunes with Barnacle Bob as his accompanist.

She leaned in. "That evening, Pierre was facing the ocean, watching a school of dolphins frolic just beyond the breaking surf. I was looking in the opposite direction toward the Indian River Lagoon. I had a pair of binoculars. I wanted to make sure I had a good view of the Mystical Merfest Boat Regatta when it passed. I was focused on a pelican and an osprey fighting over a floundering fish, when I heard shouting come from the top deck of *Queen of the Seas*. It was then that I saw them."

"Who?"

"Branson, Dorian's son and that Wren girl with the huge eyes, the one Susannah calls a freeloader. Branson was screaming something at her and she just stood there, taking it."

"Was anyone else on the boat?"

"No, they must have been the first guests on the ship because a few minutes later I saw the rest, including Captain Netherton, coming up the dock to board."

"Did you tell Agent Pearson?"

"If you think I should say something, I will." Nervously, she wrung her hands together. Liz never saw anything ruffle Greta. It seemed Wren was setting off warning bells everywhere she went.

"Is there something you know that we don't?" Greta asked.

Liz broke her gaze.

"Mr. Rhodes was poisoned, wasn't he? That would explain the sheriff's cars. If it was an accident they wouldn't be here." She leaned in and looked in Liz's pale blue eyes. "Would they?"

"Let's just say it's a suspicious death. I'll tell Charlotte or my dad, whomever I see first, what you told me. Just keep your eyes open. If you don't want to talk to Charlotte, you can always talk to me or Ryan. Just leave Aunt Amelia out of it, she's upset enough because of her friend."

"I feel so bad for that lovely Dorian Starwood. Do you know that yesterday when I went to her tent, she read my cards for free. Everything she told me about the past was spot-on and I hope what she told me about my future comes to fruition. I'm happy she has Amelia to help her through all this."

"They've been friends for decades." Liz wanted to ask Greta more about Branson and Wren, but time was tickin' on how long Wren might stay in the meditation garden. "Greta, have you cleaned the Swaying Palms Suite yet?"

"You, sly dog," Gretta said. "No, I haven't had a chance. Go to it! Pierre and I will see you before brunch, then after the cleanup we'll meet up with you at the park. I want to be there to cheer Katie on at the closing ceremonies with the mayor. What a lovely mermaid she makes."

Liz agreed. "I'll catch you later. If you do bump into my dad or Charlotte, please be sure *not* to tell them where I am. I might need you as an alibi sometime down the road."

"You have my word Nancy Drew. Too bad mystery writer Betty can't be here to help you solve your latest caper."

"Don't you worry, she's coming home tomorrow and I've got her working behind the scenes."

"I'm sure you do."

Liz turned toward the laundry room. "Greta, can you do me one more favor? If Wren walks in, make sure she tries one of those pastries Grand-Pierre has in the oven." She winked. "Even offer her a spot of tea or coffee."

Greta winked back and said, "Now, can you please do something for me? While you're up there, can you keep your eyes open for my pearl earring? That ferret of Ms. Starwood's is adorable, but she's a kleptomaniac. I don't think she spends as much time in her cage as she does slinking around like a bandit. I have a feeling when everyone leaves, we'll find a hidden cache of her booty. Including my earring."

"Will do."

Greta returned to the kitchen and Liz went to the left of the old service elevator and entered the laundry room. She grabbed the maid's cart, piled the top with clean linens and towels, and took the elevator to the second floor. Stopping in front of the Oceana Suite, she pressed her ear to the door. Either Dorian was sleeping, or she was with Aunt Amelia. The cart made loud creaking noises as she rolled it to the Swaying Palms Suite. She went to put the key in the door, but there was no need because it had been left unlocked. Wren must not be worried about getting murdered in the middle of the night. Could it be because she was the murderer? Or perhaps because the sheriff's department searched the suite earlier and there hadn't been a need for Wren to lock the door.

Liz called out, "Maid service. Anyone here?" Then she walked into an empty sitting room. Wren was a neatnik.

The bedroom was also neat. No clothing, papers, or personal items in sight. The room had the same OCD feel to it as the sitting room and balcony. Wren had even made her bed with military precision. Her one piece of luggage was a large duffel bag sitting on the luggage stand. Liz knew it was a vintage piece of Louis Vuitton, made way before Wren, or for that matter Liz, was born. She knew all about its age because Kate had scored a Louis Vuitton bag at an estate sale. Kate's bag dated from the 1980s and had the same signature monogram and gold padlock.

There was no key in the padlock of Wren's bag.

Kate's estate sale Louis Vuitton bag had also been padlocked without a key. Liz remembered watching her open the lock by poking one of the teeth from a metal hair pick into the keyhole. Inside the bag was a second edition of Hemingway's *The Old Man and the Sea*. The bag itself had a higher resale value than the book. But to Kate, it was the book that had the most value.

Liz didn't have a hair pick or a bobby pin, but inside a cup on top of the cleaning cart was a small metal skewer that Pierre used when trussing chickens. It was perfect for opening small locks, like Liz watched Greta do when someone once locked themselves in one of the hotel's bathrooms.

She only hesitated for a moment before she took the skewer and jiggled it in the small opening. Left then right. Then in a circular motion. She heard a click and tugged on the lock. Abracadabra! It opened. Being the daughter of a lawyer, she knew what she was doing was illegal, but that didn't stop her from sliding the lock from the zipper and looking inside the bag.

Cotton print floral dresses were neatly folded, a clear bag held minimal cosmetics. Trying not to disturb the order of the clothing, she gently stuck both her hands inside until she felt the bottom of the bag. Her fingers found a file folder. Before extracting it, she went to the outer door of the sitting room and turned the deadbolt. If Wren came back, Liz would have time to put things right.

Hurrying back to the luggage stand, she reached inside the bag and extracted the file folder as deftly as a bomb squad technician disarming a landmine. When she opened the folder, her mouth fell open.

Surprise didn't describe her reaction. It was a contract between Julian Rhodes and Wren Wagner saying that they were co-owners of the Sunshine Wiccan Society Water Bottling Company. Only instead of Wren, her name read Renee Wagner. And it was dated and notarized yesterday. Was that what was in the folder Wren had been angrily pressing into Julian's chest on the beach Friday night?

Liz took out her phone and took pictures of all four pages of the contract, then put the folder back in the bag.

During a quick cleaning of the bathroom, she'd had a small mishap, knocking over a bottle of perfume and spilling half its contents onto the countertop. Making up for the spilled liquid she added a little tap water. Even with the added water, the scent of gardenia and roses was overpowering. One of Liz's pet peeves was when a woman's—or for that matter a man's—fragrance lingered long after they'd left the room. Ryan smelled of soap and citrus. It didn't get much better than that.

She did a little spot cleaning in the bedroom and realized she hadn't brought the vacuum, so she got on the floor in the bedroom and picked up by hand every speck of lint from the Persian rug. In the corner, under the rattan wardrobe, something winked at her. She reached out her arm and grasped a pearl earring. The little weasel must have been on the loose. At least she's solved the mystery of Greta's missing earring. Now if only they could solve the mystery of who killed Julian Rhodes.

Taking clean towels and linens off the cart, she placed them on the credenza in the sitting room, then checked to make sure the coast was clear and pushed the cart out of the room.

Halfway down the hall, she realized she hadn't snapped the lock on the luggage shut.

Too late. Wren was walking toward her from the other end of the hallway. The Nieve Blanca orchid was missing from her right ear. *Murderer.*

Liz kept her head down. There was no reason for subterfuge because Wren didn't even acknowledge Liz as she passed. The girl seemed preoccupied with something. It seemed the benefits of her mediation must not have lasted too long because her hands were balled in fists and her chin jutted forward in anger. Liz normally would wonder what had riled her up. Maybe even question her. But the thought of the open luggage lock spurred her down the hallway toward the elevator—glasses and cleaning supplies rattling as she went.

The creaking of the cart's wheels was no match for the frenetic beating of her heart.

Chapter 17

"If it was antifreeze, isn't there some way of tracing it?" Liz sat in a leather armchair in the hotel's mammoth library. Charlotte and her father were on the leather sofa across from her. She looked first at Charlotte, then her father. "Do you think someone was out to get Dorian and Julian ate some tainted food or drank antifreeze from the blue bottled SWS water? Did Auntie tell you that she saw Julian holding a letter meant for Dorian? He was quite upset about it."

"Yes, Charlotte knows all about it," Fenton said, glancing at his tight-lipped detective fiancée.

"Did you ask Dorian about it?" Liz asked.

"Dorian's in no shape to answer much of anything right now," Fenton said, drumming his fingers on his knee, worry lines on his forehead. "I don't know about this idea for the brunch Dorian insists on giving in memory of Mr. Rhodes." He looked at his fiancée.

Charlotte wore an off-white blazer and matching skirt. Under the blazer was a lime-green sleeveless tank top and at her neck a trio of delicate gold chains in varying lengths. Her attire screamed Palm Beach but her determined hazel eyes and tone of voice shouted Agent Pearson, tough homicide detective for the Brevard County Sheriff's Department. "I've posted someone to keep an eye on things once the food leaves the kitchen, I don't think she'll let us down."

Liz smiled. "Susannah Shay, I'll bet. Nothing will get past her. I know she's devastated after finding Mr. Rhodes near death. Have you got any of our suspects in your crosshairs, Charlotte?"

"It's early days," her father answered for Charlotte. "We're looking into everything involving both Ms. Starwood and Mr. Rhodes. We're not saying that you shouldn't get involved, but for now, Charlotte is in the preliminary stages of the investigation and still waiting for lab results on Dorian's stomach contents. Legally, Charlotte can't make anyone stay at the Indialantic. However, before they realize they're free to leave we need to learn as much as we can about each of them and at the same time keep Dorian safe in case she was the original target. Plus, after what Charlotte told me about someone chasing you last night."

"He wasn't exactly chasing me."

Her father looked down at her skinned and bruised knees but didn't say anything. She'd considered opting for a long skirt but decided against it, and instead wore white shorts and a silk-screen T-shirt with a beautiful underwater mermaid surrounded by tropical fish and coral. The shirt was made by Home Arts' mixed-media artist, Minna. It was like wearing a one of a kind piece of art. She'd let her long strawberry-blonde hair do what it did best, go wild, like Daryl Hannah's in the movie *Splash,* trying to stick to the Mystical Merfest theme.

"How about your search of the hotel?" Liz asked. "Did you find any antifreeze?"

Charlotte wore a frown. "Not a thing. The hotel and entire grounds have been searched and we haven't come up with anything out of the ordinary. Certainly not a container of antifreeze. We do think it had to be put into a sweet drink or dessert. It has a very sugary taste on its own."

"Lovely," Liz said, thinking about Julian's contorted face when she'd seen him on the stretcher.

The pear-shaped diamond engagement ring her father had given Charlotte on Christmas Eve sparkled when it caught the early morning sunlight from the window, sending rainbow prisms onto the table. Liz thought about her mother's engagement ring that she kept safely hidden away in a book safe at her beach house. Her father had given it to Liz when she was twelve. Recently and annoyingly, Aunt Amelia kept reminding Liz about it in front of Ryan. *Too soon*, she thought, especially after what had happened on New Year's Eve.

"Have you gone over all the photos that Ashley took?" she asked Charlotte. "It might show someone near Dorian and Julian's table?"

"I looked them over quickly and I didn't see anything unusual. When we figure out by what method he'd ingested the antifreeze, we can analyze the photos further. We do know something specific about the type of antifreeze found in Mr. Rhodes's system. It hasn't been produced since the nineties. If you bought a bottle of antifreeze from an auto supply store today, it wouldn't contain the ingredient that killed him."

"So, we're looking for old antifreeze?" Liz asked. "How would someone know that only the older version was enough to poison someone?"

Fenton answered, "Well, there was quite a public case of a woman who poisoned her husband with a combination of antifreeze and oleander. There's even an entire book about the murder and it was featured on an episode of *Law and Order*. As I found out, all it would take is an online search."

"Oleander? There're tons of oleander in Florida. You aren't even allowed to burn it as part of yard waste. One leaf could kill a dog. Auntie's told me all about the hazards of oleander. You won't find it anywhere on the Indialantic's property. Did Julian have any in his system?"

"No, he didn't," Charlotte answered. "Just antifreeze."

Is it possible Julian was trying to kill Dorian, but the poison got switched like in an Agatha Christie book?"

"We have to keep every avenue open," Charlotte said standing up. "Dorian is a very wealthy woman but I don't see how Mr. Rhodes would benefit by killing her *before* they were married." All five foot ten of her went to stand next to the huge fireplace in the corner of the room. Next to the fireplace was a large window with a view of the glass summerhouse. All the other walls in the library were covered with rows and rows of antique books in floor-to-ceiling mahogany bookcases. Charlotte reached her hand to the mantel and ran her fingers over a bronze bust of Chaucer, the father of English literature, then spoke. "I suppose he might have been trying to poison her. Like I said, we need to keep an open mind."

"I know they didn't have a prenup," Liz said. "I heard it in that argument between Dorian's financial adviser Garrett and Julian that I told you guys about yesterday."

There was silence for a moment, then Liz turned to Charlotte. "Why are the two of you being so forthcoming? You don't usually share the particulars of a homicide investigation with me."

"Depending on how things go, we might need you, along with Ryan, to get closer to the limited number of people that were on the boat for the rehearsal dinner. We'll do the investigating into their backgrounds…"

She told them about the argument Greta had witnessed between Branson and Wren on the *Queen of the Seas*. "How did Auntie take it when you told her about the poison?"

Fenton said, "Aunt Amelia was very adamant that we find out what happened to her friend's fiancé."

"We didn't tell her the specifics of the poison, but we did tell her he'd been poisoned," Charlotte added. "I want to keep that under wraps for the time being."

"Dad, how about Dorian? You told her too? Right?"

"Yes. But it didn't seem to sink in. She's convinced there's some curse that someone put on her fiancé and she's all upset she can't communicate with him on the other side to find out who caused his death."

Charlotte raised her brow at Fenton's last comment and came to where they were sitting, taking her handbag off the rectory table. As she took a step toward the door, Charlotte said, "We still haven't found out much about Wren Wagner. Her prints aren't in the system. It's like she's a ghost."

"Well, thanks for keeping me in the loop. I assume you've already talked to Ryan." Finally, Liz felt like Charlotte was taking her seriously. Should she tell them about the contract for the water company that made Julian and Wren/Renee partners? First, she'd talk it over with Ryan. What she'd done earlier in Wren's suite was illegal and she didn't want to jeopardize being a part of the investigation. Perhaps Ryan could tell Charlotte on the down-low to have one of her deputies check out Wren's Louis Vuitton bag, no questions asked. Charlotte and Ryan had always gotten along and even more so since he got his P.I.'s license. If not, she would come forward with her reconnaissance work. It could wait for at least an hour until she talked to Ryan. Now that she thought about it, she had a breadcrumb to give to Charlotte in order to stay in her good graces.

As Charlotte took a step toward the door, Liz called out, "Can you hold just one a sec? I have something to show you."

She hurried out of the library and ran to the pantry to retrieve her handbag. She fed Barnacle Bob a treat, removed the invoice for the new water filtration system that Julian had shoved into Garrett's hand yesterday, then ran out the door. A litany of Barnacle Bob's curses followed her out. Oops, she realized she'd just given him a cat treat. Served him right with that potty mouth. She also realized something else. The cases of SWS water were no longer stacked in the corner. Had Charlotte taken them for evidence?

Liz was winded when she reentered the library and had to bend at the knees to catch her breath. When she looked up, she saw Aunt Amelia sitting with a very determined look on her face. Draped around her neck was Farrah. The ferret's eyes were closed, obviously comfortable on Aunt Amelia's wide shoulders.

"Lizzy, there you are," she said, "I just wanted to tell Charlotte something. Maybe you should hear it too. I just had a talk with Phoebe, and she told me something about Garrett that I thought I should pass on. He's been with Dorian for ages and it's hard to believe he would ever kill anyone, but Phoebe said he's madly in love with her mother. He even proposed to Dorian right before Mr. Rhodes came into the picture. Phoebe says before Dorian could give him an answer, Dorian was swept off her feet by Mr. Rhodes, and we all know how that turned out. I remember an episode of *Mannix*, I think it was 1967, when I played Joe Mannix's temporary secretary for a day, after his secretary, Peggy, had to stay home with her sick son. It had a similar storyline about a wealthy businesswoman and her financial advisor. That Mike Connors sure made this girl's heart throb." She finally took a breath and pounded a fist against the left side of her ample chest.

"I remember that scene. You spilled coffee all over Mannix's desk and he rolled his eyes, obviously missing trustworthy Peggy," Liz said.

Her father and Charlotte laughed.

Aunt Amelia joined in, causing the large fuchsia ball dangling from one of her earrings to whack Farrah on her tiny ferret nose. Startled, Farrah high dived from Aunt Amelia's shoulders onto Fenton's lap, ricocheted down to the Persian carpet, then scampered out the library's open door.

"Oh dear. Oh dear," Amelia moaned. Dorian will have my hide if her prized pet gets lost. She jumped up and scurried after her. Liz had no doubt she'd catch her, owing to her tri-weekly Zumba classes. Liz's eighty-year-old great-aunt could probably beat Liz in a relay race.

"What was that? Some kind of drive-by visit?" Charlotte said with a smile.

"That's interesting what she said about Garrett," Liz said. "I've seen the way he looks at Dorian. I have a feeling he would protect her with his life. But I don't know about killing someone. Does he have any kind of record or anything?"

Charlotte ignored Liz's last question. She wanted Liz's help but didn't seem or wasn't legally able to share much of anything else.

Liz handed the crumpled paper to Charlotte, then explained how she'd gotten it yesterday after the argument between Garrett and Julian. "I know the labels on the Sunshine Wiccan Society's water states that the water is bottled at the source in Jacksonville, where Dorian says the SWS grounds are. However, that paper," Liz pointed at the bill Charlotte had smoothed out on the coffee table, "says the new filtration system will be in Ocala. I know Ryan told you about Betty going to the address in Jacksonville. What if the whole Sunshine Wiccan Society is a sham?" Liz said, excitedly, heat flushing her cheeks. "Dorian never visited the grounds, and she told Aunt Amelia she'd only known Julian for six months. Six months!"

"We have talked to the local authorities in Jacksonville," Charlotte interjected. "They're getting back to us on anything they can find on Julian Rhodes and his Wiccan society. There is a natural spring on the property. At least that part is true. We'll check out this address in Ocala," she said, referring to the invoice for the water filtration system. "It will have to wait until tomorrow, when the courthouse opens, to get any concrete information."

A few minutes later, Liz left them. More confused than when she'd walked in.

Chapter 18

Liz had planned on leaving the courtyard before the guests showed up for the memorial brunch, but everyone filed in early. They looked like a group of mourners, except for Wren, who now wore a gleeful smirk when she caught Liz's gaze. What had changed? Did she guess Liz had broken into her luggage? Where was the downtrodden girl she'd just passed in the hallway?

The sun highlighted the thirty-foot palm in the center of the courtyard. It was another glorious island morning with temps hovering in the low seventies. Glancing around, you would never know they planned to lament a life instead of celebrating a marriage. All the flowering plants meant to flank the aisle for the outdoor wedding filled the courtyard with color and fragrance. All that was missing was the altar. She wondered who'd moved it, reminding her of the jar of sharp objects that she'd seen last night on the shelf under the altar. She shivered in the temperate air.

Laughter came from the corner of the courtyard where Branson and Garrett stood at a small rattan bar flanked by two giant elephant ear potted plants. When Liz first came to the Indialantic by the Sea the plants had been her height; now they stood eight feet tall. Dorian's son was pouring a bottle of Jack Daniel's into Garrett's tumbler, then he poured a good amount into his own glass. It was only eleven, a little early to be drinking. The bottle reminded Liz of her ex, Travis, and how after a couple drinks he'd turn into someone unrecognizable. Jekyll and Hyde, she'd thought. She also remembered that Branson had been arrested for selling hallucinogenic mushrooms and sent to a rehab. He and Garret seemed to be companionable, no animosity between them like she'd seen between Garrett and Julian yesterday. It was hard to believe that only last night Julian had been murdered. And most likely, one of the people in this room had done it. The only suspect missing was the person in the black baseball cap.

Aunt Amelia, Dorian, and Phoebe sat at one of the round marble topped bistro tables. Liz took a seat on an iron bench. A tall, wide leaf alocasia plant separated her from the threesome and there were gaps between the leaves making it perfect for eavesdropping, and at the same time making her invisible. She leaned in as close as she could without being noticed and heard Phoebe say, "Mother, you know from reading my book that you have to release Julian's spirit before you can communicate with him."

Dorian put a tissue up to her leaking eye. "He should be coming in clearly." She sucked in air. "Someone on that boat killed him. It wasn't me or my children, Amelia. But I have a good idea who it was." Liz saw her turn her gaze toward Wren who was sitting alone at a table in the center of the courtyard. Wren was smiling and busily tapping the screen on her phone. Seemingly, not a care in the world.

"Let's review how to set Julian free," Phoebe said in a singsong child's voice. "You, yourself, Mama, told me what to include in my book *Superstitions—Warnings from the Universe or Pure Bunk?!* On how to efficiently release a spirit from its earthly plain, freeing it so it can pass to the other side and find peace. After we leave here, the three of us…" She looked at Aunt Amelia, "will set all the clocks to the time of the death, unlock all the doors, open all the windows, cupboards, and drawers in the hotel…"

Liz couldn't help herself from thinking the *Queen of the Seas* would be the best place to be doing all these things seeing that's were Julian died. Not the hotel.

Continuing, Phoebe said, "untie any knots, turn all the mirrors to face the wall, light candles, and ring bells."

After Phoebe said the word "bells," Barnacle Bob, who was in his cage behind Aunt Amelia, started to frenetically ring his bell. Farrah, who was coiled around Dorian's neck, opened her eyes, and let out a little squeal. Phoebe gave Aunt Amelia, not Barnacle Bob a look, then said, "Julian should be receptive to the routine, mamma. After all, he knows the drill, for gosh sakes, he was a Wiccany Witch!"

That set Barnacle Bob off. He belted out a perfect imitation of a munchkin singing, "Ding, dong, the witch is dead! Witch-o-witch. Wicked Witch. Ding, dong, the Wicked Witch is dead…" until Phoebe finally asked, "Can't you shut that obnoxious bird up?"

Aunt Amelia looked like she'd been slapped. But she deferred to Phoebe by saying to Barnacle Bob, "Behave, BB, or no kiwi."

Rightly chastened, or so Liz thought, the macaw retreated to the back of his cage.

Liz got up from the bench, not learning anything new about the murder, and went to their table. Leaning over Aunt Amelia's shoulder, she whispered that she was leaving for the closing ceremonies of the Mystical Merfest. Dorian grasped Liz's wrist with her blue veined hand. Liz was surprised at the seventy-year-old woman's strength. "Lizzy, oh Lizzy, you must find out who killed him. My vision's even more clouded than before. I know you've helped solve crimes in the past, just like I have. But I must be too close. That same veil I told you about Friday, is clouding my psyche. Only this time it's like a liquid red curtain occluding the clairvoyant screen of my mind, blinding me with blood and death. There will be no rest for Julian until you find out who did this." There were no tears, just anger in her eyes. "And I want you to start, by talking to her." She pointed to Wren, who looked up from her phone, innocence in her large eyes. Wren chuckled, then went back to her phone.

Liz removed Dorian's grip from her wrist and said in a soothing tone, "I promise Dorian, we're all going to help find out what happened. Maybe you should sleep with Auntie tonight."

"I think that's an excellent idea," Amelia said.

"But what about Farrah? She won't be able to sleep a wink with Mr. Bob in the same room. I'm sorry, Amelia, it's for your own pet's protection, more than Farrah's."

"BB will be fine in the lobby for the night. He likes to hang out in the old nonworking Otis elevator."

"Are you sure Amelia?"

"Your well-being is all I care about right now."

"Then I'd like to ask a favor. Phoebe came up with a wonderful idea. We want to have a séance. Would it be possible to meet in the enlightenment parlor? She pushed her plate away. I don't know if I'll ever eat or drink again. Unless I get a sign at the séance…"

A séance? That sounded like a recipe for disaster. Liz tried to give her great-aunt the "not-a-good-idea" glare, but Aunt Amelia didn't hesitate to say, "Oh, course Dorian. If you think it will bring you closure. I'll have Susannah arrange the room, we can even bring in the old poker table…"

A dark room. Dorian as possibly the killer's original target with a motley group who are the sheriff department's only suspects. And it was Phoebe's idea. Again. Recipe for disaster. Unless…"Sounds like a good idea!" Liz said with a huge grin. "Only, I would suggest doing it on the screening room stage. There's not much room in the enlightenment parlor—too many pillows."

Dorian waved her hand in the air, then closed her eyes. "Fine. I was in the enlightenment parlor a few times yesterday and nothing worked anyway to get rid of the shrouded black cloud pressing down and smothering me with its deathly weight."

Liz shivered. Perhaps Aunt Amelia had a role Dorian could play in *The Sea Witch,* not that she didn't think Dorian's grief was real, only that she had a theatrical way of delivering her words that would add a lot of gothic atmosphere on stage.

Liz turned to her great-aunt. "What do you think Auntie?"

Aunt Amelia searched Liz's face. She knew the last place Liz would ever want to be was at a séance.

"I suppose," she answered with trepidation in her voice, surprising, seeing Amelia Eden Holt never passed up a new experience.

Phoebe's eyes lit up like she'd just swallowed a firecracker. "Excellent idea, Liz. Whaddya think Mama? Can I lead it? Pretty please."

"We'll see. In the meantime, I'll let you read my cards after we leave here. You can ask the question to the cosmos as to why all this is happening. I sure haven't been able to channel any answers."

A sting operation was in order. She would text her father to get Charlotte on board and maybe Liz would sit at the séance table next to Dorian. Her father could hide out behind the velvet curtains on the stage. Also, someone, maybe Ryan, could watch from above in the old projection booth with the pair of night vision goggles she'd bought him for Christmas.

Liz glanced at her watch. "Oh, it's getting late, I better run. She kissed both Aunt Amelia and Dorian on the cheek, nodded at Phoebe, then she turned to Barnacle Bob whose beak was pressed against the bars of his cage, his eyes on high alert. "Don't cause any more trouble, BB."

She might as well have said, "It's opposite day, BB." Because as she walked toward the French doors leading to the lagoon, she heard him humming the Wicked Witch tune from *The Wizard of Oz.* Liz guessed he'd technically listened to Aunt Amelia because he wasn't singing, just humming. She tried to keep from smiling, knowing it wasn't appropriate in front of Dorian. Aunt Amelia liked to recite a quote from Bob Newhart, one of her great-aunt's favorite comic actors, "Laughter gives us distance. It allows us to step back from an event, deal with it and then move on." Thank goodness for BB's sense of humor in times like these.

Before heading for the open doors, she surveyed the courtyard. Again, it struck her how small the gathering was. Uncharacteristically for Susannah, she had been following Greta's directives to a T. Susannah's blue-blood insistence on calling Greta by her last name, Mrs. Kimball, because she was the "help," had been forgotten and the two worked together like a well-oiled machine—instead of a couple of clogged gears—their usual dynamic. She supposed, death, or in this case, murder, had a way of bringing people together.

Passing the courtyard's center fountain, Liz headed for the door leading to the rear parking lot. She noticed Branson had joined Wren and her table. As she passed, she heard Branson say, "I refuse to stay here a moment longer. We aren't legally bound to this old hotel."

Liz took backward baby steps and hid next to the fountain.

She heard Wren say, "I don't think the sheriff's department will be too happy. It's all quite exciting don't you think? I'm going to check out that Merfest, this thing is a bore."

Branson grinned. "Maybe I'll meet you there."

"That would be nice." She gave him a wink, then grabbed her handbag and whizzed out the door.

Liz glanced over at Branson, whose face was flushed. The only spot that wasn't red was the deep dimple in the center of his chin. She followed Wren outside. There was no sign of her in the rear parking lot. She trotted toward the emporium's side lot just in time to see Wren jump inside a cherry-red Kia Soul with a large black bumper sticker on the back, saying, I WATCH FOR MOTORCYCLES. Liz only had a second to memorize the license plate number before the car peeled out, burning rubber, then turned south on A1A, heading in the direction of Vero Beach. The car hadn't been a rental and the plates displayed a Jacksonville car dealer logo. *Aha!* Jacksonville. The home of the phony Sunshine Wiccan Society.

Something niggled at Liz's brain. She wanted to get to the park and see Kate but instead she turned around. There was something she had to check out first, especially after overhearing the conversation between Dorian's son and Wren. She entered the hotel through the kitchen entrance. No one was inside. Then she grabbed the key to the Swaying Palms Suite and took the service elevator to the second floor. She tiptoed down the hallway and stuck the key in the lock, turned it, and walked in. *Good.* Wren's Louis Vuitton bag was still on the luggage stand. The lock, locked. For a panicked second, at the way Wren had peeled out of the parking lot, she wondered if she'd lied to Branson and had left for good.

Liz stepped into the bathroom and saw a damp towel draped over the chair at the dressing table. Wren's cosmetic case was on the sink. Inside the soap dish was a ring, a large opal in a gold setting. She recalled what

Aunt Amelia had said when she'd begged to wear her great-aunt's opal necklace to her high school graduation. "Oh, no, lovey. Opal's can only be worn by someone born in October." Then she recited a poem:

> *October's child is full of woe*
> *And life's vicissitudes must know.*
> *But lay an opal on her breast,*
> *And hope will lull those woes to rest.*

Liz assumed that Wren, like Aunt Amelia, had shared an October birthday. A small clue to pass on to the powers that be, seeing Charlotte was having a hard time finding anything out about Wren aka Renee Wagner. A clue, regardless.

When Betty came home tomorrow, there would be a full house of murder suspects. Was it wrong to feel a twinge of excitement at the prospect of a reunion of the three detectiveteers?

Maybe.

But there it was, nonetheless.

Chapter 19

Ponce De Leon Park was a mile away. She could have taken one of the hotel's golf carts, but she needed the extra time to clear her head.

When she reached the sidewalk that ran parallel to scenic Highway A1A. She paused for a line of cars to pass before crossing the road, then tilted the brim of her floppy straw hat to view the ocean panorama in front of her. The view of the glittering Atlantic and the calls of the island's plethora of birds were a soothing balm to her jangled nerves—better than a tranquilizer—or even a glass of wine. Wearing a hat on sunny days was still a necessity because of her scar. Even with sunscreen she had to be careful of the fragile skin. Makeup helped to camouflage it, but even after three surgeries, due to the depth and width of the wound, her badge of courage as her therapist called it, would always be visible.

The festival was in full swing when she reached the park entrance with its large commanding statue of Spanish explorer Ponce De Leon who was thought to have first landed in North America on their barrier island. A plaque at the base of the statue read: *While there is disagreement among scholars, it is believed that this site may be in an area where Juan Ponce de Leon made landfall in April 1513. It has long been thought that this event took place near St. Augustine, based upon studies of de Leon's compass headings that did not account for the inability of 16th century navigators to accurately determine longitude, magnetic compass deviations, or the effect of the Gulf Stream and prevailing winds.* Ponce de Leon's landing may still be up for interpretation, but most historians agreed that Ponce de Leon's search in Florida for the fountain of youth was just the stuff of legend. Liz still liked to believe the legend was true. She knew island life was rejuvenating, not like her hectic Manhattan lifestyle that had probably added years. Hopefully it would all even out.

She pushed her way through the crowd. Upbeat calypso steel drum music filled the air. The lead singer of a band called Crabby Joes, wore a hat topped with a pair of red, jiggly crab claws. Liz watched him jump down from the stage, grab someone from the crowd, and start dancing, as everyone around them clapped to the beat. There were smiles on all the big and little ones dressed as mermaids and pirates. It was a good turnout and she was thrilled no one knew about the murder.

Yet.

Across the street from the park was a vacant field were carnival rides had been set up. On such a clear summer day the Ferris wheel would give breathtaking views of both the Indian River Lagoon and the Atlantic. As every islander knew, June was the beginning of the hurricane season. But for now, the only storm that Liz saw brewing was the one back at the Indialantic, especially after Charlotte had her news conference where she planned to announce to the world about Julian Rhodes's death.

After grabbing a cup of fresh mango juice from a juice stand, she made her way to the park's small wooden boardwalk. Placing the cup on the railing, she glanced down at the beach. There were almost as many people on the sand as there were at the park. Mermaid tail wind sockets danced on the ocean breeze. Adolescents attempted to balance on wave boards, only to get thrown off, then resurface, laughing as their parents looked on in worry. Sandcastles littered the shoreline and people toting metal detectors searched for gold coins washed ashore from the 1715 fleet shipwreck. If you found treasure on one of Florida's public beaches it was yours to keep. The same wasn't true if you found gold or silver at the bottom of the ocean past the tide line.

Two manned lifeguard stations were set up. Melbourne Beach wasn't immune to shark sightings, and a few unfortunate people had the bite marks to prove it. But it was hard to worry about such things this afternoon—the perfect ending to the Mystical Merfest.

Finishing her mango juice, she threw her cup in a bin overflowing with trash and made her way to the pavilion. "Liz, over here!" Kate shouted, her face flushed with excitement. "How fabulous is all this?"

Kate and Alex sat on their mer-thrones. By the raising of Alex's eyebrows, followed by a wink, Liz could tell Kate's merman prince boyfriend had thought it was all too much. A professional surfer, Alex was used to having his bare, tanned upper torso exposed, but not like this. He looked like the perfectly molded Ken doll Aunt Amelia had bought Liz for her seventh birthday. Bathing Suit Ken came with his own surfboard, which Liz stole and gave to Barbie.

Next to Alex, a gaggle of mermen followers stood to the right of the small stage, drool pooling as they stared at the handsome world-renowned surfer. Kate seemed to have her own male admirers. And rightly so. The costume Francie, co-owner of Home Arts, had made Kate was exquisite. Each sequin on her tail had been hand sewn. Kate's long dark glossy hair trailed over one shoulder and she wore a gold crown covered in rainbow-hued albacore shells, pearls, and sequins. The pair made a striking couple and she was thrilled her best friend might have finally found her soulmate. Liz had fixed them up, knowing when she'd first met Alex that Kate and he would make an excellent match. Both were athletic, both competitive, and both huge readers. Although, she didn't think Alex talked to characters in his books like Kate did. Kate had been talking to books since Liz first introduced her to the Indialantic's huge library at age eight.

Kate coaxed Liz up the pavilion steps with a flip of her tail. Liz felt bad Aunt Amelia wouldn't be able to join in the closing ceremonies, but she'd naturally chosen to stay by her grieving friend.

Unlike Kate, whose legs were tucked inside her tail, Alex was able to stand in his costume. The bottom of his tail was stuffed with batting but there was a slit up the back enabling him to walk. He grabbed a folding chair for Liz to sit on.

After she sat, she leaned over and asked Kate a question. "Susannah said she saw Julian and Dorian in Books & Browsery on Saturday. Did they buy anything?"

Kate waved to a little mermaid and threw a flower lei toward her.

"Kate," Liz said. "Promise, just one question."

"Sorry. Wasn't that little blondie the cutest merchild? This is so much fun! Maybe next year you can play Meribel?"

"Not my kind of thing."

"Because of your scar?"

"No, it has nothing to do with that. I just don't like the limelight since what happened in New York and then last January."

"But you're a *New York Times* Bestselling author. No one down here cares about what happened in New York. You're a hometown island girl. You grew up here."

"Okay, okay, I'll think about it," Liz said laughing. "Now back to my question?"

"Oh, about them coming in the shop. Yes, they did. Yesterday morning Julian bought a book I was happy to get rid of...It was one of those dry business books on how get to the top no matter who you had to step on to get there."

Liz smiled, "I was worried you were going to say it was a black magic book of evil spells or something."

"Wow. I can't believe you said that, because I did sell a book of spells to Ms. Starwood."

"Phoebe Starwood?"

"No. Dorian Starwood," Kate said. "It wasn't the best book for a beginning witch. I warned her that I didn't like my conversation with the author in the preface. But she wouldn't listen."

"Do you remember the name of it," Liz asked.

Kate gave her a *don't you know me* look and said, "It was called, *Not Your Mother's Book of Spells.*"

"Catchy title." Liz's mind wandered to Dorian. She must have been the one to make the jar of sharp objects. What she didn't know was, who the jar was meant for. She told herself Dorian wouldn't kill Julian. But did she really know that?

Before Liz could ask more about the types of spells in book, she watched the town's mayor go up the steps of the pavilion and come toward them. Liz scooched her chair back, away from the limelight.

The mayor stepped in front of Kate and Alex, holding a microphone in one hand, and a large key covered in aqua glitter in the other. He looked over at Kate, then Alex, and said to the crowd, "It is my pleasure to present the key to our little seaside town to this year's mermaid princess Kate Fields and her merman prince Alex Russell. The pair raised the most money in the festival's history that will enable the Barrier Island Educational Center along with government grants to continue its sea turtle research. Well done, you two."

There was thundering applause and Liz stood to give them an ovation. When she glanced out at the throng of festival goers she was startled when she saw the man with the black baseball cap staring directly at her.

Liz charged off the stage and pushed her way through the crowd. Glimpsing his black cap disappearing down the wooden ramp leading to the beach, she followed. When she reached the sand, he was nowhere to be seen. Even if he tried to hide next to a group of sunbathers, his black getup would surely tip her off. She turned and took the wooden steps back up to the park.

On the fourth step up, she felt a hand grab her ankle from the gap between the steps. She teetered, then screamed, flailing for the railing to keep from falling. When her hand got a hold of the railing so did a huge wood splinter. "Oww!" She screeched.

Regaining her composure, her panic turned to anger. Even if it was a kid playing a joke, she didn't think it was funny. Slowly, she stepped backward until she was on the sand. At eye level she peered between the gap in the third and fourth step and saw two hazel eyes looking back at her. They didn't belong to a kid, but a full-grown rough looking man. A man wearing a black baseball cap.

The man put his fingers to his lips and said, "Stop following me." Then he took off toward another set of steps, climbed them two at a time and disappeared from view.

A lifeguard must have heard her scream. He came up behind her and asked, "Are you okay? What happened?"

"Just lost my balance. Thought a snake touched my ankle, but it was just a dried palm frond. Silly me."

She wasn't sure the lifeguard believed her. "That was quite a howl." He smiled. Perfect white teeth gleamed against his tanned face. "Let me escort you up. We don't have many snakes directly on the beach." He grabbed her elbow and guided her up to the boardwalk.

"Thank you," she managed, "I was being a sissy."

"It's always good to be cautious on Florida's beaches. We do have man o' war and jellyfish, not to mention land crabs that could latch onto a toe or two." He noticed her hand. "Hey, you're bleeding."

Blood dripped down from her right hand.

"Just a splinter from the railing," she said, maneuvering the piece of wood back and forth until she managed to free a piece the size of a wood barbeque skewer from her palm. Tears welled at the pain.

"You need some soap and water, and a topical antibiotic."

"I'm good," she said, getting out a wad of tissues from her bag to staunch the blood. "I'll take care of it. Thanks for saving me from a palm frond attack." What she really wanted to do was looked for the guy who grabbed her ankle and give him a piece of her mind.

He smiled back, white teeth glowing against his tan angular face, his hair naturally highlighted from the summer sun. "Any time ..."

"Liz."

"Liz," he repeated. "I'm Josh."

She glanced toward the set of steps a hundred feet away. The guy was long gone.

"I'll better meet my friend. Thanks again, Josh."

"No problem," he said, going back down the steps to the beach.

Before heading back to Kate, she paused for a moment before heading to the pavilion, the man's words repeating in her head, *Stop following me.* It would be a fat chance in Hades before she listened to the creep. Whatever he was up to must have something to do with Julian Rhodes murder.

Chapter 20

The crowd had thinned, and she had no problem spotting Ryan. Relief set in. Not that she needed rescuing, but she wouldn't mind collapsing into his ex-firefighter's chest for some hugs and reassurances. Ryan stood next to Alex, holding an Island Sunset IPA in his hand. He grinned when he saw her, excused himself, and came to her side.

"Ryan! So glad you're here. The guy. The guy in the black cap is, or was, here. He just grabbed my ankle."

"He what!"

"He grabbed my ankle from under the steps to the beach, then whispered, 'Stop following me.'"

Ryan turned toward the stairway. "Where was this?"

"He's long gone. I'm sure."

"Did he hurt you?" He nodded his head at her hand where red was seeping through the wad of tissues. "He do that?" If Ryan was a cartoon character, steam would be billowing out of his ears.

"No. A splinter from the railing about the size of a two-by-four. The guy just surprised the heck out of me. You can lose the scowl, great protector. I'm fine and I might have left out the fact that I was chasing him, not the other way around. So, how did things go at the Deli-casies tent?"

"Good try at a distraction, Elizabeth Holt. Things went great. All the shopkeepers from the emporium did a brisk business in their tents. I think they made at least what they would have if the emporium had been open."

Ryan put his arm around her shoulder. "Let's get back to..."

"Look!" Liz pointed.

Opposite the pavilion, standing next in line at the beer and wine truck were brother and sister, Phoebe and Branson.

"Dorian had mentioned they didn't get along, but she had a vision they would connect. It sure looks like they're friendly now that their mother's fiancé is dead."

The pair were laughing about something. Phoebe wore a hot-pink sundress that said, *Look at me*, and there was a henna mermaid tattoo trailing down her arm. Branson had taken off his shirt and wore a pair of shorts that hit below his knees. He was in good physical shape, with washboard abs, but his skin was a milky white, like he hadn't spent time outdoors. Already there was a pink cast to his shoulders from the afternoon sun.

"You would think they would be back at the Indialantic with their grieving mother," Ryan said.

"I agree. Instead of Aunt Amelia having to miss the tail end of the Mystical Merfest, they should have stayed with Dorian. They're probably celebrating that the wicked, wicked warlock is dead. They both had motive, seeing their mother and Julian didn't have a prenup."

He raised a roughish eyebrow. "I know you've known Ms. Starwood for years. How about her kids?"

"I've met them a couple times. But it was years ago. They were nice enough. Well, at least Branson was. Phoebe seemed to have her issues."

Ryan looked into the distance, like he was weighing telling her something.

"Come on. Why are you asking?"

"It's about what I learned yesterday about Branson."

"You mean about the drugs in high school?"

He laughed. "Should have known you would already be on everyone's trail. After what you just told me about that guy grabbing your ankle in broad daylight, I think you should back up a little and let the professionals handle things."

Liz stuck out her bottom lip.

"No pouting. Don't you have to go over your copy edit of *An American in Cornwall*?"

"Yes."

"And don't you want to get started on your synopsis for the next book?"

"Well, yes." Then she explained about her snooping in Wren's suite and the contract making Wren and Julian partners in the Sunshine Wiccan Society Water Company. "I sent you a copy of the contract."

He got out his phone and tapped the screen. "I can't open the document, need Wi-Fi. Speaking of documents, I also found out that Garrett McGee's in the middle of an IRS audit. From what I can gather, someone sent in a tip that he was skimming clients' money."

"I wouldn't be surprised if it was Julian Rhodes who gave them the tip," she said. "Guess what else I found? Wren Wagner's first name. Drumroll, please. It's Renee."

Ryan started typing something on his phone. "I just sent Wren's real first name to Charlotte, and I didn't mention your involvement, though I will have to show her the contract. I'll say it was an anonymous source. But I'm sure she'll guess it was you."

"Thatta boy," Liz said, grinning. "You know we make a good team. Admit it. I'm the wind beneath your sails and you're the h-mmm...,"

"Love of your life, blue eyes?"

"Exactly," she answered.

He grabbed her to him and kissed the top of her head. Then he looked at her and said, "So now you're breaking and entering murder suspect's rooms?"

"No, I was just there to deliver towels and bed linens," she said coyly.

"Then I suppose the document was just laying around in full view?"

"Not exactly. As part of the Three Detectiveteers," she said, "I thought you'd be happy about my sleuthing. The contract was in a locked Louis Vuitton bag. I opened the gold padlock with a metal chicken skewer because Wren must have had the key..."

"Louis Vuitton?" He asked, looking puzzled.

"You're such a guy! You've seen Louis Vuitton luggage; it's always got the LV logo stamped all over it."

"I don't do logos, you know that."

"Well, there was one slight glitch. When I left the suite, I forgot to lock the padlock."

"Nice work, Nancy Drew. I give up trying to keep you from the investigation, but it would be prudent not to rile up a cold-blooded killer. Remember, we're talking poison, a terrible way to go. And, you know better than most what happens when a killer feels trapped. Who do you think he or she will lash out at?"

"Who?" she asked, fluttering her eyelashes. It didn't work.

"The person snooping around for evidence to put them in the electric chair."

"We don't have capital punishment in Florida."

He gave her one of his smirks. He was amused but she could still tell he was worried about her getting involved.

She gave him a quick peck on the cheek. "And you wonder why I sometimes keep things from you. I don't want you to worry about me."

"Is that true, or you don't want me squashing your dreams of catching a killer?"

"If I do have dreams of catching them, it's for an altruistic reason; I want Dorian to find peace and closure, and I want to stop someone before they kill again, possibly snaring Dorian or someone else in their web."

He smiled. "You're starting to sound like your auntie, with your descriptive wording.

"The Sheriff's Department still hasn't ruled out that the poison wasn't meant for Dorian instead of her fiancé." She then told him about her conversation with her father, Charlotte, and Aunt Amelia and what she'd just overheard between Wren and Branson. "There you have it. Full disclosure, partner. I'm not holding anything back."

He didn't say a word, just stared off toward the ocean.

"Okay! Got it. If it makes you feel better, I'll leave it up to the professionals." She put quotation marks in the air. "But first I want to find out who the guy in the black cap is. I almost fell down those steps."

Oops. Not the right thing to say. Ryan clenched his jaw and said, "You should've let me go after him. I'd get you the information about what he's been up to and it would only take a single punch."

"Oh, my. Is that a professional response to the situation, Mr. P.I.? Violence?"

"When it comes to your well-being, it becomes personal. Finding out Wren's first name is a good lead, scout. He took his large hand and rustled the hair on top of her head like he did to Blackbeard.

She stomped her foot like a petulant child. "Pushing my buttons, Mr. Stone? I'm not your puppy."

"Calm down, tiger." He grabbed her hand and kissed it. "Not at all. I'm your biggest admirer."

She believed him. Laughing, she said, "This isn't a competition, you know."

"I know. After what happened in January, I just want to keep you safe."

Her eyes filled with moisture at the thought of the last murder at the Indialantic. Through the blur of tears, she saw Ashley, Deli-casies' barista. Thankful for the distraction she pointed. "Look, there's Ashley. I think we should talk to her about the night of the rehearsal dinner."

"I'm sure she's turned over all her photos to the authorities," he said.

"True. But what about her impressions about the night. Photographer's make the best witnesses because they're so focused on the details of their surroundings." She grabbed his arm and pulled him in the direction of Ashley.

"So much, for leaving everything to the professionals," he mumbled under his breath.

Ashley spotted them approaching and waved. When they reached her, she said, "Wow! What a fantastic last day! How'd you handle things in the Deli-casies' tent without moi?" she asked Ryan.

He gave the young barista a grin. "We barely managed. But Pops was a champ, even got interviewed in the *Beachsider*. And, surprisingly enough, he gave them my grandmother's recipe for blue crab salad."

"Get out!" Ashley said laughing. She made a fist and lightly tapped against Ryan's upper arm.

Liz smiled. "Ash, do you have time to talk about what went down on *Queen of the Seas* last night?"

Ryan added, "We don't want to take you away from your work."

"I think I have a few million shots the newspaper might like for tomorrow's edition. After the exposure I got photographing the literary ball at the Indialantic, my portfolio is bursting. And it's all thanks to you Ryan."

"Just in time for college," Liz added. "We're gonna miss you, Ashley. Compared to yours, Ryan's barista skills are sorely lacking."

Like Liz, Ashley's skin was fair. Her cheeks were pink with sunburn and the top of her freckled nose had started to peel. Dark auburn hair had been pulled back with a large butterfly clip, a few dark tendrils escaping. Liz recognized the cotton sundress with the circle skirt she wore as one from Francie's dress patterns. Francie had been teaching Ashley to sew in Home Arts, and it looked like she'd done a marvelous job of it.

Ashley laughed. "Oh, I think you'll be surprised. By the time August comes around he'll be a pro. I'll teach him everything I know. If Pops can get the hang of the new BUNN machine, so can Ryan." Ashley grasped the camera hanging from around her neck and took a few photos of Liz and Ryan.

The handsome lifeguard Josh, with the million-dollar smile, passed by. He mouthed, *How's your hand?* Liz held it up and mouthed back, "*Good.*" Even though the blood was still showing through the second wad of tissues she'd just added.

"Why don't we go over to the picnic table to talk?" Ryan motioned to a shaded table under a huge palm.

After they sat, Ashley looked across at Ryan and Liz. "I know you want to talk about the night Ms. Starwood's fiancé died. I've told Agent Pearson everything and I turned over my memory cards. I can honestly say there's nothing that stands out in my mind on how he could have gotten a hold of anything with shellfish. Ms. Shay and I were totally aware of his allergy. I even made sure when I was in the galley that not even a single utensil ever touching the shrimp came near his plate. Plus, Ms. Shay was standing behind me when I did the plating of the appetizers and main dishes. There was little room for error."

With Susannah there, I bet, Liz thought. "Do you remember anyone near their table when you and Susannah served their food? Did Branson Arnaud, come over to check on things?"

Ashley looked off into the distance. When she turned her head toward them, she said, "I do remember him standing close to Mr. Rhodes after the appetizers were served, but we were there too, and I know he didn't touch anything on the table. I have no idea what happened during the time we were below in the galley getting their main dishes ready."

"Susannah told me Julian wasn't there when you brought up his main dish."

"That's true. Just Ms. Starwood was there. Funny, because when we brought their appetizers to the table she was gone and just he was sitting there. Musical chairs."

Liz and Ryan looked at each other. Ashley noticed. "I don't know much about what happened to him, but I do know the police seemed pretty interested in everything I told them. And Agent Pearson wants to meet with me tonight."

"How about beverages?" Liz asked. "What were Ms. Starwood and Mr. Rhodes drinking?"

"They were both drinking that water in the blue bottle. There was a big bucket of it on ice. Wren, that blonde with the childish dresses and big eyes kept having me fill her glass with the blue-bottled water. She sure seemed to like it."

"So," Liz said, "The appetizers and main dishes for Phoebe, Branson, Garrett, and Wren were served buffet style?"

"Yes. I wish I could tell you more. Luckily, the photos I took earlier of the Mystical Merfest emporium tents weren't on that same memory card. Amelia wanted me to take them for her to promote next year's festival."

"Oh, wow, that's fantastic," Liz said. "Can you send those photos to my email?"

Ashley chuckled. "Why do I have déjà vu?"

"Because your photos helped us big-time last January," Ryan said.

"And your photos might just help us again," Liz added.

"I have them in the cloud," she said, getting out her phone. She tapped a few places on her screen and Liz heard bells ring on her phone telling her she got an email. Liz looked at her phone and grinned.

"Your wish is my command," Ashley said. "Now, tell me what's really going on with that man's death?"

Ryan reached across and covered Ashley's hand with his. "All will become clear in about an hour when Agent Pearson has her news conference. Suffice it to say, whatever you can think of that seemed out of the ordinary might be important. Even little things that struck you as strange. Do you have any recollection of what part of the evening Julian Rhodes went below deck?"

"As I just said, he wasn't on deck before we served the main course. But I do recall Ms. Starwood's daughter, uh…"

"Phoebe," Liz offered.

"Phoebe wanted to give a toast, but Mr. Rhodes was MIA. She told her mother she would go and find him. I remember watching her go to the staircase and meeting Big Eyes at the top of the staircase. One bumped the other in the shoulder," Ashley continued. "I thought they were gonna go flying down the staircase. Phoebe won but the other woman waited a few moments, then she went downstairs too."

"Did you tell all this to the sheriff's department?"

"No. They just seemed concerned about me handing over the memory card from my camera."

"Hey, you two," someone said from behind Liz. She turned and saw Phoebe minus her brother.

"I just wanted to remind you that Mama wants the séance to start at five." The skin under Ryan's left eye twitched. "Séance?"

Phoebe said excitedly, "We're bringing not-to-be future stepdaddy front and center, so he can learn to move on in peace. I'm sure you can come along too." She smiled at Ryan, but ignored Ashley, then moved to the end of the table.

Ryan didn't respond.

Liz took his arm, and said, "He can't make it, but I can." She didn't have to glance up at him to see the look of relief on his face. She pinched his thigh when he didn't answer.

"Ouch! Wish I could, but I uh…have that thing. Liz, you know that thing."

"Yes, the case you're working on for Dad."

"You're a lawyer, too?" Phoebe asked.

"No, a private investigator."

She looked flustered at his answer. "Well," she turned to Liz. "I'll see you at five."

"Anything to…uh… help out your mother. Who will be there?"

"Garrett, Amelia, Mother, Branson, and even Julian's cousin, Wren. She overheard Branson and me talking and insisted she attend. Apparently, she has a message for him. I can only imagine, what it is." Then she bent over and whispered so Ashley couldn't hear, "I have my own question for him, like who was the real target of the poison, him or mother?"

Before they could react to Phoebe's words, she turned and walked away. They heard her calling out to a mermaid with a dozen shell necklaces on her arm, "Hey there, how much?" When the woman answered, she said. "That's highway robbery. Do you take credit cards?" The woman shook her head no, and Phoebe got lost in the throng of people standing in front of a mobile ATM.

Ashley whistled, "Wow. I hope she didn't hear me talking about her. Seeing her just now reminded me of something. At the very beginning of the cruise, I saw her arguing with the dead guy. It was something about money, and how things were going to change once he married her mother. She gave it right back to him but after he walked away, she seemed quite upset."

"Thanks, Ashley. It seems Dorian is the only one missing the guy," Ryan said.

Liz leaned in. "That's for sure. This séance should be a real free-for-all."

Thanks for not making me go," Ryan said with a smile. "Although I would like to be a fly on the wall."

"I think it would be fun," Ashley said, obviously enjoying how uncomfortable her boss was at the prospect.

Liz grinned. "Oh, you'll be going, Mr. Fly. You won't be on the wall or sitting at the table." She looked over at Ashley. "I'll explain later."

He gave Liz his Ricky Ricardo eyes, *Lucy-y-y*, just as Josh, the lifeguard came up to their picnic table toting a first aid kit.

"Let me see your hand, palm up," he said to Liz, then winked at Ashley.

Liz did as she was told, watching him use a wet wipe to clean the wound before adding a topical antibiotic and a gauze pad. Then he wrapped an entire roll of gauze around and around her hand. It was a little overkill, but she realized what he was doing when she saw him looking in Ashley's direction. Ashley was returning his gaze.

When he was done, Liz said, "Josh! You're the best." He would be a perfect match for Ashley. Then she realized Ashley would be off to college in a few months. But still in driving distance. Why did she have such an obsession with pairing everyone up? She was starting to annoy herself. She supposed she just wanted everyone to be as happy as she was with Ryan. Or it could be she'd been watching too many vintage TV sitcoms with her great-aunt. All with happy endings, except for shows like *The Twilight Zone, Night Gallery,* or *Alfred Hitchcock Presents.*

Ashley stood and took her camera from the table. "I better get back to work, almost time to pack up. Enjoy your séance," she said. "See you tomorrow at Deli-casies. I'm so happy Pops is leaving in the morning to visit his sister in Brooklyn. Even though he worries about his grandson handling things while he's gone, I think you're doing an excellent job, Ryan."

"That's because I know you'll be there full time for the next week," he said.

After Josh put everything back in the first aid kit, he looked shyly at Ashley and said, "Need help, packing up your camera equipment? I saw you brought a lot of gear with you. I'm off duty and heading home myself."

Ashley gave him one of her easy laughs. "Actually, I wouldn't mind the help. I have a wheelie cart but there's so much and it's hard to maneuver."

"Thanks again, Josh," Liz said.

Ryan stood. "Ashley, we'll talk tomorrow. Don't lose any sleep over anything we were talking about. Everything will work out."

"I know it will, boss." She gave them a thumbs-up, slung the camera around her neck, then disappeared into the sea of merpeople, Josh following behind her like Blackbeard wanting a treat.

"You're going to miss her when she leaves for college," Liz said.

"You got that one right." He sat down, raised an eyebrow, then pierced her with his searching dark-eyed gaze. "So, what's all this about a séance? Thought I was the P.I. and you the fiction writer. Why do I get the idea this whole séance thing was your idea, not Dorian's?"

"Definitely Dorian's. My idea was to have it in the screening room, so you can hide out in the projection booth with those goggles I got you for Christmas."

"Are you staging some scene from one of your auntie's old *Twilight Zone* episodes?"

"More like one of Grand-Pierre's Agatha Christie novels. There's the *Sittaford Mystery, Peril at End House, Dumb Witness,* and the book Grand-Pierre and I are reading right now, *The Pale Horse.* They all feature séances. From reading Christie's biography, I learned that her mother, Clara, was known to have the power of 'second sight'. I'm reading *The Pale Horse* for the hundredth time. It's that good."

"Hundredth?" He asked, adding a laugh.

"Oh, and I almost forgot, Christie had a short story titled *The Last Séance*. I always meant to read it, but it's hard to get a hold of. Then there's Dorothy L. Sayers's novel *Strong Poison...*"

He threw his hands in the air. "Okay, I get it. You've read a lot of books with séances in them. But have you ever attended one?"

She didn't answer, averting her gaze from his handsome face.

"And have you told Charlotte about this séance where you're hoping to snare a killer?"

"Not yet. Plus, she's doing a news conference about Julian Rhodes's murder around the same time as the séance. But I'll tell my father. I planned on putting him on stage behind the curtains."

"Will he be packing a gun?"

"Father doesn't carry a gun."

"I'm surprised. Most defense attorney's do. It comes with the territory."

"Not Dad's. Remember he's semiretired. How about you? Now you're a licensed P.I. do you have a license for a gun?"

"Nope. No reason to on this sleepy barrier island. Then again, you do seem to have your fair share of murders here."

"Hey, this is your island too. You should have said, '*We* have our fair share of murders.'"

He put an arm around her shoulder, and they met up with Greta, Pierre, Kate, and Alex, for the last half hour of the Mystical Merfest.

Liz had almost invited Kate to the séance but realized she might not be a good fit. Like Aunt Amelia, Kate was too impulsive. There was no avoiding having her great-aunt at the table, but she could eliminate her best friend, who always had good intentions, only with disastrous results. Plus, Liz knew Kate would be exhausted from her marvelous Mystical Merfest mermaid duties.

When Liz went up to Kate to say goodbye, she asked if it was okay to borrow a couple of books from her shop. "No problem," Kate responded. When it came to books, Kate wanted to share them with the world. After all, to her they were living, *speaking* things. On second thought, maybe Kate would be an asset to the séance because of her otherworldly ways? If she could carry on conversations with characters in books, perhaps she could do the same with the dead?

Kate took off her crown and asked, "How is Ms. Starwood doing? Have they found out what happened to her fiancé?"

"Well, that's kind of complicated. Charlotte's making an announcement soon. You might as well know. He was murdered. Poisoned."

Kate's large chocolate eyes showed surprise. "I just saw Mr. Rhodes's cousin a while ago. It looked like she'd been crying."

"That's strange, she didn't seem too upset at the memorial brunch," Liz added.

Ryan came over to them and looked at Liz. "Ready?"

"Yep." She hugged Kate and promised to call her later that night. Then they said goodbye to Alex, Greta, and Grand-Pierre and walked back to the Indialantic.

Liz planned to be forearmed for the séance and possibly snare a killer.

Chapter 21

With the help of an unenthusiastic team consisting of Ryan and her father, they'd managed to set up a round table on the screening room's stage. Charlotte was busy giving her news conference and her father was already waiting in the wings behind the velvet curtains in case anything went haywire. Which, Liz had a hunch, it would. Ryan was hiding up in the projection booth until the lights went out. They all agreed that a dark room might be dangerous if Dorian was the killer's intended target. Thankfully, Charlotte, who seemed more open-minded lately, had even loaned a few deputies to the operation. They would be stationed outside the screening room doors once the séance began.

"What's the food in the center of table for?" Dorian asked. She looked better than she had at brunch. She'd added color to cheeks that complimented her violet hair. Both she and Aunt Amelia wore diaphanous chiffon caftans with billowing sleeves. Aunt Amelia's had hot-pink and tangerine paisleys. Dorian's had violet and chartreuse geometric shapes. Both looked like they'd shopped at the same 1960s Haight Asbury clothing co-op.

Liz's main reason for having backup, which included her father and Ryan, had nothing to do with anyone's motive for murdering Julian Rhodes. What she wanted to find out was if the killer had mistakenly killed Julian when his or her real target was Dorian. Hopefully when the lights went out Dorian would still be alive when they came back on because Dorian was determined to have the séance whether there were people watching out for her or not.

Aunt Amelia hadn't said a word since she'd sat down. She had dressed in true Aunt Amelia style, but her trademark baby-blue eyeshadow, thick black eyeliner, and false eyelashes were missing from the lids atop her usually glittering emerald eyes. Her flaming red hair was pulled into an I-dream-of-Jeannie ponytail, but she hadn't wrapped a section of hair around the rubber band, then secured it with bobby pins, as she usually did. No flowing scarves around her neck, no sparkling rings on her fingers or dozens of bracelets at her wrists.

"From what I've read about séances," Liz answered to Dorian's question about the food, "aromatic food should be placed in the center of the table to entice the dearly departed craving physical nourishment." In this case Pierre had provided homemade chicken stock that he'd simmered on the stove with rosemary, basil, and sage—along with a homemade French baguette, fresh from the oven—you couldn't get more aromatic than that. She'd also added a silver goblet filled with wine, in case Julian was thirsty. When she was in Indialantic's kitchen, she'd tried a little séance humor on the chef. "Remember, no shellfish," she'd said to Grand-Pierre. Thankfully, it had gone over his head. Just as well, because the more she read about séances, the more spooked she'd become. Especially after finding out that Dorian had never performed a séance or even attended one.

"Amelia, tell us about that scene in *Dark Shadows* where they had a séance," Dorian said in a soft voice. "The one where Victoria Winters time travels."

Dorian wasn't oblivious to her friend's un-Amelia like demeanor at the table and was trying to draw her out. And it worked. Aunt Amelia's grass-green eyes sparked. "You mean the time when they were having a séance in the old house and all of a sudden Victoria Winters vanishes and ends up in the eighteenth century? Oh, how I loved when they went back in time on my show. All the costumes and hair and makeup. Then to replace Victoria," she added excitedly, "a girl from 1765 crossed over the time barrier and ended up in 1967 Collinsport, Maine. The character's name was Phyllis, Phyllis Wicke, I believe. Only she didn't fare as well as Victoria. Phyllis died moments after she arrived," she added with a chuckle, "under mysterious circumstances, of course."

"Let me guess," Liz said, laughing, "Barnabas Collins bit her neck?"

"Most likely," Aunt Amelia answered. "People never gave our show its due. It was filmed live, no editing. You try doing that five days a week for five years running."

Garrett, Branson, and Phoebe looked clueless about the American Gothic soap opera that Aunt Amelia had a role in. But Liz didn't care. Auntie's mojo was back. She could almost hear her father laughing from behind the velvet curtains a few feet away.

Liz wanted to get up and give Dorian a hug for bringing back the light in her great-aunt's luminous eyes, instead she blew her a kiss. She was sure her great-aunt's malaise had a lot to do with when Ryan, Liz, and her father had pulled Aunt Amelia aside and told her that the killer's target might have been Dorian, not her fiancé. They explained about the threatening notes. They left out that it was antifreeze that caused Julian's death, just in case she slipped in front of Dorian, who was still a suspect as far as the sheriff's department was concerned.

When Liz had returned from the park, Dorian had told her that her usual method of channeling the dead was via one-on-one readings or ciphering messages from the crystal pendulum that pointed to letters and symbols on a mat much like a Ouija board. So far, neither had worked in contacting Julian. Liz remembered it was her daughter Phoebe's suggestion that they have a séance, which should have sent Liz's skeptical spider sense reeling.

Phoebe, who sat between Dorian and Aunt Amelia, said, "I've only been to a séance once. But it was a doozy. They made it very clear that the number of candles in the middle of the table should be no fewer than three." Phoebe was dressed in a gauzy white dress with appliqued white flowers adorning a plunging neckline. A white floral headband held back her wiry, short brown hair. She'd be perfect if instead of a séance they were performing a thirty-year-old virgin sacrifice. She added, "The more candles you have the better. Spirits seek warmth and light. And at my séance, after the lights went out, the table tipped, and all the candles went sliding toward me. On second thought, perhaps three candles are good enough."

Liz had also read something similar in the only book she'd found in Kate's shop, *Reuniting with Loved Ones who've Passed into the Spiritual Realm.* It was dated 1919 and in the foreword the author explained how performing a séance was a sure way to bring back those lost in The Great War, or War to End all Wars, later know as WWI, seeing another *not*-so-Great War followed. She was surprised to read that Mary Todd Lincoln, looking to communicate with her deceased son, was involved in a series of séances that took place in the White House's Red Room.

After Liz had found out Dorian had never officiated at a séance before, she took notes from the book on the proper protocol for bringing back the dead, then transferred them to index cards for Dorian to study before the grand event. The first card read: *Our beloved Julian, we bring you gifts from life into death. Commune with us, Julian, and move among us.* Then she'd written in parenthesis, *repeat chant until spirit responds then thank them for their appearance.* Then, if things went well, Julian would inhabit Dorian's body and there would be a meet-and-greet. The other option would be for Dorian to go the route of one knock for yes, two for no. They would soon find out. Though skeptical that Julian would appear, Liz had a feeling as soon as Garrett, Wren, and Branson sat at the table, Julian's killer might possibly be among them.

Dorian said, "Even though I've never conducted a séance, I'm sure with Farrah by my side as a conduit, I'll have no problem bringing forth Julian."

Doubtful, Liz thought, seeing how unfamously Julian and the ferret had gotten along in the land of the living. Instead of being coiled around Dorian's neck, Farrah sat on her lap, her little ferret chin, if ferrets had chins, resting on the blue linen tablecloth. Earlier, she'd learned that Farrah had once again escaped her cage. Captain Netherton found her on the pet veranda curled up in the corner of his Great Dane's bed. They'd nicknamed it the pet veranda because usually on any given day that was where you would find the Indialantic's felines and canines, lounging under the veranda's shaded canopy, enjoying a cool ocean breeze.

"Where's Branson, Garret, and *that* girl?" Phoebe glanced at her watch. "I told them to be here at…"

The doors to the screening room opened and Garret and Branson hurried down the ramp leading to the stage, passing the wall filled with photos of Aunt Amelia arm in arm with mid-century television actors, her version of having a star on the Hollywood Walk of Fame.

"Branson, what kept you?" Phoebe asked. "Let me guess, you were on the phone with father's solicitors again, trying to understand why you didn't receive squat in the will."

"Shut up Phoebe, you don't know what you're talking about. Don't upset Mother. As usual your timing is impeccable."

"Oh, hush. I heard you whining to mother for more money for your restaurant. Father's second wife got everything. Why are you surprised? And if he would have left anything in his will, he would have given it all to me. You couldn't even show up to console him on his deathbed."

"Phoebe! Leave it!" Garrett said, pounding his fist on the table.

Instead of fighting it, she closed her mouth and said, "Sorry, Mama. It was just such a harrowing experience."

Dorian didn't seem to register what was going on around them. She said, "Okay, dear. Let's get this done with. I think we will have a good result, but the two of you can't be bickering."

Compared to Garrett, who was probably thirty or more years his senior, Branson seemed out of breath and out of shape. Sweat stains darkened the fabric of his aqua T-shirt and his upper lip was beaded in perspiration. He sat next to his mother and took her hand. With real concern in his gaze, he asked, "How are you holding up?"

"Much better. I only felt ill after leaving the cruise…I'm sure a lot of it had to do with…don't worry about me, darling. And thanks for always checking up on me. As soon as I speak to Julian and he tells me who killed him, we can all move on."

There was beyond-the-dead silence at the table after Dorian's last sentence, only interrupted by Garrett scraping the stage's wood floor with his chair. He chose to sit between Liz and Branson.

Garrett appeared the opposite of Branson. Calm, cool, and collected, dressed in tennis whites, a pair of Ray-Bans on top of his ginger hair, and a barely perceptible smile on his face, like this was all going to be good sport. He even made a joke, "If Mr. Rhodes doesn't show up, I wouldn't mind trying some of that soup and bread. It smells amazing."

One chair remained empty. The one for Wren Wagner, who'd told Phoebe she had a message for Julian's ghost. Liz could only imagine what it would be.

As if reading Liz's mind, Dorian spoke. "Where's that Wren creature? She's the most important person to attend."

Branson shrugged his shoulders. "Got me."

"When we were at brunch," Phoebe interjected, "she told me she had every intention of being here. I tried to dissuade her. But she insisted."

Dorian tapped the table. "Phoebe! Why would you do that? No matter. Let's begin. I need to connect to my Julian. The truth will be revealed one way or another."

Liz knew why Dorian wanted Wren at the table. She wanted to hear from Julian's own dead lips that Wren had killed him. Dorian wasn't the only one who had Wren as her odds-on top contender as Julian's killer.

You're right, Mama, we only have six. Per the séance I attended, we need an uneven number at the table."

Liz stood up. "I'll run up and check her suite."

"The food will get cold," Phoebe whined.

"I'm sure his spirit will still be able to smell it, especially the rosemary. I'll only be five minutes, tops. Promise."

Liz ran up the ramp, opened the door, then stepped through the doorway and into the hallway. Two officers from the sheriff's department sat on rattan cushioned chairs looking down at their phones, probably waiting for Ryan to give them the signal to man the door. There was only one entrance and exit to the screening room and she'd just come out of it.

"Sorry, not yet," she said to the female deputy who was double the size and height of her male counterpart. Liz was reassured she could handle anything that came her way. "Have you seen a pale blonde woman with large hazel eyes in the last few minutes?"

The male officer answered with a definite Boston accent, "No one's passed by here."

"Thanks."

She hurried to the lobby and took the curving iron staircase to the second floor. She realized she didn't have a key to the Swaying Palms Suite, but that didn't seem to be a problem because when she got to the suite, the door was open by at least ten inches. She knocked anyway. "Ms. Wagner, it's Liz Holt. Dorian sent me up to see if you're coming to the séance. We're all waiting for you."

No answer. She walked in. Worried that Wren might be in the bath, even though the bathroom door was open, she called out, "Hello? Ms. Wagner. Are you decent?"

Again, no response.

She entered the bathroom. It was empty. It was also empty of anything belonging to Wren Wagner. No cosmetic case. No opal ring in the soap dish. She darted into the bedroom. The Louis Vuitton bag was gone. The luggage stand was closed and leaning against the wall. Something reflected light under the folded luggage stand. She bent to pick it up. It was the key to Wren's Louis Vuitton bag's lock. She stuck it in her pocket and went out the open doorway of the sitting room and into the hallway. As she walked toward the staircase, she had an epiphany. What if Wren still planned on attending the séance and was waiting until the lights went out so she could make her move on Dorian? What if she was already hiding in the screening room—under the stadium seats—or in Aunt Amelia's games closet?

What if...

They would soon find out.

Chapter 22

"Commune with us, Julian. Move among us." Not exactly the script Liz had given Dorian but close enough.

Three candles flickered in the center of the table, the only light in the large room. As if choreographed by a movie set director, they heard a deafening boom of thunder. There weren't any windows in the screening room, but Liz cold tell that lightning had struck nearby.

They were all holding hands. Ten minutes had passed and there were no signs from the great beyond. Liz had an itch on the top of her nose that she needed to scratch. It was driving her bonkers, but Dorian had given clear instructions they weren't allowed to break the circle of hands. She raised her right hand which was joined with Ryan's and brought it to her nose, then she used his knuckle to satisfy the itch, wanting to moan in ecstasy at the relief. Ryan gave her one of his looks. He wasn't a happy camper or happy séancer—she'd didn't need psychic powers to discern his state of mind—the set of his jaw told everything.

When she'd returned to the room without Wren, Phoebe had insisted they invite one more to the table to make it an odd number. Six wouldn't do. They needed seven. "How about your boyfriend?" Phoebe had asked. "Who needs Julian's cousin who upset Mama this morning."

Figuring it might be better to have Ryan close by, she'd sent him a text. *You have to join us at the table, pretend you're coming in from the hallway, we need seven at the table. Wren MIA.*

He texted back. *You've got to be kidding!!!*

Liz had looked up and told Phoebe, "He said he'd love to attend."

"Spirit. Please answer my incantations." It was ten minutes into the séance and Dorian was now trying different voices and combinations of words to conjure Julian, but nothing was working. No thumping one, or two, no taking over her body with his spirit, or speaking with Julian's deep voice, no tilting of the table. Just silence broken by the occasional cavalcade of thunder.

Liz wasn't telepathic, but she could tell Ryan had had enough, especially when he kicked her shin under the table with his sneaker. "Ouch!" she called out, her voice echoing off the tall walls. The candles flickered, not from a ghost, but from her exhalation of pain. Her "Ouch" also caused Farrah to start dooking. She slithered onto the table, grabbed a chunk of baguette, then leapt onto Garrett's lap. He shrieked like an infant getting its first shot, then the ferret catapulted into the darkness.

"Don't unclasp your hands!" Dorian begged. "I think Julian is working through Farrah. She'll return, and we will have some answers."

She felt another kick from under the table, it was a kinder and gentler assault, and this time she managed to keep her mouth shut. She also managed to elbow Ryan in the ribs.

"Ow-w-w."

"Julian is that you?" Dorian asked. Thunder answered her. "We want to know who killed you? Is the person here? Rap once or twice. Or give me a sign." Farah jumped back up on the table, her tail knocked over the silver goblet filled with wine, then the goblet crashed against one of the brass candlesticks. The candlestick toppled on its side, luckily its flame was snuffed out by the loaf of bread. The goblet and the candlestick had made two distinct thumping sounds against the table. In Dorian's mind it was clear that Julian had answered "no" to the question of whether his killer was in the room, solidifying Wren as his murderer.

Dorian jumped up, still holding Branson and Phoebe's hands, causing a wave effect around the table. Phoebe held Ryan's hand, Ryan held Liz's, Liz held Garrett's, Garrett held Aunt Amelia's, and Aunt Amelia held Branson's. With the loss of the candle it was almost impossible to make out anything in the room but hazy shadows. Liz hoped Dorian, or Julian for that matter, was right that Wren wasn't in the room.

Dorian whispered, her voice raw with emotion, "So, it's true, that girl is the one who killed you? Or was she out to get me? We will find her and when we do, I'll make sure she talks."

Dorian sat, and seeing they were one big daisy chain, so did everyone else. "Now it's time to set him free." She instructed everyone to say, one by one, "We release you." So, they did. When it was Dorian's turn, she said, "Your spirit can go now to the other side. Your death will be avenged. You've just confirmed it. I knew what that woman told me wasn't true. Go in peace."

Dorian released Branson's and Phoebe's hands. Liz let go of Garrett's but still held onto Ryan's.

Dorian asked, "Can someone get the lights?"

"I will," Liz said as she shot up from her seat. The light switch was on the wall behind the velvet curtains where her father had been hiding for the last half hour. She used the flashlight feature on her phone and went to the wall. Before flipping the switch, she whispered, "Dad, you good?"

He stuck out his hand and gave her a thumbs-up. *What a sport.*

She flipped the switch. As she walked back toward the table, a spotlight illuminated Farrah sitting amid spilled wine and dried candle wax. She held something between her ferret paws. As Liz got closer, she saw it was a ring. An opal ring in a gold setting. Phoebe gasped. "Mother! Look what your weasel is holding. It can't get much worse than this."

Dorian stood and leaned toward the center of the table. "What is that? What are you holding, you little rascal?" Farrah held it up as if to show it off to everyone, then she scampered away, ready for a game of hide-and-seek. This time, she landed on Ryan's lap. But he was too quick for her, more than likely he was used to grabbing things from Blackbeard's slobbery mouth before he chewed them to death. He got a hold of the ring and placed it in the center of the table.

"Mother, it's an opal. Where did it come from? Was it brought here by Julian? Is he warning you about something? You know what they say about opals in my book."

"Yes, it must be a sign or some kind of warning…Julian wasn't born in October, plus it's a woman's ring," Dorian mumbled.

"The unluckiest of gemstones," Phoebe said. "Where did it come from? Did you know an opal can foresee an early widowhood, it can give you a cloak of invisibility, and it loses it shine when the person who owns it dies. Only someone born in October can wear it without harm. Or if the opal is surrounded by diamonds, the larger the diamonds the better, then it can negate its evil powers. There are no diamonds on this one. Was anyone here born in October?"

Aunt Amelia sheepishly raised her hand. "But that ring does not belong to me."

Branson laughed. "Phoebe, it's just a ring mother's pet ferreted from someone's personal belongings. There's no sinister aura around it. I'm sure when it's returned to its owner, the ring's evil voodoo curse you speak of will be broken." He reached to the center of the table and held the ring. "See! I was born in July and I'm not worried about any opal curse." He slipped the ring on his pinkie finger. It only slid down to the knuckle. "Branson," Dorian instructed, "give it to Amelia. She was born in October. No harm will come to her."

He took it off his finger, polishing the ring with the hem of his T-shirt, before handing it to her. "See. I rubbed off all the voodoo magic. It has no power over anyone now." If Liz wasn't mistaken, his words didn't match his shaking hand when he passed it to Aunt Amelia.

Taking it from him, Aunt Amelia said, "I'm sure it was probably left behind by a former hotel guest. I'll have Susannah check and see if anyone has called about it..."

Phoebe interrupted her. "I remembered another little snippet of info from my book, brother. Opals turn pale if brought into the presence of poison."

"Ridiculous," Branson said, "just like your dumb book."

Liz knew the opal ring had nothing to do with Julian Rhodes. It was Wren Wagner's ring that Farrah must have swiped from the Swaying Palms Suite. The same ring she saw in the soap dish this morning. "That ring belongs to Ms. Wagner," Liz said.

They all took a collective breath.

"That's surely a sign then!" Phoebe said.

"Amelia, please return it to her, immediately. I hope Farrah won't suffer from holding it."

"What about Branson, Mama?" Phoebe piped in, fake concern on her face. "I better look in my book and she how we can reverse his handling of it."

Branson rolled his eyes. "Give me a break, Phoebe."

Garrett got up and went to stand by Dorian's chair. "I think we're all tired. And Dorian needs her rest. Can I escort you up to your suite my dear? I'm sure someone can bring dinner up to you?"

"Of course." Aunt Amelia said, patting her friend's hand. "Garrett's right, Dorian. I will have Greta or Susannah bring you up something and I'll make a special blend of tea, just for you."

Dorian relaxed her shoulders, looking like she was eager to succumb to their coddling. But then she glanced over at Ryan and said in authoritative voice, "Please send Agent Pearson to my suite, as soon as you see her. I need to talk to her about something."

Then Liz noticed Dorian and Garrett locking eyes. Liz, herself, was starting to think the ring might have powers. Especially, after hearing the part about an opal's ability to render the wearer invisible. Where had

Wren gone? Was she hiding in the hotel? Somewhere in this room? Or, was she long gone, escaping justice? Liz knew during the brunch, when she overheard Branson and Wren talking, that Wren said she was staying put. And what had transpired at Dorian's and Wren's little *tête-à-tête* earlier?

Everyone headed for the door except Ryan who had whispered that he would stay behind to tell her father the coast was clear. Liz couldn't wait to get home to Bronte. She needed a snuggle and the calming sounds of the kitten's gentle purring. She was relieved that nothing had happened at the séance, just some hijinks from a mischievous ferret. Dorian was safe. The weekend sure hadn't turned out as they'd planned, but she could salvage the tail-end of it by cocooning herself in her beach house and getting a good night's sleep.

She smiled inwardly at the thought, just as Greta burst into the screening room. "Amelia. Amelia, you must come quick. There are a dozen news vans and reporters banging at our doors. Even the kitchen door. Pierre is in a frenzy and I can't find Fenton anywhere. What should I do?"

They were looking at the obvious results of Agent Charlotte Pearson's news conference.

So much for Liz's best laid plans.

Chapter 23

A short time later, Liz had walked into Aunt Amelia's sitting room. She almost swallowed her tongue. Dorian was prone on her great-aunt's "fainting couch" with her eyes closed, looking like a corpse inside a coffin. Instead of a rose, her hands held the jar of disturbing, sharp things Liz had seen under the altar.

"Dorian," Liz stammered, "what the heck are you doing with that awful thing!"

Her eyes snapped open and she pivoted her head to Aunt Amelia who was sitting beside her. In a weak voice she said, "Amelia, please explain it to her..."

"The jar was meant to..."

Dorian got up on one elbow and said in a loud voice, "Protect me from the person writing the letters and that girl. But now I see it was my Julian I should have been protecting."

Liz and Aunt Amelia exchanged glances.

"Auntie," Liz said, "why don't you get Dorian some of you special blend tea? I'm sure you'll choose the right one for the occasion." Liz thought, *the tea for people who've gone a little cuckoo for Cocoa Puffs, as BB would say.*

"Great idea, Lizzy."

After Aunt Amelia left the room, Liz sat next to Dorian. "Is everything okay? Besides the obvious," she said, gently placing her hand on her arm.

Dorian sprang into a sitting position and pushed the jar into Liz's hands. "Take this offending thing away."

She started to cry.

Liz jumped up and stowed the jar under her chair, her palms felt scorched like she'd just removed them from a roaring fire. After retrieving a box of tissues from Aunt Amelia's dressing table she sat back down and handed it to Dorian. "You can tell me anything, Dorian. What's made you so upset?"

"Agent Pearson, your dad's lovely Charlotte was here. She said the results came back on my stomach contents from when I was at the hospital. They found minute traces of crushed oleander leaves in my system. I know all about how toxic every part of the oleander plant is, even the honey made from the flowers is poisonous. What I don't understand is that Charlotte also told me that Julian didn't have oleander in his system, the poison he'd ingested was from a different source. Mine came from the bottle of SWS water."

Liz was stunned. She recalled the conversation she had with her father and Charlotte and how there'd been a true case where a wife had poisoned her husband with oleander and antifreeze.

Liz had to ask the question, "Dorian, do you ever remember drinking from Julian's glass of water the night of the rehearsal dinner?"

Dorian stared off into space. Then she clicked the fingers on her right hand. Her gaze was clear when she turned to her. "Yes! I did drink from his bottle of SWS water. I'd left for a few minutes during the appetizer course, when I came back to the table Julian was missing. I remember taking his full bottle and pouring it into my glass. So that's it. He was meant to drink the oleander and ingest the poison, not me."

"What happened to that bottle? Did you see anyone take it away?" Liz asked quietly, almost in a whisper.

She could tell Dorian did know who. But she clamped her jaw tight. "Don't you want to catch your fiancé's killer?"

"I need Garrett. Could you please go get him and have him come here? I need to ask him something important. Come to mommy, Farrah."

The ferret slunk from under the covers at Dorian's feet, and nestled around her neck.

Instead of pushing it further, Liz said, "Of course, Dorian."

She left the suite in search of Garrett. Why did Dorian want to see Garrett? Was he the one who'd removed the oleander laced bottle?

* * * *

She found Garrett in the lobby on a rattan cushioned loveseat with the local *Beachsider* newspaper on his lap. The decor in the massive lobby had barely changed since the hotel first opened its doors in 1926, the only thing from the new millennium was the fabric for the rattan furniture's cushions. The palm leaf pattern was almost an exact match from early photos of the Indialantic by the Sea in shades of moss-green and tan.

Barnacle Bob's cage was next to the loveseat. It seemed she'd interrupted a conversation between Garrett and Barnacle Bob. The macaw cackling at something Garrett had just said.

When Garrett noticed Liz, he said, "Hope you don't mind that I took his cage and stand out of the elevator?" He nodded his head in the direction of the *non*working shiny brass accordion gate elevator. Aunt Amelia said that until she had the money to fix it, the elevator would remain as is. She thought the elevator, old registration desk, and the wood cabinet behind the desk with cubbies, gave the lobby character. And Liz agreed. Also included in the lobby's timeless décor was the original revolving door that had let in Hollywood starlets and leading men, musicians, gangsters, and famous politicians—*some a combination of both gangster and politician*, her great-aunt would add with a laugh. And more recently, a few murderers.

"Not a problem at all," Liz said to Garrett as she caught Barnacle Bob's gaze, "but get near him at your own risk."

"I have to admit, I was thinking of moving him back to the elevator. He won't stop singing, *Felix, the cat. The wonderful, wonderful cat. Whenever he gets in a fix he reaches into his bag of tricks.* Over and over, again."

"You do a good imitation of him," Liz said.

"I remember the cartoon theme song from when I was child," he said, laughing. "Felix and his magical bag of tricks and the characters Poindexter and The Professor."

"It must have been Aunt Amelia who introduced him to it," Liz said. "She has not only acted in vintage television shows and commercials, but has also done the voices of a few female cartoon characters."

"That explains it," he said. "Dorian told me about her prolific television career. At first I thought the parrot was very entertaining, but after the twentieth rendition of the song, it tends to get to you. He started singing as soon as a black-and-white tuxedo cat came traipsing through, followed by a huge great Dane that looked like it could eat both the cat and the parrot for dinner in one slurp."

"Oh, Killer's harmless. He might snuggle them to death. Caro and Barnacle Bob are the ones with a tempestuous relationship. Right, BB?"

"Meow. Meow," he bellowed, as he glanced around the lobby for his arch nemesis, Caroline Keene.

She hadn't corrected Garrett that BB preferred being called a macaw not a parrot. It served him right for disturbing hotel guests and possible murder suspects.

Liz pointed her finger at the cage. Barnacle Bob sheepishly bent his head, then opened his beak. "Don't even think about!" she scolded, then took a seat in a fan-backed wicker chair across from Garrett. She said to Garrett, "Be warned. Once you get one of his repetitive jingles in your head, you'll need a surgeon to remove it."

"Polly wants a cracker. Polly wants a cracker," the macaw repeated, feigning innocence at irritating anyone. Then he added, "Who loves you baby? Who loves you?"

Liz didn't know where that last phrase came from, probably some old TV reference, but she couldn't help, answering. "We all do BB. We all do."

"He's a riot. That last ditty came from the detective show, *Kojack*," Garret offered with a grin. The lines around his eyes showed that laughter came easy to him.

There was an awkward silence which Garrett broke by saying, "How's Dorian holding up?"

"My great-aunt's with Dorian now. Her magic tea should help. Although Dorian seems kind of all over the place. I feel for her. I just hope she'll be able to move on."

"Oh, I don't think she'll have any problem moving on, once I get some proof about something." He turned away. The veins at his left temple protruded. No laugh lines now. He said, "How long did she know the guy? A red-hot minute? Julian was bad news from the beginning that's why I…"

Liz leaned toward him, "Why what?"

"Nothing. Soon it will be out in the open. I do know he thought Dorian was an ATM machine, so do her kids."

"It's nice she has someone to be so protective of her. Have you been her financial advisor long?"

He laughed, "Only for twenty-six years."

"I hope I'm not overstepping my bounds, but I did happen to overhear you and Mr. Rhodes in an argument on Saturday."

"He was impossible to deal with. Whatever his hold was on Dorian, I'm glad it's over. Not that I would wish him dead, but he wasn't what he seemed. He didn't like it that everything involving Dorian's finances had to be cleared through me first. I think Dorian was afraid of his power over her. And it wasn't a witch's spell, although she was spellbound by his fake façade. It took tons of digging, but the pieces of the puzzle have been coming together. I just need to fill in a few empty slots."

Liz leaned in and said in a soft voice, "If you don't want to go to the sheriff's department with what you have, my boyfriend, Ryan, is a P.I. and he might be able to help you. And Agent Pearson is an amazing detective."

"I'll keep that in mind." He stood and turned to Barnacle Bob. "Back to your elevator, old boy."

"I can get him," Liz said.

"That cage is pretty heavy."

Liz flexed her bicep. "I'm used to it. Maybe you should go check on Dorian, I think she can use all the friends she can get right now."

He smiled. "That, I am."

As he walked away, she felt a twinge of guilt that she hadn't sent him up to Aunt Amelia's suite right away like Dorian had asked. But she was happy she hadn't. Even though she didn't know exactly what she'd learned from their chat. She knew one thing, Garrett had Dorian's back. What she didn't know is how far he'd go to save Dorian from Julian Rhodes.

As she carried the heavy brass cage to the elevator cab, Barnacle Bob squawked, "Bet your sweet Bippy, bet your sweet Bippy."

Bippy? Another reference she'd never heard before. "Sweet Dreams, BB. See you in the morn."

Chapter 24

Early Monday morning, Liz stepped onto the Indialantic's front veranda that overlooked the Atlantic and was assailed by a ragtag menagerie of pets, just like she'd been assailed by a gaggle of reporters when she'd walked over from her beach house. Charlotte had two squad cars stationed at both the entrance and exit of the circular drive leading up to the hotel's main entrance. There was a gentle breeze and the temperature hovered around seventy. Cooler than most Junes in her memory and Liz was loving it. Even with an ocean breeze, summers on the barrier island could be quite brutal. The veranda was on the south end of the hotel with only a view of flora, fauna or the occasional egret, heron, or crane stopping in from the Pelican Island Sanctuary Nature Preserve.

"Morning, Grand-Pierre." The chef had his nose stuck in his e-reader, lounging on a cushioned wrought iron chaise.

She placed Bronte, who was snuggled in her basket under a potted palm. The kitten kneaded her cushion a few times then settled in. Killer commanded a spot in the shade. His large Great Dane body served as a pillow for Betty's cat, Caroline Keene. The two shared the same black-and-white tuxedo coloring. Captain Netherton had been taking over Caro's care while Betty was away, letting her bunk in his suite alongside Caro's canine boyfriend, Killer. Barnacle Bob didn't usually hang out with the rest of the pet crew. He wasn't a fan of Caroline Keene and no doubt blamed the feline for the loss of feathers on the top of his head. And rightly so. Liz hoped Farrah was with her owner. She knew one thing, after a stressful, life changing event, there was no better salve than the love of a pet.

Venus, Greta's sphinx cat gave Liz a dismissive blink. She was used to being the baby in the bunch, and still hadn't forgiven Liz for bringing

Bronte into the fold. Venus had been sunning herself on a pink princess velvet cushion, her hairless body matching the color of the bed she lounged on. Liz pulled the cushion with Venus on it into the shade. "You don't want to get a sunburn, do you, goddess?"

The cat's frosty blue eyes looked up at her in irritation, then closed. Their color, almost the same as the deceased Julian Rhodes's. Reminding Liz of Susannah's graphic description of his terrible death and Liz's view of his contorted face when the blanket slipped off as they were wheeling his body to the ambulance. The juxtaposition between the cozy scene in front of her and Saturday's was hard to reconcile.

"What chapter are you on, Grand-Pierre?" Liz asked. He was reading Agatha Christie's, *The Pale Horse.* Liz was also reading it for their two-person mystery book club. The novel featured historian Mark Easterbrook and his sleuthing buddy, Ginger Corrigan. Having read all the Hercule Poirot tales many times over, Liz was trying to broaden Pierre's love of Christies to the author's lesser known works. Ones that didn't just involve the Belgian detective Hercule Poirot, Chef Pierre's look-alike alter ego, or the elderly Miss Marple with her knitting bag of tricks.

"It seems I've lost my place, Lizzy dear." He said. "I'm trying to recall the last scene I read. There was something to do with a man in a wheelchair..." Recently, Pierre had been having problems with his memory and under the care of both a medical doctor and a homeopathic practitioner. Liz had seen a rapid improvement in the past few months and had hoped things would remain that way.

She stepped over to his lounge chair and took the eBook from him, swiping through it until she came to the part introducing the wheelchair bound character, Mr. Venables. She handed it back and took a seat on the adjoining chaise.

"*Merci.*"

"Are you enjoying the book?"

He laughed. "Of course, *ma petite.* I know I was stubborn about trying one of Dame Christie's standalones, as you called it, but it is refreshing to have a new, younger sleuth afoot. I see a little of myself in Mr. Easterbrook, and there is even a resemblance to you in mademoiselle Ginger."

"I'll take that as a compliment. Has everyone had breakfast?"

"Yes. Greta forced me out here as a pet sitter."

"You wouldn't happen to have seen Wren Wagner leave the hotel yesterday?" she asked.

"Greta told me she was gone. It's a shame. I had such a nice discussion on Saturday morning with the petite Wren. She came up to me when I was waxing Agatha." If Pierre wasn't cooking or reading mysteries, he could usually be found in the garage tinkering with his motorcycle he'd nicknamed Agatha.

"Said her *le petit ami*, boyfriend, had a motorbike. She even fetched the leather conditioner from the garage for me, so I could clean the interior seats of the sidecar. Seemed to know a lot about motorcycles."

Liz took a deep gulp.

Garage!

Antifreeze!

"Grand-Pierre, you don't know if we have any antifreeze on the grounds, do you?"

He didn't notice the excitement in her voice and said, "A strange thing to ask, *ma cherie*. But yes. There's a can in the garage. I think it was left over from when the hotel had a valet and they used to park guest's cars inside."

Snap! Vintage antifreeze.

"Why do you ask?" Grand-Pierre questioned.

"Uh, you know Kate and her vintage shop of oddities. She told me old automobile signs and advertising cans were an up-and-coming thing." It wasn't a total lie because last week she'd seen a school bus yellow Pennzoil tin sign hanging in Books & Browsery by the Sea.

"Then Katie should check out the other stuff in there," Pierre said. "I think the antifreeze can was next to a crate of old license plates."

"Thanks. I'll be sure to tell her. So, what else did Wren tell you?"

"Said I reminded her of her *grand-pere*. Even gave me a kiss on the cheek when she left."

"That's interesting. I never took her for the sentimental type," she said sarcastically.

"We talked a lot about gardening. She knows a lot about herbs and flowers, and medicinal cures. Said she lived on some type of farm co-op at one time."

"Did she say the name of the town or city where she lived? Or where her family came from?"

"Oh dear. She might have. But I don't recall." He pinched the skin between his bushy white eyebrows as if it would help him remember.

"It doesn't matter Grand-Pierre, I was just curious. But if you think of anything that might help us find her, let me or Auntie know. She left behind a piece of jewelry."

"Oh, that's a shame."

"Yes. It is. Now, you get back to *The Pale Horse*. Ryan and I are going to pick up Betty later from the Melbourne Airport. She's coming home today."

"I've missed her," he said. "But I'm sure she's had a wonderful time in Jacksonville with her great-grandkids."

"Oh, I know she has." Liz just hoped Betty had more intel to share with her and Ryan.

Before racing off Liz grabbed the teapot from the tray next to him and poured some steaming Island Bliss mint tea into his cup. "Talk to you later, Grand-Pierre. Please keep an eye on Bronte. I don't know what might happen if she met Farrah the ferret. She's such an innocent." Betty said Liz coddled the kitten, but didn't everyone?

"Of course, *Ma petite sirene.*"

"*Sirene?*"

"Little mermaid," he answered.

She looked over at his hunched form. Probably from standing over stovetops for so many meals or reading mysteries for a good portion of his eighty-one years. She suddenly felt very protective. "If any nosy reporters, or people with cameras show up, call Greta right away. You have your phone, right?"

He patted his apron pocket. "*Oui.* But why would there be reporters?"

"It's a long story. Something to do with Dorian Starwood. They want to interview her. She has such a following. Aunt Amelia wants her all to herself."

Not exactly the truth, but close to it.

"I'll be fine," he said. "But before you go, Lizzy, can you tell me again how to make notes on this machine?" He held out the e-reader.

She showed him how to highlight the section he wanted, then tap the word NOTE. "And don't forget to tap SAVE," she said, handing it back to him.

In the past, he would keep all the clues from his mystery novels in his head until he came up with his lead suspect. Now he was able to keep track of the clues as he read, then peruse them later. Liz did the same thing, only she didn't have memory problems. She kissed him on the top of the head, blew a kiss to Bronte, and went to the iron gate.

Her face must have betrayed her excitement at her upcoming trip with Ryan, because he called out, "Don't get in trouble, *cherie.*"

"I won't. Promise, Grand-Pierre. Let me know when you get to the end of the next chapter. We'll compare notes."

He didn't answer, already lost in his book.

A few minutes later she entered the butler's pantry to check on Barnacle Bob. BB was taking his morning siesta. Greta had moved him from the elevator to the pantry to give him breakfast. Liz saw that Barnacle Bob was not only a dirty talker, but also a dirty eater. Below his cage was a plastic mat to catch the overflow of food he liked to spit through the bars of his cage.

Aunt Amelia had been trying to introduce something new to his diet in the form of food pellets that looked like mini hockey pucks, hoping in time to eliminate the less nutritional diet he coveted. Five pellets were lying on the mat along with some of BB's breast feathers. He must have struggled to get the pellets through the space between the bars. Her great-aunt was always up on the lasted health food trends for the pets at the Indialantic. Which would've been fine, if she'd been the one that had to feed him, not Liz or Greta.

Liz stepped toward Grand-Pierre's desk and saw the handwritten menu he produced rain or shine, memory or no. From what he'd written, she could tell Greta could handle it without her help. Ryan had called at six a.m. to tell her they were taking a surprise road trip and to be ready at ten. When she'd reminded him that she had to get Betty from the airport, he'd said they'd pick her up on the way back.

Blown away by the fact Dorian had poison in her system and forgetting about the sleeping macaw, Liz looked up at the ceiling and said, "Julian Rhodes, who planned on giving you a double whammy of poison? Someone bewitched a witch. But who?"

At her words, Barnacle Bob snapped into action, "Bewitched, bewitched. Bewitched, bewitched, bewitched, duh-duh, du-duh…" first singing the words, then humming to the tune of the 1960s *Bewitched* sitcom theme song.

Having had a witch at the hotel, it was only a matter of time before the insufferable bird came up with that one from his mid-century television mind vault.

He then broke out into another of his favorite chants, "Kiwi, kiwi, kiwi."

Bending down, she took one of the mini-hockey puck pellets from the mat and pushed it between the bars of his cage. "Tootles, BB. Catch ya later."

As she walked out, she heard his usual litany of curse words. She turned and said, "Wish I could twitch my nose like Samantha on the *Bewitched* sitcom and make you disappear, you foul mouthed, incorrigible parrot." She purposely addressed him as a parrot instead of a macaw, wanting to incense him further.

In all fairness, she couldn't imagine eating one of those things either.

She left the pantry, then exited through the open doorway at the back of the kitchen and stepped into the hallway. She made a left, passing the hotel's old dumbwaiter. At her father's apartment door, she knocked, then called out, "Dad. You home?" When he didn't respond she turned the knob and walked inside.

He wasn't in his office, so she placed a note on his desk that she'd be going out with Ryan, then picking Betty up from the airport. She left via the office door, then took a path that lead along the lagoon, which ended at the hotel's garage. There was something she had to check out.

Actually, there were two somethings she needed to check out.

Chapter 25

Between the dock and the emporium's parking lot was the hotel's old garage, a sturdy structure that had survived every storm the Atlantic threw at it. Adrenaline hit and she broke into a run. The side door was open. She stepped inside and flipped the light switch. Dust motes filtered down from the windows on the far side of the large space. At one time the building could house twenty cars. And not just any cars, but big cars like Studebakers and old-school limos. Now it held lawn equipment and a mammoth workbench littered with an assortment of tools. In the past, Pierre did most of the small maintenance jobs around the hotel and emporium, but since moving into the caretaker's cottage Ryan had taken over.

When the Indialantic was under hurricane warnings, the center of the garage was left empty and used to store the hotel's outdoor furniture. She searched the perimeter of the garage, looking for the box of license plates Grand-Pierre had mentioned. On the northeast corner she spied a plastic milk crate on a wooden bench next to a couple of rakes. She went up to it and found a stack of license plates dating from the 1930s, even a New York World's fair plate featuring the World of Tomorrow's Unisphere. She thought of snatching it to give to Kate for her shop but knew better than to touch anything; because next to the crate on the bench was a rectangular dust free impression of where a container had once stood. A can of antifreeze as Grand-Pierre had said?

She was disappointed but not surprised. No wonder the CSI's couldn't find anything. Whoever poisoned Julian, had taken it. Her money was on Wren, especially after Grand-Pierre just told her that Wren had been inside. She supposed the crime scene team could check for Wren's prints inside the garage. But what would that prove? She'd been asked to go inside and get the leather cleaner for Pierre's motorbike. Thinking of Wren, something else was bugging her. If she had left the Indialantic yesterday, how likely would it be that she would leave the opal ring behind? It would make sense to at least ask Greta or Susannah if they'd seen it. Why did she have to leave in such a hurry, especially after telling Branson she planned on staying?

Last night before bed, she'd gone over all the photos Ashley had sent from Saturday's Merfest in the emporium's parking lot. Nothing stood out. She did see who she thought was the man in the black cap standing next to Dorian's tent. But she couldn't be one hundred percent sure it was him. She'd also spied Wren talking to Phoebe and Branson and had sent both photos to Ryan, along with a selfie of her lips kissing her phone screen. *Hehe.*

* * * *

A few minutes later she was standing outside the glass door to the orchid house. It was the only entrance or exit to the structure. Now that they knew Dorian had ingested oleander leaves, Liz wanted to see why Wren had been wearing an orchid that came from inside a locked building that only Liz, Pierre, and Aunt Amelia had a key for.

Looking at the shattered pane of glass next to the doorknob, she got her answer. She didn't know if it was a concrete clue but whoever reached through the hole in the glass had a much smaller hand than Liz. She used her key to unlock the padlock and walked into the temperature controlled room. The sides of the narrow room had three bleacher type benches with potted orchids. Above the benches were rows upon rows of hanging orchids whose roots were too long to keep in pots. She took in a deep breath, inhaling the familiar scent of earth and flower and marched toward the far wall with the sink and potting bench. Obviously, this was where Wren had performed her decapitation of the Nieve Blanca orchid. Liz didn't believe Wren would break into the orchid house just to get a flower to wear in her hair.

Even though they called the space the orchid house, it also doubled as a greenhouse/garden shed. Next to the sink was a marble mortar and pestle used by Liz and her great-aunt to gently release fragrance from dried lavender, gardenia, or rose petals. Had someone used it to make a powder or oil from the oleander? Then they added it to Julian's water bottle that Dorian drank from?

Before leaving, Liz pulled out the small trash can beneath the sink and noticed a crumpled paper towel with a residue of dried brown leaves.

Grand-Pierre said Wren had knowledge of flowers and herbs. If she had, it was important to find her.

Doing an analysis on the leaves on the paper towel and any residue on the mortar and pestle would take time. As Charlotte often told her, the instant results on DNA and other forensics didn't happen as fast as shown on television. She left once again without touching anything except the doorknob.

As she walked past the summerhouse on the way back to Ryan's she mused that instead of trying to find Julian Rhodes's murderer, she should be planning a midnight rendezvous under the stars with the man of her dreams. Soon, she thought. Things must come to a head soon. Perhaps Wren's leaving was a good thing? It solidified her guilt. Now the others could leave and then they could get on with their lives. The dress rehearsal for *The Sea Witch* was Friday and she and her father had tried to convince Aunt Amelia to postpone. A consummate actress, she wouldn't hear of it. The show must go on, she'd told them.

She took out her phone and sent a group text to Charlotte and her father, telling them what she'd discovered in the garage and orchid house. She continued past the cutting garden, then made a left and followed a path west toward the caretaker's cottage. Ryan said he wouldn't tell her where they were going until she got in the car. Wherever they were going, she hoped they'd find the missing pieces they were looking for.

Rosy, the Indialantic's semi tame rosette spoonbill tern greeted her on the grass bordering the rear parking lot near the lagoon. "How's it going, Rosy? What ya doing on the grass—no minnows for breakfast?" Liz must have reminded her. She stretched her rosy wings and took off for her favorite piling on the dock. Looking to her right Liz saw her father's cabin cruiser *Serendipity* bobbing in the gentle waves of the lagoon. Had it only been two days ago that they'd sat watching the Mystical Merfest Boat Regatta pass by?

At the end of the dock, Liz spied Captain Netherton on the top deck of *Queen of the Seas*. Her watch read nine forty-five. She had at least fifteen minutes until she needed to meet Ryan. The past couple of days, Liz and the captain kept missing each other. She'd never talked to him personally about what happened the night Julian was poisoned. She knew he would have shared everything with Charlotte, but still, he might remember something two days later with a clearer vision of the events. And now with the news that Wren had left town, it seemed even more important than ever to glean any kind of clue as to where she might have gone.

A few minutes later, Captain Netherton said to her with a weak smile, "So that's everything. I'm sorry I don't have much to add. Susannah and Ashley prepared and then served Ms. Starwood and Mr. Rhodes food at their table. Ashley even helped with the cleanup when she wasn't taking photos."

He'd basically reiterated the same thing Susannah and Ashley had told them.

Captain Netherton put his pipe in his mouth and gnawed on the stem as he gazed out across the lagoon. Betty had talked him out of smoking it, but old habits were hard to break. After a few moments of silence, he said, "I did notice poor Ashley had a hard time of it when she tried to get any shot with Mr. Rhodes in it. He always turned away or told her there'd been enough photo taking for a lifetime. I overheard Ashley ask Dorian if she wanted to video portions of the rehearsal dinner. Mr. Rhodes got really angry. You know what? Now that I think about it, that might be the time he went down to the stateroom. He did stomp off somewhere before dinner was served, but I had to return to my post, so I have no idea where he went."

"Do you mind showing me the stateroom where the uh...body"—technically he'd been alive at the time—"Julian was found?"

"Of course not. The police are done. I was just about to tidy it up. Come with me." He put a kind hand on her shoulder. Like Betty, Greta, Pierre, and Susannah, the Indialantic's permanent guests, Captain Netherton had become family. He and Betty were an item, even though Betty wouldn't admit it. Just like Betty's cat Caroline Keene and Captain Netherton's dog Killer were best buds, so were Betty and the captain. With his lean, erect posture, white goatee and mustache, the retired coast guard captain reminded Liz of a nautical man from another age, or as Aunt Amelia said, "He's the spitting image of Captain Daniel Gregg from the 1960's TV sitcom, *The Ghost and Mrs. Muir*." Liz had viewed the old show many times and had to agree.

As they walked to the stairs leading down to the stateroom, she asked, "Doesn't it make sense that Branson should have been the one prepping and serving Dorian and Julian's food?"

Captain Netherton turned and looked at her. "I specifically remember him saying he would look over the buffet, but he didn't seem concerned about his mother's and Mr. Rhodes's plates."

"Do you know if he prepared the meal himself at his restaurant?"

"No, we specifically talked about that. Mr. Arnaud is no chef. He said the chef de cuisine at The Soulful Sea prepared everything ahead of time."

When they entered the stateroom, Liz noticed black fingerprint powder on every smooth surface. There wasn't a chalk outline on the wood floor to tell her where Julian had fallen. Just as well, she thought. Ashley had said Wren and Phoebe had come down the stairs to the room the night of the poisoning. Susannah had found him, but what no one knew was why Julian was down there in the first place?

Up until last fall, the *Queen of the Sea's* stateroom had been used for storage. With Aunt Amelia's permission, Captain Netherton tackled cleaning it out, discovering a vintage jewel of a room buried under decades of junk. Two forties style sofas flanked a table big enough for eight. On the teak walls were framed nautical maps and vintage photos yellowed with age. In one of the teak cabinets, the captain had found photographs proving that at one time the room had been used by VIPs for clandestine meetings when they needed a private place to discuss the politics of the time, which included the turbulent time period during WWII and the Cold War. Liz smiled. That was one of the things she loved about growing up at the Indialantic; there were so many stories and so much history attached to it. They were still discovering things and it had been almost a hundred years from when the hotel first opened its doors.

While Captain Netherton looked on, she went to work checking the cushions in the sofa, then got on her hands and knees near the chair where Ryan said he found the SWS water bottle and looked underneath. Nothing. She even riffled through the cupboards. Again, nothing.

When she glanced up at the captain, he had his hands on his hips, a smile on his face. "I've checked everything a hundred times myself. I've had a chat with Amelia. I promised her we would find out what happened to her friend's fiancé."

"I made the same promise."

"Hey, don't look so glum. With Charlotte on the case, along with you, Ryan, and Betty, I'm sure there will be an answer soon."

"I hope so," she said, standing up. "Can I see the galley where the food came from before being served?"

"Sure."

They went back up the narrow steps. The galley was a half level below the main deck and a half level up from the stateroom. The galley and stateroom were the only cabins below deck. The galley was small but efficient; the same fingerprint powder was on all the surfaces. She looked in the refrigerator. As she thought. It was empty. On the table was a wrinkled copy of the rehearsal dinner menu. She picked it up and asked, "So everything on this menu was served at the rehearsal dinner, correct?"

The captain leaned over her shoulder. "Yes."

"Along with the blue bottles of the Sunshine Wiccan Society's water, right?"

Yes. Only the water wasn't in here. It was in a tub of ice next to where the tables were set up."

"So, if a bottle of water was found in the stateroom, Julian must have brought it with him." She glanced at the menu again. "That's it!" She pointed at the paper.

"What's it?"

"The mango mermaid margarita intermezzo!"

"The inter-what-zzo?"

"Intermezzo is a term used for a palate cleanser. Usually it's a sorbet, but in this case a margarita. It would be the perfect place to hide the poison. Was it served by Susannah or Ashley?" She didn't let it slip that the poison had been antifreeze, but she did remember Charlotte's words that the antifreeze had a sweet taste. Now that she thought about it, the SWS water had just a hint of orange, not enough to mask the antifreeze Charlotte described, only oleander, she thought sadly.

"No. There wasn't room in this refrigerator for the margaritas and glasses, so Mr. Arnaud used the one up on deck, off the main cabin. He brought the tray out himself and served everyone at their seats. I remember because he came down here to the galley to cut some lime slices."

"Did he have the drinks with him?"

"I don't believe he did. The girls were getting the dinner course ready to bring up to Ms. Starwood and Mr. Rhodes. There really wasn't room."

Captain Netherton's account of the dinner matched Susannah's and Ashley's, with one exception, the fact Branson had left a tray of margaritas on deck when he went down to get slices of lime. "That means when he came down to the galley, the margaritas were just sitting there…unattended!" Excitement made her words come out in spurts.

The captain looked at her. "I suppose…It was a hectic time, seeing I was the only member of the boat crew. I didn't even have time to taste the food, even though Mr. Arnaud offered."

"Looks like that might have been a good thing," she said.

"I hope if there was any residue of poison in the margarita glasses the authorities will find it," he said. "The man was poisoned, and we've now calculated that it could have been anyone."

Liz grinned, "We've? Wow. Betty's wearing off on you Captain Netherton. I see your point but if it's found that the margaritas were the conduit to the poison, we can ask more questions on where and what people were doing when they were served. It would still be good to find out how many glasses the sheriff's department collected. If it's six, there you go."

"Do you know how easy it would be to dump Mr. Rhodes's glass into the lagoon?"

"True." Liz glanced at her watch. She had to leave in a few minutes but had one last thing she wanted to ask. "Captain, how about Dorian's daughter, Phoebe? A witness said she and Wren had gone down the steps, either to the galley or the stateroom. Did you notice her?"

"No, sorry. I never talked to Ms. Starwood's daughter that night or Wren. I did have a conversation with Ms. Starwood's friend, Garrett. Seemed a nice man. He was very interested in the course the boat was taking, and how long we'd be anchored at the inlet for dinner."

"Anything else that seemed strange or out of the ordinary with Garrett?" So far, she'd been forgetting about Garrett and his possible motives or lack of motives for murdering Julian Rhodes. She knew one thing; he sure had a crush on Dorian. And then there was the little detail that Julian had threatened Garret, saying soon he would be taking over Garrett's job as financial advisor and agent.

"I don't know if it was out of the ordinary, and I told Agent Pearson about it, but Garrett had asked me if there was a private place he could have a word with Ms. Starwood before dinner was served."

"And…"

He raised an eyebrow. "I told him my small office that doubles as a storage closet would be adequate for a private talk."

"Do you mind showing me your office?"

"Liz, are you sure you should be snooping around? Look what happened last January." He finally said it. She was surprised he hadn't said it earlier.

"Don't worry. This time there's no one after me. It's just you and me, right? No stranger danger." *Except the man in the black cap*, she thought.

He arched a white brow, then said reluctantly, "Come with me." Before continuing up the steps, he grabbed his cane. After being injured in a Coast Guard rescue mission in his active days, he occasionally relied on his ornate headed cane. It wasn't just any cane. Aunt Amelia had given it to him last Christmas. It had been gifted to her from the prop department after the last episode of *Dark Shadows* aired in 1971 and had been one of the canes used by the show's main character, Barnabas Collins played by actor Jonathan Frid. The handle of the cane resembled a silver wolf's head. Liz never understood the logic of a vampire needing a cane. If he was eternal, as most vampires were, didn't that mean he never aged? Why the cane? And why a wolf head? Wouldn't a werewolf sport a wolf's head cane?

She remembered voicing her concerns to Aunt Amelia who'd sighed, then told her, *"Oh Lizzy, that's what's interesting. The wolf's head on the cane was made from pure silver. Barnabas used it to fend off the show's werewolf, Quentin, or any other werewolves who came his way. There's no love lost between werewolves and silver. And Barnabas might have been* eternal *but he'd been alive or one of the living-dead for 175 years. As I can attest, life has a way of wearing you down when you get on in your later years. It's not easy for us oldies."*

Liz didn't remember her exact words, but knew it was something along the lines of, "You're not old, Auntie!"

She and Captain Netherton went up the stairs to the main deck. The sky, which had started out as a clear blue when she'd driven over to the Indialantic, was now covered with gray, ashy clouds. She'd had so many good memories of riding on the *Queen of the Seas* over the years that she hoped this one tragic incident wouldn't mar those memories. The boat was a must-do with tourists visiting the island. She knew that Charlotte hadn't mentioned the name of the boat in her news conference last night, but with all the reporters lurking around, it was sure to get out.

They walked through the seating area of the main cabin where cushioned benches lined both the port and starboard sides of the boat. There were ten rows of seating with a wide center aisle, enough to accommodate sixty guests. The pilot house was open and during his eco-history tours of the Treasure Coast, the captain would point out interesting facts; the location of sunken treasure, famous pirates, while identifying the large assortment of seabirds roosting nearby or at the Pelican Island Nature Preserve, not to mention all the sea life, including manatees, sharks, and dolphins.

Captain Netherton stopped at a door, inserted a key, and opened it. Holding it open for Liz, he followed in from behind, then flipped on the light switch. It was a good sized room with shelves lining both sides of the rectangular space. His desk was on the far wall, neat and tidy, just like his suite at the Indialantic where he did his own housecleaning and laundry. There was a small loveseat next to the desk, a nice quiet place for Garrett and Dorian to talk without anyone overhearing them. In the corner was a table with a coffee maker on top and a single coffee mug. Written on the mug was: *Rule #1 The Boat Captain is Always Right. Rule #2 if the Boat Captain is Wrong refer to Rule #1.* Next to the table was a refrigerator.

They turned to each other with the realization that the refrigerator that held the mango margaritas was also in the same room Dorian and Garrett had met. She voiced the obvious. "Now it seems Garrett and Dorian had access, along with everyone else. Do you know if they were here before the margaritas were served?"

"That, I have no idea."

"Do you know if Branson filled the glasses here or on deck?"

"I would assume here. He had a large serving tray with glasses that already had a salt rim. That's why he needed the extra space in the fridge for the frosted glasses and the premade margarita mix."

"I don't see how Garrett or Dorian could have added the poison while here in your office," she mused out loud. "How would they know which one would go to Julian? The best case scenario would be someone did it while Branson went down for the limes, or they sidled up to the table when no one was looking."

"Or Branson did it here before he carried the tray upstairs and delivered it personally?" Captain Netherton added. "I have a feeling, Liz, you're missing the forest for the trees, or the possible murderers for the margaritas. Knowing that it could have been the margarita that contained the poison doesn't help now that we've realized everyone had motive and opportunity."

"Wish it could have been videotaped."

"Ashley took photos," he said, "I would look for anything that shows the guests near the bride-and-groom-to-be's table. As you know I've been spending a lot of time with super-sleuth Betty, I would talk to the ones who *don't* admit talking to Julian that night."

"You would, would you?" she said, smiling. He was right, though. Nothing could be proven, especially in court. *Well, your Honor, I submit this photo showing where Ms. Wagner is talking to the deceased Julian Rhodes. Oh, and here's one with...*

"How did Dorian Starwood end up in the stateroom after Susannah found him?" Liz asked on her way out of the room.

"She heard Susannah's screaming, I'm sure. I do know when Ms. Starwood came to the stateroom and saw her fiancé's body, she kept repeating it was all her fault and she was sorry, over and over again."

That wasn't anything new. It was easy to feel responsible when someone dies and there are unresolved issues. Liz had had the same feelings, recently. "Did you tell Charlotte or anyone from the sheriff's department that she said that?"

"Why, uh, no."

"I'm sure Dorian didn't kill him and I'm going to help Aunt Amelia prove her friend is innocent." She didn't want to say there was still a chance Julian had tried to kill Dorian and it backfired. "I know Dorian was getting threatening anonymous notes."

"Notes, you say?" Captain Netherton asked. "Now that's interesting. Saturday, before the Merfest Regatta I was in the lobby checking my mail slot. Mr. Rhodes was there peeling off an adhesive strip to a white envelope and sealing it. When he saw me, he startled. I winked at him and looked at the envelope. It had Dorian's name on it. He shoved it in his pocket and murmured something about it being the flower bill for the wedding."

"How was Dorian's name written?" she asked, remembering what Aunt Amelia had told her. Also, there was the little fact that Aunt Amelia planned to supply all the flowers. They'd never hired a florist.

"Printed." He looked puzzled.

"Don't worry. I don't have it figured out, but I think you've been a big help. And I'll be sure to fill you in after meeting with Betty and Ryan. Speaking of which. I better vamoose. Ryan and I have an errand, then afterward, we'll get Betty from the airport."

"I know Caroline Keene will be happy to see her."

"Not you, Captain?" she said, raising an eyebrow.

He blushed.

She kissed him on the cheek. "Don't worry, you'll see her soon."

Chapter 26

Betty's Blue Bomber Cadillac Deville had been on loan to Liz since the day she came back from Manhattan. She meant to buy her own wheels but hadn't gotten around to it. Plus, as Betty always said, the Indialantic by the Sea Hotel and Emporium was its own ecosystem. Everything you needed from food, shelter, clothing, home décor, surfing gear, and even boyfriends, like the one sitting next to her, were all within arm's reach.

They were supposed to use Ryan's Jeep for his secret trip, but the oil light wouldn't turn off after he'd started the car. They'd left Pierre with his head under the hood trying to fix the problem.

"I think we'd be better off using Pierre's motorcycle and sidecar than this thing," Ryan said, buckling his seat belt.

Liz looked at him and grinned. "Then what would we do with Betty and her luggage? Maybe next time Pierre can show you how to successfully change your oil, city boy." She pushed the button on the console to lower the top. The frame to the canvas groaned and stopped halfway. She got out, folded it the rest of the way down, then snapped the cover in place to keep it from springing up.

Back inside, she started the car and put it in drive. "Which way, boss? A right or left on A1A? Hope it's the opposite direction of those rain clouds."

"Boss? I like that."

"You would," she said, tapping his arm with her fist.

"Make a right."

After a few sputters and a couple of backfires, she left the parking lot and took off down the highway. Glancing at the turbulent ocean to her left, she realized she'd probably made a mistake putting the top down. The cloud cover was heavier than when she'd walked over to the Indialantic. At least she didn't have to worry about wearing a hat to shade her scar. Her long strawberry blonde hair tended to contract exponentially into masses of ringlets based on the humidity in the air. She'd worn a white sleeveless sundress, and a peach chiffon scarf Aunt Amelia had given her from the set of one of her TV shows. The long tails of the scarf occasionally whipped Ryan on the cheek. She was channeling her best Grace Kelly from the movie *To Catch a Thief,* the scene where Frances Stevens is tooling around the Cote d'Azur in her sky-blue sports car (in Liz's case the blue bomber). She glanced over at Ryan and saw a resemblance between him and Grace's costar, Cary Grant. They both dressed in black, and just like John Robie, Ryan had been known to break into homes cat-burglar-style if the occasion called for it. Which it had.

It felt empowering to feel the wind on her face and the freedom under the open sky. For a moment she was unencumbered by the heavy malaise that had settled on the Indialantic. She refused to think about psychics, witches, and warlocks, and concentrate instead on happy things like the man next to her, and welcoming calm minded Betty Lawson back into the fold. "Okay, where are we going?" she shouted over the wind.

"Charlotte called last night. Thanks to you, and your discovery of Wren's real first name, she was able to get an address for her parents. Wren/Renee does have a record, but it's sealed because she was a minor at the time of her arrest. Talking to her parents might shed some light on what the arrest was for and, if nothing else, maybe we'll find her hiding at their house."

"True."

When they reached Highway 510 Liz made a right. They traveled west, under the I-95 overpass and found themselves in Florida farm country. Passing a herd of cows lounging on the grass, she asked, "I wonder if it's true what Auntie always told me growing up? That cows lay down when it's going to rain?"

"Hmmm, you would have to Google it," he said.

"I think it's more fun just to believe her. I'm really worried about the effect these past couple of days have had on Auntie. She has dress rehearsal for *The Sea Witch* on Friday."

"Hopefully we'll be able to find something soon," he said. "Tell me about your morning. You sound like you've been busy."

She told him about everything she'd just learned from the garage and orchid house. Then filled him in on her time with Captain Netherton. "We think the poison was put in the mermaid mango margaritas."

"We? Mermaid margaritas?"

"Okay, *I* think," she said. "With all the recent developments that Dorian had oleander in her system and Julian Rhodes didn't, I'm leaning to say he was the intended target. Dorian told me she drank from his SWS water bottle during the rehearsal dinner."

"Unless…" Ryan said, turning to her. The wind in his dark, glossy hair and his unshaven face made him appear like a roguish pirate. All he needed was a knife between his lips and a headband.

"Unless what? Don't say it," she said.

"Okay, I'll just think it," he answered.

"Dorian would never ingest poisonous oleander to throw suspicion off herself for killing her fiancé with antifreeze. You have to trust me on this. Plus, I found the crushed leaves in the orchid house and saw Wren with an orchid in her hair. The glass pane by the door had been shattered by a rock and broken into. The hole was so small I couldn't put my hand through. But Wren could have."

"Liz, I know you think that's what happened, but until the CSIs confirm that it is oleander on the paper towel and the mortar and pestle, we can't do a thing. Plus, Dorian Starwood is on the small side herself."

"You're right."

"I'm what?" He cupped his hand to his ear and leaned in.

She grinned. "You're right. We have to wait. But not about Dorian."

"Eyes ahead. Our turn is coming up. Make a right, at that horse farm. Pleasant Lane."

"I hope Wren's parents are pleasant."

"That reminds me. And don't take it the wrong way. Charlotte said that seeing I'm on retainer with the sheriff's department, I'm to do all the talking."

"But I…" She made the quick turn onto a dirt road.

"Ah, what did I just say?"

Before she could protest further, they pulled up to a white farmhouse with a red barn behind it.

Liz whistled. "I feel like we're somewhere in the Midwest instead of Florida."

Ryan pointed to a tree in the distance. "Subtract the palm tree, and I'd say you're right."

After Liz parked in the circular drive, they saw a man in overalls coming from the barn. Liz felt relief when she noticed his big smile.

They got out of the car and Ryan made introductions.

"Will Wagner. Nice to meet ya. So, you're trying to find our Renee? Hope she's not in trouble."

Liz opened her mouth, then shut it, trying to remember the role she'd been assigned as a mime from Cirque de Soleil.

Ryan took something out of his pocket. "We run an inn that your daughter was staying at. She left this ring behind. We didn't have a forwarding address but remembered her saying you lived close by."

Wow, smart thinking, Liz thought.

"Renee told you we lived nearby? Wonder why she didn't come see us? Yes, that's her ring. She said someone gave it to her for high school graduation. If I know Renee, she probably stole it. I bet she skipped out on the hotel bill, too? We've stopped paying her creditor's years ago. Part of the tough love meetings my wife went to after Renee graduated high school."

"Will!" A woman stood on a wraparound porch complete with two large rocking chairs that looked like they'd been swiped from the front of the local Cracker Barrel. "Don't be so rude. Invite the lady and gentleman in for some coffee." Her thin salt-and-pepper hair was pulled back in a ponytail. Her face dark from the sun. Confirming the sun exposure were numerous lines on either side of her mouth and eyes.

Liz followed Will and Ryan to the porch. The Wagner's had a lot of land, but it didn't look like much of it was in use. The screen door creaked as Mrs. Wagner opened it and ushered them inside. The interior of the house was as she'd suspected. Lost somewhere in the 1950s, complete with granny-square afghans and early-American décor sporting *E. Pluribus Unum* eagles on the sofa cushions and wall clock. Kate would have a good time finding things here for her emporium shop Books & Browsery.

Mrs. Wagner held out her hand toward Liz. "Maureen Wagner."

"Liz Holt."

Then she turned to Ryan, and he said, "Ryan Stone."

Will was already in his Lazy Boy, the footrest extended. He looked old enough to be Wren's grandfather. Maureen also. They either had Wren late in life or life on the farm hadn't been a bed of roses.

"They've come about Renee," Will said. "They have her opal ring someone gave her before..."

Before what? Liz could tell by Ryan's expression he was also interested.

"What's she done now?" Maureen asked in a tired voice.

Ryan repeated what he'd told Wren's father.

"How kind of you," Mrs. Wagner said. "Have a seat, I'll get some refreshments."

"We don't want to put you out," Ryan said, "just seeing if you had a forwarding address?

"No. Sorry. It's been a while since we've seen her. Right, Will?"

"Been three years, I think." Will grabbed a mug large enough to double as a soup bowl from a TV tray and waved it in the air. "I wouldn't mind a touch-up, Mo. And I'm sure these kids would love to sample your lemon squares. I know I would." He rubbed his protruding belly and smiled with affection.

"It's settled then," she said. "I'll be right back."

When she was out of sight, Liz asked, "Do you mind if I use your powder room?"

Will chuckled, "I thought Mo was the only one who called it that? Last door on the right."

She got up from the sofa and winked at Ryan. He returned a scathing look. Liz ignored it. Like on every crime show she'd ever watched Liz did her best sleuthing using the bathroom excuse. It was impossible to turn down someone who needs the restroom, no matter what you might be hiding. Even a daughter.

It seemed there was nothing to hide in the Wagner home. All the doors on the way to the bathroom were open. The master bedroom had a red, white, and blue patchwork quilt on top of the double bed. The next bedroom must have been Wren's. It belonged in a time capsule. Dust free and smelling of furniture polish. Over a desk in the corner was a large corkboard adorned with concert stubs, hunky heartthrobs torn from magazines, and photos of young Wren wearing her high school cap and gown. There was conversation coming from the living room and she figured she had a few extra minutes to look around. She checked under the bed and pulled out a pink photo box with the word PRINCESS written in silver glitter. She opened the box and found it was filled with letters.

The letters were written by Wren and addressed to her parents. Liz thumbed through them. They were in date order. She pulled out a letter near the end of the stack and opened it. Inside was a photo of a young Wren standing next to Julian Rhodes!

Above the pair was a wooden sign like you'd find at a dude ranch, SUNSHINE SERENITY SPRINGS. The same name Ryan had recently mentioned. She read the letter. It was from Wren/Renee to her mother. Her last lines read: *I'm counting the days to getting out of this cult-like concentration camp. Elder Jay is a fraud. This is involuntary servitude. I would have rather gone to the paid rehab you claim you couldn't afford, other than this "free" chance for rehabilitation the judge suggested. I bet the judge is getting a kick-back from turning us into slaves.*

Elder Jay must be what Julian was calling himself back then.

"I should have known," a voice said from behind her. "If Renee was involved, this was no innocent visit to return a lost ring. What do you want? We have no money. Renee's taken it all. My husband has a shotgun. Should I have him fetch it?"

She turned slowly to see Maureen Wagner holding a knife in her right hand.

Liz prayed it was to cut lemon squares.

Chapter 27

"So much for keeping out of it and letting me handle things," Ryan said, as they sped out of the Wagner's yard.

"Oh, but look what we found! A connection between Wren and Julian." Excitement flushed Liz's cheeks. After Mrs. Wagner brandished her knife at Liz, she was led out of Wren's bedroom and ordered to come clean in front of her husband about the true nature of their visit. After Ryan filled them in and showed them his P.I. license, the Wagner's didn't seem too surprised that their daughter was possibly involved in a murder investigation and had left town. Mrs. Wagner had allowed Ryan, not Liz, to take the box of letters if he promised he'd return them. As they'd stepped off the porch, heading to the car, Mrs. Wagner called out, "On second thought. You can keep the letters. It will save me from going through them year after year to see if we could have done anything differently. I know now we couldn't. And it's time for us to let go of the guilt." Then she'd waved, turned, and walked into the house. Her posture more upright, her steps more sure than when they'd first seen her.

"Don't forget what we didn't find. Wren/Renee Wagner," Ryan said.

"Glass half-empty, Mr. investigator? Elder Jay was the leader of Wren's rehabilitation program. An apparent cult leader one minute, fake white witch the next. I bet Wren was blackmailing him with the true nature of his phony Sunshine Wiccan Society so she could become part-owner of the water company, threatening to spill the beans to Dorian about Julian's checkered past."

"Left. Make a left to the highway," Ryan said, pointing, "remember we have to pick up Betty at the airport. If Wren was blackmailing Julian, then why would she poison him?

Liz thought for a moment. "Because she got what she wanted as in the SWS water company, then simply killed him because of what he'd done to her at the camp. She spoke of abuse. A good motive in my humble opinion. In her mind it could also have been an altruistic way of saving Dorian from being married to him."

"From the short time we spent with Wren's parents," Ryan said, "Wren didn't come off as altruistic."

"True. I take back that theory."

It was a thirty-minute drive to the airport. The Blue Bomber kept up with the other cars going eighty in the seventy-mile-per-hour speed limit, but there was no chance for conversation. "Can't wait to tell Betty everything," she shouted. Her scarf was long gone, her hair whipping against her face. "I'm so glad the Wagner's let us take that box of letters."

"What?"

"Never mind," she shouted back. They took to their own thoughts. Puzzling out Wren's motive for killing Julian. Revenge for her work camp service and wanting to be sole owner of the Sunshine Wiccan Society's water company, seemed the best theory. The Sunshine Wiccan Society was now a party of zero. Maureen Wagner had explained that Renee had gotten in trouble right after graduating from high school when she was seventeen and was sent to Sunshine Serenity Springs, a type of boot camp rehabilitation center. Mrs. Wagner hadn't disclosed what her daughter had been arrested for, only that drugs and theft were involved. The Wagner's only option had been to send her to the boot camp, the other choice would have been juvenile detention. "We didn't have the money for a fancy place," Will Wagner had said sadly. "Farm life isn't easy."

Maureen had told them that parents who'd sent their children to Sunshine Serenity Springs were only allowed visitation once every three months for an hour. When Mr. and Mrs. Wagner went, they didn't see anything wrong, and hadn't believed their daughter's complaining because Elder Jay had been so charismatic, giving them a tour of the produce fields, gardens, and natural spring. It wasn't until Wren/Renee's letters started arriving that they looked into it further.

Their daughter claimed that Sunshine Serenity Springs was far from serene, more of a cult-type work camp with corporal punishment run by Elder Jay for the sole purpose of turning them into slave labor in order to support Sunshine Serenity Spring's booming produce and flower stand outlets. Other parents got together and told the Wagners that their children were complaining about the conditions at the camp. That's when they saw the camp for what it really was.

Then, a local paper got a hold of the parents' allegations and plastered Elder Jay's, aka Julian Rhodes', face all over the press in Jacksonville. *That would explain why Julian didn't want Ashley taking pictures of him on Queen of the Seas.*

Wren/Renee was sent to serve six months in an Indian River Juvenile Correctional facility because her parents didn't have the money to send her to a dual-diagnosis rehab. From that time on, she blamed her parents for her time spent inside. She'd cut all communications with her family until a few months ago, when she'd called all chirpy and happy things were turning around for her. She even asked if they needed money.

"Next exit," Ryan shouted, breaking into her thoughts.

When Liz pulled up to the baggage claim exit, eighty-three-year-old Betty Lawson was sitting on a bench next to two large suitcases. She knew one of her suitcases held only research materials for book two in her London Chimney Sweep mystery series. Her white, shiny hair was in a chignon and she was dressed as elegantly as ever in a turquoise long cotton tunic, topped with a strand of coral beads. White capri pants and red ballet flats completed her timeless look. Liz hoped she looked as classy when she reached Betty's age.

After hugging her hello and having to be told to release her grip, Liz loaded the suitcases into the Blue Bomber's trunk. Betty didn't ask why Ryan was sitting in the back seat, just gave him a hug and a kiss, and got in the front. Then they took off for home.

The first ten minutes in the car, Liz did a quick recap of everything she and Ryan learned. It was the first time since Liz knew her that Betty seemed speechless.

When they stopped at the railroad tracks for a train, Betty chided, "Wow! I leave for a couple weeks and look what happens. Told you, no murders without me. I need inspiration for my next book."

"You should have enough inspiration for a lifetime," Liz said. "I don't know if Sherlock Holmes would have had fun at the séance we had yesterday, or what he'd make of that jar of razor blades and barbed wire Dorian was clutching to her breast last night."

"Pshaw. I think you'd be surprised to know that Sir Arthur Conan Doyle, author of the Holmes tales, was very into mysticism. Especially in his later years. Even attending séances and trying to commune with the dead."

"Ugh. Why did you have to say that?" Ryan whined from the backseat. "He was a physician, wasn't he? Can't believe he was into ghosts and spirits."

The lights stopped flashing and the crossing rails raised. A few minutes later they were flying over the causeway above the Indian River Lagoon.

On Fifth Avenue they passed restaurants, beach shops, clothing and toy stores, and Island Books.

Once they hit A1A the wind had picked up, the charcoal sky matching the color of the Atlantic's towering swells.

"Maybe you should pull over and put the top up," Ryan shouted from the backseat. "You two have the windshield for protection, I'm a sitting duck, soon to be drowned duck."

Lightning flashed over the water, followed by deafening thunder.

"Too late!" Liz shouted. "I'll slow down and try to lower the top while we're moving."

"What?" He asked, as the first torrent of rain hit.

Liz pushed the switch on the console. Nothing. She tried again.

"Ryan, hand me an umbrella. There should be one under the passenger seat," Betty called out.

He passed her an army green umbrella. Betty opened it, then, resembling a sea turtle, she crouched low in the seat.

With the wipers on high and rain sluicing down her long bangs, Liz could barely make out the road. They were probably only a half mile away from the Indialantic. She tried the button for the top again. Not even a groan. "I'm going to pull into the old abandoned Sebastian Beach Inn and try to do it manually."

She made a left into the parking lot filled with hills of sand and chunks of broken blacktop, finally stopping on a section of cement. The nose of the car faced a wood-railing fence. Beyond the car was the ocean and a sheer drop to the rocky beach below. A few more feet forward and they could reproduce the ending scene to *Thelma and Louise.*

Keeping the car running, she and Ryan got out, each grabbing one side of the frame to raise the canvas top.

"Betty! Push the button!" Ryan shouted.

They watched a hand come out from under the umbrella, then there was a groaning sound. They tugged on the frame until it finally started to move upward. When the top met the latch at the windshield, they heard Betty securing it from inside.

As Liz fought her way back to the driver's door, wet sand that felt like specks of sharp glass stung her bare legs. She reached for the door handle just as a huge gust of wind pushed her bangs off her face. In front of her, parked next to a bright green industrial sized dumpster was a car.

A red Kia Soul with a bumper sticker that read, *I Watch for Motorcycles.*

Liz sprinted toward it, fighting the elements, even slipping a few times in the muddy sand.

Wren. Why was her car here? Liz opened the driver's door and looked inside. Empty. Just a bunch of gum wrappers littering the passenger seat. She felt someone behind her and whipped around.

"Ryan! You scared me to death" Liz screeched.

"I scared you!" He shouted. "I couldn't understand where you were running to. But now I see. This is Wren's car."

Betty joined them. "Who's car?"

"Wren/Renee Wagner's," Liz answered.

Betty's long hair was glued to her cheeks, mascara ran, making her look like Farrah the masked Ferret. Betty pointed and shouted. "Look over there! There's a section of broken railing."

Liz grabbed her hand, then Ryan's, and they slowly made their way to the gap in the fencing. Glancing down at the beach they saw Wren's body. She was laying on her back, her head resting on a boulder like it was a pillow, her torso in repose. There was no way she could have fallen from where they were standing and land in such a position. It was obvious by the amount of birds and carrion surrounding her body, and the sand covering the same dress Wren had worn at brunch yesterday, that she'd been there for a while. Liz's first thought was of Mr. and Mrs. Wagner. She felt frozen, unable to jump into action.

It was Betty who said in a calm voice, "Call 911. It's too late for anything else."

As another bird landed, Liz gladly turned away.

This wasn't the first murdered body Liz had seen on the beach, but she prayed it would be her last.

Chapter 28

An hour later, holding the box of letter's Mrs. Wagner had given her, Liz pushed against the revolving door. "Where's her luggage? Her Louis Vuitton bag? It wasn't in her car?" Liz shouted, but Betty and Ryan couldn't hear her muffled questions through the glass that separated them. And it was a good thing, because as they filed out one by one into the Indialantic's lobby they saw Aunt Amelia, Dorian, Garrett, and a stranger seated in front of them.

Liz stopped dead center under the lobby's crystal chandelier and glanced again at the stranger and realized he wasn't really a stranger. It was the ankle grabbing guy in the black baseball cap. The man had a black goatee, reminding her of Ryan's dog, but there was nothing adorable about the rest of his face. If he was a character in an old dime-store novel, he would be described as "craggy" or even having an ex-prizefighter's face.

Aunt Amelia got up and rushed toward them. "I am so glad you're back. You wouldn't believe what this gentleman has been telling us about…" she paused, glanced back at Dorian who was now holding hands with Garrett, then leaned in and whispered, "Julian Rhodes. It is all quite astounding. And Jarvis also has something to say about Ms. Wagner too, but Dorian insisted we waited until you were here." Her great-aunt's excitement seemed at a feverish level but calmed when her gaze fell on Betty, a sopping wet Betty. She ran and gave Betty a bone crushing hug, then picked her up in the air. "Boy, am I happy to see you. You wouldn't believe what's been going on here. Though I'm sure Liz and Ryan have told you everything. I…"

"Take a breath, Amelia," Betty said as her friend lowered her to the floor. "I don't want to have to get a paper bag for you to blow in. Why don't we go…" Betty turned to Liz.

Liz shrugged her shoulders and said, "The kitchen." That way they could all sit at the long farm table.

Liz was dying to get out of her wet clothes, but she was also curious about what ole Jarvis the stalker had to say that was so important.

As she walked to the kitchen, she replayed the scene at the beach. After Wren's body had been brought up, it was quite clear, at least to Liz, Ryan, and Betty that she'd been pushed to her death and her body rearranged. They weren't allowed anywhere near her after the CSIs arrived. Maybe, it had been an accidental shove? Maybe a hit on the head? Whichever way it happened Wren/Renee Wagner was dead. And so was Julian Rhodes.

They could have given Charlotte the box of letters and the photo showing Julian and Wren together at Sunshine Serenity Springs, but they agreed that turning the box over before they could look through it was not an option. Ryan figured he was still on the case about who murdered Julian and if he did find anything important, he would disclose it to Charlotte, personally.

Only Greta was in the kitchen when everyone entered, telling them that Pierre had gone off for his late afternoon nap and Susannah was having a costume fitting for *The Sea Witch*. Meaning she'd decided not to find another theater company. As if she ever would.

Where Branson and Phoebe were, Liz had no clue.

Greta brought over the glass-domed plate holding Pierre's cinnamon beignets and set it in the center of the table, then she took coffee and tea orders. Ryan got out the cups, and plates, while Aunt Amelia and Dorian talked in low voices with bent heads.

Liz sat at the table, placing the box of letters in front of her. It was as if the box contained a living, breathing thing—Gizmo from the movie *Gremlins*, waiting to pop out with more surprises. She gazed at Ryan, her fingers itching to delve into the box's contents. She reached for it and Ryan gave her an almost imperceptible shake of his head. He was right. Now wasn't the time.

"Tell us who you are," Liz said tersely to the stranger, "and what you want, and more importantly, why you grabbed my ankle at the park? I could have broken my neck!"

"He did what!" Aunt Amelia exclaimed.

Instead of the man explaining, Garrett spoke up, "After Dorian got her first threatening letter, I hired Jarvis to keep Dorian safe. He's a Palm Beach P.I. I thought it was strange that for each letter received it was only Julian who intercepted them. Also, the letters didn't start coming until six months ago. The same time Dorian met Julian."

"At first I didn't believe what you said was true," Dorian interrupted, looking at Jarvis, "but when you showed me photographs of the same envelopes and paper used in the notes that you found in Julian's car..."

Liz jumped in. "Captain Netherton told me this morning that on Saturday he saw Julian sealing an envelope with your name on it, Dorian. Did Julian tell you there was another threatening note that had come to the hotel on the day of the rehearsal dinner?"

"Yes," she said in a quiet voice, shaking her head. "Do you think that's what he meant when he told Ms. Shay, to tell me he was sorry?"

"I suppose that's possible," Liz answered.

Garrett's eye's blazed with anger. "Don't feel sorry for Julian, Dory. The only reason he faked the letters was so you would be totally dependent on him. Tell them, Jarvis, about Wren's and Julian's meetings."

Jarvis took a bite of his beignet and mumbled, "He's met Wren on numerous occasions. But as I told you and Ms. Starwood. I don't think they had a romantic relationship. If anything, she had some kind of hold on him. Maybe blackmail?"

Liz elbowed Ryan. "Time to tell them."

"Wren Wagner is dead," Ryan said.

"She's what?" Dorian squeaked.

"Her body was found on the beach behind the abandoned Sebastian Beach Inn," he said.

Jarvis, who looked nothing like the English butler that his name conjured, was reaching for another beignet.

Liz had enough. Bedraggled and emotionally drained from the past five hours, she stood, grabbed the box of letters from the table and said, "Charlotte, Agent Pearson, will be here soon. Maybe she'll have more information about Wren. Right now, I need a shower."

Betty and Ryan also stood.

Ryan said, "Good idea. Betty, I'll get your luggage from the car and bring it up to you."

Betty blew him a kiss, then the three of them headed for door. Ryan held open the door and Liz and Betty walked under the threshold and into the dining room.

Branson and Phoebe entered from the opposite side of the room. When they reached them, Phoebe asked, "Where'd everyone go? You see Mama?"

"They're in the kitchen," Liz answered, then she introduced Betty to the pair.

Branson whistled, looking at their damp clothing and bad hair days. "What happened to you?"

"They'll explain inside," Ryan said.

"Nothing happened to my mother, I hope." Branson looked stricken.

"No. Not your mother," Liz answered. "Someone else."

"What's in the box?" Phoebe asked.

Liz realized she was clutching the box like it had treasure inside. She stumbled on her words, "Uh, just some...research for my, uh..."

"Next book," Betty added.

Liz hoped the psychic gene had skipped Phoebe. Especially if she'd killed one or both of their murder victims.

As Branson and Phoebe scurried to the swinging doors leading to the kitchen, Liz felt one of Susannah's migraines coming on. The only cure would be a hot shower and Bronte's furry presence at her serene beach house. A lot more serene than Sunshine Serenity Springs Boot camp had been for Wren/Renee Wagner.

After they separated in the lobby. Liz grabbed an umbrella from the bamboo stand and stepped outdoors. It was not only still raining, but there were bolts of lightning piercing the ocean, followed by ear-splitting thunder. Standing under the hotel's main awning, she took out her phone and texted Ryan and Betty.

One hour. The bell tower, I'll bring the box. Tell no one.

Chapter 29

Thirty minutes later Liz was showered, dressed, kissed the cat, and was ready to tackle the letters and talk over the latest developments with Ryan and Betty. The rain had stopped, but storm clouds still blanketed the sky. Rather than getting caught in another monsoon, she took her golf cart to the Indialantic and parked under the awning at the lobby entrance. It appeared no one from the sheriff's department had arrived. They were probably still processing the crime scene.

The only car parked in the circular drive was a white Nissan Altima with Vero Beach plates. She assumed it was Branson's, which she confirmed by peeking inside and seeing a stack of The Soulful Sea restaurant menus on the front seat. In the backseat was a closed cardboard box.

She entered the lobby. No one was around. Which was good because she had an ulterior motive to look through the box of letters before the others arrived. Barnacle Bob was in his cage in the elevator. "Hey, BB, how you doing, bud? Did you do something naughty and that's why you're quarantined once again?" There was a crack of thunder and Liz saw the macaw tremble. Barnacle Bob wasn't a big fan of thunder.

"Snap, crackle, pop! Snap, crackle, pop!" he repeated.

Aunt Amelia thought his fear of thunderstorms had something to do with the way he'd been abandoned outside a bird rescue center during a storm. Her heart swelled when another boom of thunder had him bouncing around his cage, wings aflutter. When Liz was small, she had a rescue dog named Molly. Molly would shake and pant through every storm, not calming until hours after it abated. It was only when you held Molly and wrapped her tightly in a blanket that she would quiet. "Oh BB, what can I do to help you?"

He replied between his trembling and sang in a high-pitched voice bordering on hysteria, "Stormy weather…Stormy weather."

"Okay, I know Auntie is busy with Dorian and you feel abandoned. I'll bring you with me to the bell tower. We've tried this before. Don't let me regret it." She removed her earrings and necklace and put them in her mail cubby behind the registration desk. Slowly, she walked toward the cage and opened the door. Instead of sticking her hand in, she turned her back and aimed her right shoulder near the opening.

"Stormy weather… Pretty bird."

"Hop on, BB. I've gotta get up to the bell tower before the others so I can preview the letters. Maybe I'm psychic, I just know there's some tie between them and the two murders."

BB did as he was told for a change. The weight of his body and his bird feet clutching her shoulder was a feeling she wasn't used to. When they got to the top of the curving staircase he seemed to have finally found his footing. Still leery of his beak, she kept her head tilted to the left to avoid any earlobe nipping.

They passed through the hallway without meeting anyone and then climbed the narrow staircase to the bell tower. Once inside, she tilted her body and Barnacle Bob transferred from her shoulder to the tripod that held a telescope Ryan had bought her for Christmas. And yes, Ryan had even bought her a star and named it Bossy Pants.

"Good bird. Maybe we can trust each other from now on?" He didn't answer, nervously looking out from the curved half moon opening that had a view of the rough Atlantic. There were a few flashes of lightning, miles in the distance, followed by low growls of thunder.

Liz sat at the old scarred wood table and opened the box of letters. Most were as the Wagners had said. Wren complaining about the workload and poor quality of food and health care. The young adults lived in bunkers, woke at five, and were sent to the fields or kitchens to make the baked goods to sell for the farmer's market. There was no air-conditioning except in Elder Jay's quarters. "Idle hands make idle minds," seemed to be Elder Jay's response to criticism from his unhappy campers.

In later letters, Wren became obsessed with pointing out Elder Jay's posh lifestyle. His new model automobiles, jewelry, and bags of cash he took to the bank every Monday from the spoils of the weekend's market. In one letter she mentioned that someone who was in charge of the baked goods table was accused of pocketing half of the proceeds. They never saw the kid again. Afterward, the entire camp had to sit through a two-hour lecture from Elder Jay on the sins of stealing.

Liz glanced at her watch and told herself, *one more letter before Ryan and Betty come.*

And what a letter it was.

She immediately sent a group text to Ryan and Betty, put her phone back in her purse, and reread the letter. In the letter Wren talked of meeting a new friend. The two of them planned to escape together. The friend's mother was a famous psychic and had lots of money and was going to take care of them.

The last line had been the Ah-Ha! moment.

"Whaddya have there?"

Liz placed the letter down, then reached for her phone. Darn! She'd just put it in her bag. She didn't have to turn around because she knew the voice. What she didn't know was if they'd killed Wren or Julian. Or both.

Chapter 30

She turned and faced Branson. "Just working on my next book. It's going to be based on a bunch of old family letters."

He came to the table and looked over her shoulder. She quickly covered Renee's (Wren's) signature with her hand, but it was too late.

Branson grabbed the bottom of the letter, Liz the top. It ripped in half. After examining it Branson said. "I didn't know Wren wrote to her parents when we were in Stalag Serenity Springs. She always said she hated them but not as much as our fearless leader Elder Jay." He pulled a chair next to her. "So, I see you guessed that she killed Julian, the fake witch, and Mother's fiancé."

Liz looked him in the eyes. "Did she do it alone or did you help?"

"Don't get me wrong. I hated the guy too."

"Then why did you introduce him to your mother?"

"I had to. He walked into the restaurant. Said he would spread the news about my past and the fact the restaurant was mortgaged to the hilt. Then he threatened to plant something drug related in the restaurant and call in an anonymous tip. It would not only hurt me, but Mother, too. He wanted on the gravy train. Her gravy train."

"Where does Wren come into all this? Have you been with her since you met at Sunshine Serenity Springs?"

"No," he said calmly. "After the compound closed, she went to serve six months in juvenile detention. She told me she'd been looking for Elder Jay/ Julian Rhodes for years, so I told her where he was. Then like an idiot, I fell for her, like I'd done back then. We reconnected, so to speak."

"I take it your mother never saw Elder Jay/Julian when you were at Sunshine Serenity Springs," she said, checking her options for escape.

"No, I went inside at the end, right before it got closed down. Wren was there a lot longer than me. If you ever saw the way we were treated, you'd understand her wanting payback."

"Why did she kill him?" She reached around the back of the chair for her purse.

He grabbed it and tossed in on the floor, then continued, "After she got Julian to turn over half of his water company, I think she realized he'd find a way to take it back once he married my mother. Plus, Wren knew how upset I was about my mother marrying him and his blackmail. It might have been her way of helping me."

"You had no idea she was going to kill Julian with the..."

"Antifreeze. No."

There it was. Liz broke out in a sweat. She glanced at Barnacle Bob who'd been eavesdropping as usual. He started repeating, "Antifreeze, Antifreeze."

Branson locked his eyes on Liz's. He'd figured out his mistake. No one knew Julian had been killed with antifreeze. Not even Dorian. He advanced toward her. "I didn't kill him. Wren did."

"No, but you're just as much as guilty as she was. You knew what she was going to do."

"He deserved it anyway. He was evil to the core. The way he treated everyone at that camp. The way he treated my mother. I heard that those threatening letters to her were written by him. No surprise there. He reveled in having people dependent on him." He stepped toward her.

She stood and took a step away from him, her back pinned to the half wall below the arched opening. If he pushed her, it would be a sixty-foot drop. "You probably told her to put the antifreeze in the Mermaid Margarita. I just realized that on the first menu you gave us on Friday, the margaritas weren't listed. But the new menu had them. I'd call that premeditation. Did you and your pal Wren put oleander in Julian's SWS water?"

"Not Me. Wren. She almost killed my mother. She told me it was a spur of the moment decision. When she looked up how much antifreeze it would take to kill someone, she saw something about this other case where a wife had killed her husband with antifreeze and some kind of flower." He looked feverish. "The water was meant for Julian, but Mother drank it. That's why I told Wren we should take a break. She went berserk. It was an honest mistake she said, but she didn't seem upset. I saw then that if we ever married, she might kill again, either me or my mother. It all came down to money with her."

"How did she take your breaking up with her?" Liz asked, taking a baby step toward him, away from the opening.

"Not well," Branson said. "I told her to wait until things cooled down. What happened next was an …"

"A what?" a voice said from behind Branson. Ryan was standing there.

Branson frantically glanced around for an exit. There were only three, down the stairs, or out the open stucco archway on both sides of the tower.

Ryan stepped closer.

"Accident," Branson said.

"Ryan held up a gold lock in a plastic bag. Etched in the metal were the initials LV for Louis Vuitton. The same lock that matched the small key Liz had found on the floor in Wren's suite.

"What's that?" Branson asked.

"Found it in your car. You know what it is," Ryan answered.

Because of the stack of menus she'd spied on Branson's front seat, Liz had sent Ryan and Betty a text to check his car before coming up to the bell tower. The menus reminded her of what she'd realized when talking to Captain Netherton that the poisoned margaritas weren't on the first menu, only the second.

"It's the lock to Wren's missing luggage," Liz answered, happy she'd told Ryan about the key to Wren's Louis Vuitton bag that she'd found after Wren had *supposedly* left the hotel. "Wren never left the hotel with her luggage, did she? You'd already killed her before you came to the séance. That's why Wren didn't show up. I remember how sweaty you were and out of breath when you came in for the séance. The coroner said Wren's time of death was sometime early afternoon on Sunday. And when we saw her on the rocks, she was wearing the same dress from the brunch."

Her words must have hit home, because Branson came and pulled her to him and put his arm around her neck in a chokehold.

She gasped for air.

"I wouldn't do that," Ryan said, gritting his teeth.

She felt Branson's hot breath on her neck, the panicked trembling in his grip. "Stay back," he said to Ryan. "If I jump, I'm taking her with me. I didn't kill Julian. I swear, Wren did. Yes, she told me about her plan. I couldn't stop her. You didn't know her like I did."

"You did stop her though, didn't you son?" Betty and Dorian had come quietly up the stairs and were standing behind Ryan. Dorian said, "It sounds like you did it for me." She stepped toward him. "Come, dear. I know your aura is pure. But hers wasn't. I knew it from the séance. Maybe that's why I felt her presence, she was already… Darling, release Liz. I am here. We'll work it out."

But he didn't have to because Barnacle Bob stretched his wings and started to dive-bomb Branson's head, pounding against his forehead with his pointy beak like Woody the Woodpecker. In order to protect his face, Branson released his hold on her.

Liz sprinted away. Ryan sprung forward, grabbed Branson, and twisted his arms behind his back, then pushed him face down on the floor. WWE wrestling-style, he kept a knee to Branson's tailbone. "Liz? You all right?" Ryan asked, not even breaking a sweat.

"I'm good. BB, you're my hero!"

He squawked, "Duh-duh-du-duh, du-duh…Batman!" Then flew to her shoulder.

"What about me?" Ryan asked, trying to make a joke but she could tell he'd been more than worried about her fate.

"Yes," Liz said, still trembling, "both of my caped crusaders, you saved the day. And Barnacle Bob, you even did it during a thunderstorm."

Betty came to Liz's and Barnacle Bob's side, then put her arm around Liz's waist.

Dorian went to Branson. She got down on her knees and said to Ryan, "Please don't hurt him Ryan. He's no killer."

Branson looked at his mother, his eyes filled with tears. "You're wrong Mother, I did kill her. But it was an accident. I told her we shouldn't see each other and she laughed, saying as a precaution she'd put the empty can of antifreeze somewhere in my restaurant where the police would find it, along with the glass that held Julian's poisoned margarita. I lost it. I shoved her against the railing, it broke, she went flying. Broke her neck, I think. I tried to give her CPR, nothing worked."

Betty elbowed Liz, and pointed to her bag, where she showed Liz that her iPad was facetiming the entire conversation. Liz saw her father's face looking up at her.

A few minutes later, Fenton, Charlotte, and one of her deputies entered the room. Branson was handcuffed and led down the stairs by the deputy. Dorian followed behind. She seemed surprisingly calm. Maybe she had a glimpse of Branson's rosy future, or maybe just a mother's intuition that things would turn out okay. Liz didn't see how.

Liz had no such positive feelings toward Branson. Yes, maybe killing Wren had been an accident, but she believed he could have prevented Julian's death. She guessed there was no way to prove he knew Wren's plans ahead of time. The only part of the conversation that had been recorded was when he'd confessed to pushing Wren.

Justice would prevail, as her father always said. They'd have to wait and see.

Chapter 31

"By the way," Ryan said, as the last curtain closed on Aunt Amelia and her cast of *The Sea Witch*, "Phoebe is on her way to Paris to face charges for stealing some statue of a ballet dancer."

"Not just any statue, a Degas." Liz's palms were hot and itchy from all the standing ovations they'd given Aunt Amelia and Susannah. The pair had even held hands at the play's end and bowed. Liz had to commend herself. The changes she'd made to the script had made both her great-aunt and Susannah happy. She was also happy she'd talked Aunt Amelia out of the idea of building a cyclorama water tank like they'd used on *Voyage to the Bottom of the Sea*. Even Aunt Amelia's boyfriend, Ziggy, owner of the theater, had vetoed that idea. Something he never did when it came to his Amelia.

Now they had a few months before the next production. And Liz would make sure she had nothing to do with it.

Liz explained about the statue. "It was supposed to be her and Branson's inheritance from their father. It looks like greedy Phoebe stole it and then tried to sell it. Garrett's P.I. found out from someone at one of our local pawn shops. Dorian bought it back and Phoebe's in Paris, pleading to the authorities, saying that following her father's funeral, it mistakenly found its way into her luggage when she returned to the States. Doubt if that defense will fly."

"I think before the next event at the Indialantic, everyone should go through a diligent background screening."

Liz laughed. "Please. Don't even say the word event."

Ryan handed his playbill to Liz and she stowed it in her handbag. He said, "I guess things could have turned out worse for Branson now that he's been arraigned for manslaughter. The other charges of him being an accomplice to murder have been dropped for lack of evidence. And did you hear Dorian and Garret are planning to go to Bali after the trial?"

"I'm glad Dorian has Garrett. And the IRS audit of Dorian's finances were cleared without a single red flag. I just hope the pair don't plan on getting married at the Indialantic by the Sea. A nice quiet ceremony in Bali would be so much better. Or even London, when Aunt Amelia, you, and I meet up with them for Betty's book launch of *The Insensible Equation*."

"Little matchmaker. By the way, I ran into Ashley and lifeguard Josh at Squidly's. Looks like you struck again."

Liz laughed and squeezed his hand, "I had nothing to do with that, it was Karma. But I know a good guy when I see one. I picked you, didn't I?"

"You picked me...I thought I picked you."

"We picked each other," she said, pulling him to her and giving him a long, hard kiss.

"Ms. Holt, I'm surprised at you. This is a public establishment."

"Well Mr. Stone, are you saying you never want me to do that again?"

"No, I'm saying..." He pulled her to him.

The lights in the theater went off.

"I guess it's time to go see Auntie," she said with a laugh.

They got up from their seats and made their way to her great-aunt's dressing room.

A long line of well-wishers was waiting in the hallway to congratulate Aunt Amelia. "Everyone from the Indialantic must be inside already," Liz said, "there will be a mutiny if we cut ahead. You know Auntie and her admirers."

"How big is our star's dressing room?"

"Not that big, and she has to share it with Susannah. Maybe we should go to the lounge for a glass of wine."

"Not a bad idea."

"I'll text Betty not to let Aunt Amelia leave before we see her."

* * * *

In the lounge, Ryan brought her a glass of rosé and sat next to her on a red velvet settee. Aunt Amelia and her boyfriend-owner Ziggy had decorated the theater's lobby in 1930s deco style, using some items stored at the Indialantic. Scattered on the walls were posters of past plays. All had Amelia Eden Holt playing one part or the other. The poster for *The*

Sea Witch not only had her name listed at the top of the cast, but also as the playwright. Raising her glass, Liz said, "Here's to Auntie."

"And, here's to keeping the drama on stage, not at the Indialantic," Ryan answered.

"I'll toast to that." She looked at the pale pink liquid in her glass and thought about what Dorian had told Aunt Amelia after visiting her son at the sheriff's station. He admitted that after Wren fell off the cliff, he'd returned to the hotel, packed up her things, he stuck her ring in his pocket and it fell out during the séance, where Farrah found it. He'd stowed the Louis Vuitton bag with the open lock in the backseat of his car. Later, he dumped the bag in the trash container at the back of his restaurant.

"Okay," Ryan said, standing, "Aunt Amelia's dressing room should have thinned out by now."

"Her plant! I left it under my seat in the theater. I got her a new orchid for her collection."

"Speaking of orchids. Charlotte did find Wren's fingerprints in the orchid house and traces of oleander. Looks like I might have to give you part of my retainer from the sheriff's department."

"Sounds good, partner. Maybe I should get a P.I. license too."

"Might as well have Betty get one also," he said. "You can get a group rate."

"The three detectiveteers! All for one, and one for all."

Chapter 32

Fifteen minutes later they opened the dressing room door to what could only be described as pandemonium.

Feathers floated in the air and a loud cacophony of squawking caused Liz to cover her ears before stepping inside. Betty, Charlotte, Fenton, Captain Netherton, Susannah, Greta, Kate, Alex, and Pierre were all clustered in the corner. Aunt Amelia was in her canvas makeup chair, Ziggy next to her. Her face was slathered in cold cream and her hair was still in medusa-style spikes. She looked at them in the reflection of her vanity mirror, a huge grin on her face. "Oh Lizzy, you'll never guess! Looks like we'll have a wedding to celebrate very soon!"

She and Ziggy? Dorian and Garrett?

"Meet Brazilian Bombshell Carmen Miranda!" Aunt Amelia bellowed in her stage voice.

Liz glanced to the other side of the room where Barnacle Bob's brass cage stood. But he wasn't inside. A blue-and-yellow macaw was.

She heard Barnacle Bob's shrill squawking from above. Looking up, she saw him hanging from the chain to the light fixture.

Liz was speechless.

But Barnacle Bob wasn't. "Well, shiver me timbers!"

Recipes

Island Eats Food Truck Savory Grilled Cheese

Ingredients:

    Two slices thick sliced Rustic Italian hearth-baked bread
    Four slices prosciutto (thin sliced)
    Four "Peppadew" peppers, sliced thin
    2 oz. gorgonzola cheese (sliced or crumbled)
    2 oz. brie, sliced
    2 oz. fig spread
    2 oz. grated parmesan
    4 oz. unsalted butter
    2 oz. mayonnaise

Butter all sides of each bread slice; you may use up to 2 oz. butter
Sprinkle grated parmesan on one side of each slice (the outer side, if you will)
    Spread fig spread on one inside side
    Spread mayonnaise on the other inside side
    Layer brie on top of mayo
    Place "Peppadew" peppers on top of the brie
    Layer gorgonzola cheese on top of Peppadew
    Layer prosciutto on top of gorgonzola
    Place fig spread side on top of prosciutto

Melt remaining 2 oz. butter on medium-low heat in non-stick pan. When butter stops foaming, add assembled sandwich to pan. Cover pan to help heat through and melt the cheese. Turn when bread is golden brown. When second side is golden brown, and cheese is melted through, you're done.

Island Eats Food Truck Chicken Sandwich

Ingredients:

One 12" hoagie roll or similar bread roll
1/2 lb. leftover roasted or BBQ'd chicken meat, de-boned,
de-skinned, and shredded
2 tablespoons chicken stock/broth
1 red onion, thinly sliced
12 slices pickled jalapeno
1 cup shredded lettuce (about 1/4 to 1/2 small iceberg head)

Aioli:

1/2 cup mayo
3 cloves garlic, crushed
1/2 teaspoon cayenne
1/2 teaspoon five-spice powder
1/2 teaspoon ground allspice
1/2 teaspoon ground pepper
1/2 teaspoon dried thyme, crumbled
1/2 teaspoon grated nutmeg
1 tablespoon soy sauce
Squeeze of lime

Directions:

Combine all the aioli ingredients together in a bowl and thoroughly mix together. Set aside and allow flavors to come together for 15 minutes or so if possible.

Gently heat the shredded chicken and chicken stock in a microwave for 30 seconds on high; mix thoroughly when heated.

Slice hoagie roll along the side, leaving one side attached; open the roll and scoop out the bulk of the bread, leaving a "dugout" in the roll.

Generously spread the aioli on both halves of the roll. I mean, *generously.*

Add sliced onions and sliced jalapenos to both halves of the bread.

Add all the chicken with some of the stock (to keep it very moist) to the bottom half of the roll.

Put four dollops of aioli on the chicken spaced equally along its length.

Cover the meat with shredded lettuce.

Bring the two sides together and slice in half, leaving two six-inch halves.

Island Eats Food Truck Apple Pie Fries

Ingredients:

    1 package of refrigerated pie crusts (two crusts) or
homemade
    1 10 oz can of apple pie filling (or make from scratch)
    1 egg
    1 tsp cinnamon
    1/4 tsp nutmeg
    1/4 cup sugar
    Sparkling sugar
    Caramel sauce for dipping.

Directions:

Preheat oven to 350. Spray a cooking sheet with oil.

Dust work area with flour and *slightly* roll out crusts.
Pulse in food processor a couple of times or use a knife to chop pie filling into smaller pieces.
Spread apples over top of 1 crust leaving about 1/8″ uncovered at edges.
Place other crust on top.
Cut into 1/2 inch strips and then cut to resemble french fries.
Beat egg in a small bowl.
Mix together sugar, cinnamon, and nutmeg.
Brush tops with egg wash and sprinkle sparingly with sugar mixture.
Add sparkling sugar to resemble salt (optional)
Transfer to prepared baking sheet.

Bake for 15-20 minutes or until golden brown.

Serve with a bowl of caramel dipping sauce or put dipping sauce in a squeeze bottle and drizzle on top.

About the Author

Kathleen Bridge is the author of the By the Sea Mystery series and the Hamptons Home and Garden Mystery series, published by Berkley. She started her writing career working at *The Michigan State University News* in East Lansing, Michigan. A member of Sisters in Crime and Mystery Writers of America, she is also the author and photographer of an antiques reference guide, *Lithographed Paper Toys, Books, and Games*. She teaches creative writing in addition to working as an antiques and vintage dealer in Melbourne, Florida. Kathleen blissfully lives on a barrier island. Readers can visit her on the web at www.kathleenbridge.com

Don't miss MURDER BY THE SEA by Kathleen Bridge!

When a murderer crashes a masquerade ball, it's up to Liz to unmask the killer...

It's been quite a year for novelist Liz Holt. She's overcome a lot and is finally feeling at peace with her new life at her family's hotel, the Indialantic by the Sea, on the beautiful barrier island of Melbourne Beach, Florida. She's ready to ring in the New Year at the Florida Writes Literary Masquerade Ball.

But when her ex-boyfriend surprises her at the ball, she can't disguise her anger, and the two engage in a very public argument. When her ex turns up on the hotel grounds, shot through the heart, Liz finds herself topping the suspect list. With the help of family and friends, she needs to clear her name before the real killer waltzes away scot-free...

Look for MURDER BY THE SEA on sale now.

Printed in the United States
by Baker & Taylor Publisher Services